Advance Praise for Timothy Woodward and *If I Told You So*

"A romantic coming out tale simply told and engrossing. As Sean's gay identity emerges, Woodward poignantly captures the evolution in his relationships with family, an old girlfriend, a new boyfriend and, most importantly, himself."

—Lee Bantle, author of *David Inside Out*

"Reading Timothy Woodward's *If I Told You So* ought to be a rite of passage for every LGBTQ and straight young adult. It is a potent reminder of just how powerful first love can be—and how irresistible."

—James Lecesne, author of *Absolute Brightness*

"Woodward writes from the heart—a genuine, honest story about the joys and pains of first love, and realizing that no one is as alone as it sometimes seems."

—Robin Reardon, author of *A Secret Edge*

"A touching story about navigating the sometimes treacherous waters of first love and first loss."

—J. H. Trumble, author of *Don't Let Me Go*

If I Told You So

Timothy Woodward

KENSINGTON BOOKS
www.kensingtonbooks.com

KENSINGTON BOOKS are published by

Kensington Publishing Corp.
119 West 40th Street
New York, NY 10018

ISBN-13: 978-0-7582-7488-5
ISBN-10: 0-7582-7488-2

First Kensington Trade Paperback Printing: September 2012
10 9 8 7 6 5 4 3 2 1

Printed in the United States of America

For my mother, who always knew.

For Lynn Safford, who planned the parties and
provided my inspiration. You are missed.

ACKNOWLEDGMENTS

Thank you to the readers of the partial drafts, the early drafts, and the almost but not quite final drafts. Jenny Rainville, Julia Bruce, Stacy LaBella, Amanda Maselli, Jo Anne Frazier, Tiffany Pelletier, Elizabeth Foscue, Meg Costello, Stephen van Ness, and Renée Bouchard, your insight and enthusiasm were invaluable.

Thank you to my students, so many of whom appear in these pages, especially Drew Doucette and Erica Louise Loughlin. I hope you can see yourself and like what you see.

I owe a great debt to the faculty at Southern New Hampshire University. Your guidance shaped this story from page one. Thank you to Rick Carey, Gretchen Legler, Kim Ponders, and Bob Begiebing. Thank you also to my three mentors who each suffered through the earliest drafts: Merle Drown, Diane Les Becquets, and especially Katie Towler, who suffered most of all.

Jade Hale, Susan Kennedy, Mike Hancock, Linda Butler, Robert Perreault, Peggy Newland, Patrick Bernard, Anne Botteri, Kevin Sheahan, and Meg Bieniek were also there from day one. You are my writer family. And Lynn Safford, who we all miss, thank you for giving me the ice-cream shop.

Thank you to Kelly Stone Gamble for celebrating each milestone with me along the way.

Thank you to Greater Boston PFLAG and Pam Garramone for everything you do for all of the Sean Jacksons in the world. This book could not exist if not for the impact you make every day.

Thank you to Suzanne Brockmann for introducing me to my incredibly patient agent, Deidre Knight, who never gave up.

And a special thank you to my editor, John Scognamiglio, for making things so easy.

Kristan Watson has waited the longest to see this book happen. Let's hope the next one doesn't take so long.

Finally, thank you to my parents for their unconditional support and love.

Prologue

"Where have you been?"

So much for the stealthy entrance. My plans of sneaking in unnoticed are crushed when my mother turns on the hallway light. She's standing at the top of the stairs like a sentry, and her eyes bore through me better than any spear she could brandish at my throat.

"Out." I try not to sound too insolent.

"Do you know what time it is?"

"Late?"

"Two A.M. *late.*" She starts down the stairs with her arms folded across her chest. Her eyes never leave mine. "Sean, I like to give you a lot of trust, but you're making it really difficult."

"I'm sorry. I would have called, but there wasn't a phone where we were."

"And who is we?"

"Jay and Becky."

She's made it to the bottom of the stairs, but she purses her lips and takes a step toward me before responding. "Jay again?"

I don't say anything because behind her question is an accusation. I'm not sure what I am being accused of, but her tone says, "I don't think I like Jay."

She grabs my chin, her thumb pressing hard below my lip. I want to turn away, but her grip is strong. She looks at my eyes carefully, examining.

"Mom," I say, "we weren't doing drugs."

She keeps looking for several seconds, but finally convinced, she lets go.

"Should I even ask what you were doing, then?"

I think back to Jay's boat, the camp, and the escape in the canoe. I think about Jay pulling me out of the water and holding me to his chest. I close my eyes, afraid my mother might see through them and read my thoughts. I don't say anything.

"Sean . . . ?" She puts her hands on my shoulders, and before I can resist she pulls me toward her. "Honey, I just love you so much and I worry, you know?"

I can feel the cool damp of my shirt where she presses it against my back. *Don't notice. Don't notice.*

"You're all wet."

"Yeah." I had thought the interrogation was about to end, but this little detail has opened a whole other line of questioning. *Think quick. Why am I wet?* Certainly, I can't tell her about Jay and me and the canoe tipping over. But it's two A.M., and my brain is fogged with thoughts of Jay. I take too long to formulate an answer.

"Why are you all wet?" She's noticed that it's not just my shirt, but my cargo shorts and sneakers, too.

"Um, I went canoeing."

My mom folds her arms, waiting for more.

"And . . . we . . . just . . . tipped over."

"Oh my God! Are you okay, were you wearing a life jacket? Where were you?"

She should see that I'm standing in front of her in one piece, but she has hit panic mode. She starts to check my arms and legs for life-threatening injuries.

"Mom, calm down. Jay took me out in his canoe, but we hit a

sandbar coming in to shore and while we were trying to get un-stuck we tipped over. The water was, like, two feet deep. I'm fine." And it's kind of close to what really happened. The two feet of water part, anyway.

"People drown in two feet of water. You're not supposed to be on the lake at night in a canoe. Does Jay even have running lights?"

"Mom, look at me, I'm fine!"

"I'm not sure I want you hanging out with Jay anymore. This is the second time you've come home with some ridiculous tale to tell."

"Mom, you can't. I mean, Jay's my boss."

"All the more reason why you shouldn't hang out with him."

"I'm sixteen. You can't treat me like a little kid."

"I'm treating you like my son who still lives under my roof. Sean, I want to trust you to make the right decisions, but . . ." She looks away and exhales through her nose with enough force that I can hear it.

I open my mouth to defend myself, but all I can get out is a sarcastic gasp.

"I don't want you hanging out with him. You can see him at work, but other than that—"

"Mom, you don't understand."

"Then explain it to me."

"I, I . . . I can't."

"Until you can, the only way I can trust you is if I know you're not with him."

"Mom!" I can feel the tears pressing on the bottom of my eyes. *Don't lose it, Sean.*

But I can't hold it back any longer. The pressure behind my eyes is too much, but I don't want my mother to see me cry. I plow past her, and her guidance counselor instincts have been alerted to a teen in crisis. She catches me by the shoulder and uses my own momentum to spin me toward her.

"Sean?"

"You don't understand."

This time her voice is soft and absorbent, a tissue to dry my eyes. "What? What don't I understand? Try me."

I look into her eyes, only inches from mine. It occurs to me that her prediction that I would be taller than her has finally come true. At five nine I practically tower over her petite, five-four frame, but despite my height advantage she still holds power over me, and I can feel the words being dredged from my throat. "I'm in love with him."

She just stares for a second, and then her eyes close as she makes connections. I can see the pieces clicking into place for her. She opens her eyes and, just to be sure, says, "Sean?"

I open my mouth to speak, but the words are frozen again. I thought I was past this. It doesn't matter; she heard me.

Her hand drops from my shoulder and goes to her mouth. Now her eyes are shiny and wet. Tears of sadness? Grief? Anger? I don't stay to find out. I turn and bolt up the stairs to my room. My mother doesn't try to follow.

I slam the door behind me and lean against it, my knees folding underneath me. I slide to the floor and sit. I try to listen for my mother, but all I can hear is my heart throbbing in my ears. I wait. My hands are shaking; I can't face her right now. This wasn't how I intended to tell her.

I want to call Becky. I hesitate, not sure I should leave my post by the door. I look at the doorknob. Nothing. I decide if my mom hasn't come pounding down my door yet, she's probably not coming. I crawl to the phone where it lies halfway under my bed. I start to push buttons, but I stop. Who am I kidding? It's two A.M. I put the phone down and lean my head against my mattress and close my eyes. My tears seal my eyes shut, and it takes too much strength to open them again. I touch my cheek and realize I've been crying for a while. I use my sleeve to wipe my face, but the effort is exhausting. The adrenaline from a few minutes ago has started to slip away. There's no longer a bass drum thumping through my head; I can actually hear myself breathing. I concentrate on breathing for a few minutes and try to figure out how I got here, a crumpled, wet, crying mess on the floor of my room.

Chapter 1

"Sean!" My mother's voice cuts through the cocoon of morning warmth and sunshine. "You are not going to sleep all day!"

I roll over and hug my tattered quilt tighter around my shoulders. The quilt, a handmade gift from my grandmother, is as old as I am. The stuffing has leaked out in places so that it doesn't provide much warmth anymore, but it's perfect for sleeping in on a Saturday in mid-June.

"I'll be up in a minute," I say, loud enough for her to hear. I crack one eye to read the red digital numbers on my alarm clock. 10:07. Twenty-three minutes doesn't seem too much to ask.

"A quick minute." I hear her retreat from the bottom of the stairs, apparently satisfied that I am still among the living.

It's the first Saturday of summer vacation, the first Saturday of an entire summer of lazy Saturdays to look forward to. The phone rings, disrupting my half dreams, but my mom answers after only two rings, and I close my eyes, thinking the distraction should be good for a few more minutes of shut-eye. With any luck it'll be Aunt Maureen.

"Sean!" I look at the clock again. 10:11.

"I said I'd be up in a—"

"It's your father on the phone."

I roll over on my stomach and swat some dirty laundry away from the bed until I find the phone hiding under a pair of cargo shorts.

"Hello." I try to keep that just-woke-up fog out of my voice.

"Hey, kiddo. Still asleep, huh?"

"It is Saturday."

"Hey, no worries."

My dad sounds way too cheery.

"Did you catch any of the Sox game last night? I saw the highlights on ESPN, but the networks down here only cover the Braves."

"Sorry, didn't catch it." I don't have to try very hard to keep the enthusiasm out of my voice.

"That rookie pitcher from Japan is somethin' else! I'm tellin' you, he's the real deal. I picked him up in my fantasy league. I figure he'll help me in Ks and wins, and maybe ERA if he stays healthy."

"Good luck with that," I say. "Listen, Dad, I need to take a shower. Start the day, you know?"

"It's after ten; you know you won't be able to get away with that when you're down here in Georgia."

Now I'm wide-awake. "What?"

"I asked your mom to let me tell you. We decided that it would be a good idea for you to live with me for the summer."

"With you? In Georgia?"

"How does that sound?"

"Isn't it hot in Georgia?"

"You'll get used to it. I've already got a job lined up for you. A friend of mine needs help on his landscaping crew."

A shudder shoots down my spine. Landscaping means fertilizer. Fertilizer makes me feel dirty. Now I really do need a shower.

"What do you say?"

"Um, let me think about it."

"Don't think too long. I've arranged for you to fly down here next week."

What was that I was saying about an entire summer of lazy Saturdays? I decide to make a personal rule against answering the phone before eleven A.M. This is way too early to have the day ruined.

"Great. That gives me, like, seven days to pack." I try hard not to make it sound too sarcastic.

"Your mom and I still have some details to work out, so why don't you let me talk to her again?"

I am only too glad to get off the phone. I mean, it's not that I don't like my father, I just don't like talking to him. When we do talk, I feel like we should hire a translator. He goes on about RBI, ERA, and how the Red Sox need a new middle reliever. If it's football season, he wants to know what I think of the Patriots' nickel package. I feel bad for him in a way; he moved to Georgia about a year ago, so keeping track of his favorite teams is hard. I just don't want to be the one to keep him up-to-date.

My parents have been divorced for five years, so I'm used to it by now. Actually, for a while, it wasn't all that different. My dad still lived in Bell Cove, and I saw him almost as much as when he lived with us, which wasn't that much. He's a workaholic and had constant late meetings. When he was home, he'd be too tired to do much more than sit in his recliner and watch the news. Then he moved down state to a town on the Massachusetts border. I was only able to see him a weekend or two a month, and I guess that was when we really started to grow apart. Not that we were ever all that close. My dad's always been into sports and fishing, flannel shirts and work boots. I'm more of an arts and theater, polo and loafers guy. He's country and I'm country club. Now that he's in Georgia, we only talk on the phone. He does make an effort to call me every week, but our conversations are always pretty short. He tells me about the bass he caught at his favorite fishing hole; I tell him about the new play the drama club is putting on. *Okay, talk to you next week. Have a good one. Bye.*

I find my mother downstairs in the kitchen where I pour myself a bowl of Frosted Mini-Wheats.

"Uh, Mom? Dad thinks I'm living with him for the summer?"

"We both felt that working with your father in Georgia would be better than doing nothing around here."

"I can't believe you two agreed on something."

"Don't be smart. You're sixteen. You should be saving for college. Besides, your father misses you."

"Then he shouldn't have moved to Georgia."

"Sean, just because I don't get along with your father doesn't mean that you shouldn't get along with him."

"He wasn't exactly the model dad. It's not like he was home much."

"He's trying."

"Too little, too late." I push myself up from the kitchen table and drop my dishes in the sink. My spoon clatters against the stainless steel. I head for the door.

"Where are you going?"

"Out. If the only reason you're sending me to Georgia is so I can work, then I might as well get a job here." I'm out the door before she can reply. I grit my teeth and climb on my bike to ride into town. I'm serious about the job. It's either that or sweat like a pig in Georgia.

Ten minutes later, I'm standing with my bike between my legs, looking out over Bell Cove and the lake beyond. My hometown is nestled along the south shore of the lake, and it extends seven or eight houses inland at its widest point. In some places, a house has been built up on the hill away from the main town, either a rich city-dweller's summer-cottage attempt to get back to nature or an aging hippie's attempt to get back to civilization.

From here at the top of Mann's Hill, I can see everything.

Main Street runs along the shoreline, with shops and buildings on one side and a paved walkway on the other. During the summer it's crowded with walkers, bikers, and joggers enjoying the lake breeze. The chamber of commerce publishes brochures that call Bell Cove "quaint." I looked it up: small, old-fashioned, and odd. I guess it's an accurate description; I'm just not sure it's the kind of thing that should be advertised in brochures. Anyway, it's still early in the season, and there are only a few couples enjoying a stroll along our "quaint" Main Street.

Summer means everything to a town like Bell Cove. Pretty much everything revolves around the lake and the tourists it brings in during the summer. The spring is nice, but the water's too cold for swimming, so people tend to take their vacations to places like Florida or somewhere in the Caribbean. The fall brings beautiful foliage, but most of the tourists will head over toward Conway and the Kancamagus Highway, with its beautiful hiking, waterfalls, and scenic overlooks. In the winter, everyone's in the North Country for the skiing. Which leaves the summer for Bell Cove and the other small lake towns. What this means for me is that, with the first day of summer this week, I am getting a very late start on finding a job. Since the tourist season really starts to ramp up starting on Memorial Day, most kids started looking for jobs over a month ago to line up summer work. I cross my fingers that there will still be jobs left.

I ride into town only to discover that, as I suspected, most of the downtown shops have already hired for the summer, and what's left is left for a reason. The harbormaster is looking for someone to clean boats; I can just imagine myself in rubber boots, scrubbing green-bottomed hulls and smelling like bleach all summer. No, thank you. There's also an opening for a cashier at the gas station, which doesn't sound too bad until I realize that I'd be responsible for cleaning out the bathrooms. I'd rather smell like bleach.

Since I don't have a car, I can't get out to the Walmart by the highway. It's also too far to ride my bike to the McDonald's or the Burger King by exit 23. A lot of kids take boats across the lake and get jobs in neighboring towns, but I only have a twelve-foot fishing boat my dad left behind, which is no good in bad weather. Besides, my mother would never let me; she's afraid of boats. I know, I know, living on a lake and afraid of boats. Don't get me started.

All afternoon on Main Street it's the same story. I'm turned away at every pretentious boutique selling sun catchers and wooden moose carvings and at each nautical-themed restaurant with fishing nets tacked to the walls. I've come to the end of the row of clapboard façades that line Main Street. All that's left is the Pink Cone. I've deliberately avoided the local ice cream shop, as I see it as a last resort. First of all, only girls work there, and the idea of being caught in the middle of half a dozen divas fighting over boyfriends and who has the best lipstick color is only a notch above cleaning bathrooms at the gas station. And second, I've heard all the rumors about "Fabulous Renée," the crazy, bitchy owner of "the Cone."

I'm not sure I want to work for someone with a reputation for tyrannical insanity, so when I walk in the front door of the Cone to ask whether they're still hiring for the summer, it's not with a lot of confidence.

"How old are you, hon?" the woman behind the counter asks, a hand on her hip and the other pointing a plastic ice cream scoop in my direction.

"Sixteen."

"Fabulous. You got any references? A resume?" She catches me off guard. I'm hoping to get an application to fill out. "Never mind. You kids never do. You live around here?"

"Morgan Beach."

"Fabulous. I like local kids. Tell me why you want the job."

Since I really haven't thought this summer job plan all the way through, I don't know how to answer that question. Finally, I settle on the truth.

"My mom and dad are making me get a job, and if I don't

find one around here, I'll have to go live with my dad and work in Georgia." It's not exactly the best pitch for a job ever, but I do remember to smile.

She gives me a long look, but after about fifteen seconds she lets out a small snort and one corner of her mouth turns up. "Well, at least you'd be motivated to keep the job once you got it. Fabulous. We're having an orientation for the late-season hires on Monday at nine A.M. Don't be late."

It happens so fast, it takes me a second to realize I've been offered a job. "Thank you. I'll be there. Thank you!"

"You don't have a job yet. My manager will be running the training, and you'll have to pass muster with him. What's your name?"

"Sean Jackson. Thank you for this!"

"Well, Sean Jackson, it's nice to meet you. I'm Renée Bouchard, the owner here. We'll fill out the paperwork at Ice Cream Orientation—if you make it through orientation."

So this is the infamous "Fabulous Renée." She doesn't seem so scary. "Thank you. This is great! This is . . ."

"Fabulous?" Renée offers, amused by my excitement.

"Fabulous," I agree. "Fabulous."

I get home ready to gloat about my employment victory, but my mother has gone out. So I jump online, ready to IM whoever I can find signed on. Almost before my computer beeps to tell me that the sign-on process is complete, my screen fills with a message from LuvBug922. It's my girlfriend, Lisa.

LuvBug922:   What's up?

I'm about to tell her my news, but decide to kid around with her a little first.

NHBeachBoi: OMG, the rents totally shafted me today! I have to go to Georgia to live with my dad for the summer.

LuvBug922:	What!??
LuvBug922:	That sux!
NHBeachBoi:	I know. My dad says I have to help his friend with his landscaping business
LuvBug922:	I'll never see u!
NHBeachBoi:	You're going to be at your camp all summer anyway
LuvBug922:	But that's only across the lake and I get some days off.
LuvBug922:	u can't go to Georgia! ☹
NHBeachBoi:	But my rents said I can't just sit around the house all summer
LuvBug922:	What are u gonna do??

I've had enough fun. I smile while I type the next message.

NHBeachBoi:	I got a job!!!

While I wait for her reply I scan my buddy list to see who else I can tell, but I guess people have things to do on the weekend, because no one else is signed on. Bummer.

LuvBug922:	Where!?
NHBeachBoi:	The Pink Cone. Pretty crazy huh?
LuvBug922:	LOL That IS crazy! You'll probably be the only guy working there! LOL ☺
NHBeachBoi:	At least it's a job. Hopefully now that I have one they won't make me go to Georgia

LuvBug922:   I know. They can't send you to Georgia!! It's too
              hot!

LuvBug922:   j/k! I'd miss you too much

I wait a long time before I type.

NHBeachBoi: Me too.

LuvBug922:   Hey, GTG, I'm supposed to go be social with my
              cousins who are in town for the weekend. TTYL
              {{{{Hugs}}}} I Luv U

I wait for her to sign off, trying to avoid having to reply, but
her icon stays lit up in my buddy list. She's waiting for it. I feel
like a jerk, but I type

NHBeachBoi: <3 u 2. {{{{Hugs}}}} ttyl.

I decide to sign off before she can write back, just in case.

Just as I sign off, I hear the front door open, and my mom
calls up to me.

"Sean?"

"Yeah," I shout from my room, but get up to go to the top of
the stairs. My mom hates having to shout through the house.

"Can you help me with the groceries? There's two more bags
in the car." She heads toward the kitchen with a brown paper
bag clutched in one arm, her purse on the other shoulder, car
keys in her hand.

I go out and grab the two bags from the open trunk of the
car. I close it with a thud, and take a deep breath to steel myself
for the confrontation with my mother. It's time to tell her I'm
not going to Georgia.

When I get to the kitchen, her back is turned to me while she
puts soup cans away in a cabinet near the stove.

"I found a job."

Her hand pauses in mid-reach for just a moment before she continues putting cans away. "Here in Bell Cove?"

"At the Pink Cone. I start Monday." I decide to leave out the part about having to survive orientation.

I can see her purse her lips, and I'm sure she's going to shoot me down, but then one side of her mouth goes up in a wry half smile.

"Your dad is just going to love that," she says.

Obviously, my dad is going to be furious that I'm refusing to go along with his plan, but I don't see what my job at the Pink Cone has to do with anything.

"Does that woman—what's her name?—Renée something, still run that place?" Mom asks with sincere curiosity.

"The Fabulous Renée? Yeah."

And then I get it. Renée is the most prominent—heck, the only—gay person in Bell Cove, and while I wouldn't necessarily call my dad homophobic, I'm pretty sure he'd be less than thrilled to have his only son working for her. Working at an ice cream shop isn't exactly a "manly" job like landscaping in Georgia, and working for a lesbian is just the cherry on top, pun intended.

"You're going to have to tell him yourself. I'm not going to do your dirty work for you." As if to make her point, Mom gives the cupboard door a little extra shove as she closes it, causing a bang loud enough to make me jump.

I open my mouth to respond but realize I have no words that won't get me in trouble with her. The last thing I need is to have both parental units mad at me, and especially not the one I live with. I press my lips together and exhale through my nose loud enough for my mom to hear. She gives me a look that says, *You made your bed.*

"Can I at least wait until after dinner?"

I sit on the edge of my bed and punch in my father's number

on the phone keypad. I decided I wanted to be alone for this. The phone rings three times before someone picks up. A woman's voice answers.

"Hello?"

It's Jill, my dad's girlfriend. He met her up here in New Hampshire, and it's pretty serious because she agreed to move to Georgia with him. I don't really have anything against her; my parents have been divorced long enough that it's not like I have any secret wish for them to get back together.

"Hi, Jill. It's Sean. My dad there?"

"Sean! Excited about coming to visit? Your dad's right here. Hold on." I can just hear her say, "It's Sean," and I imagine her holding the phone out to my dad.

"Yello." My dad's distinct phone greeting. I guess it's a Southern thing. He's from the South originally, and he answered the phone that way even when he lived in New Hampshire.

"Hey, Dad."

"What's up, son?"

"I need to talk to you about coming to Georgia."

"Oh?"

"I really don't want to go."

"Your mom and I discussed this. It'll be good for you. I want to see you."

"But you didn't discuss it with me." I try hard to keep any anger out of my voice. I know that will get me nowhere.

There's several seconds of silence. "Let's discuss it now. Why don't you want to come?" I'm surprised how calm Dad is being. I wonder if Jill has anything to do with that.

"I have friends here."

"Your friends will still be there. Think of the stories you'll have to tell them when you get back."

"I don't need stories. Besides, I got a job."

"A job?"

"Mom said you guys thought I needed a summer job, so I went out today and found one."

"Doing what?" I can tell he's impressed that I've found a job so quickly. I may just win this battle.

"Um, working at the Pink Cone."

Dad starts to chuckle, but I can't tell if it's a good or a bad thing. After about twenty seconds, he says, "That lesbian woman still running that place?"

Mom was right. "Yeah, so?"

"So you're saying you'd rather spend a summer working for a dyke in an ice cream shop than spend it with me?" Okay, maybe a little homophobic.

"That's not what I said! What I said is I want to spend my summer here, with my friends, by the lake, and since you and Mom won't let me do that unless I also have a job, I went out and got one."

"That's not good enough. I already paid for your plane tickets."

"I'll pay you back. I'll send you the money from what I earn at my job."

"Sean, I'm your father. If I want you to spend the summer with me, you're going to spend it with me." There's a note of finality in his voice. The case is closed.

But I have one last Hail Mary. I take a deep breath and just blurt it out. "I don't want to spend the summer away from Lisa."

"Lisa?" I've caught him off guard, and he's listening.

"My girlfriend."

"I didn't know you had a girlfriend. How long has it been?"

"We were in the winter play together."

"So you're pretty serious?"

Not exactly. But if that's what you want to hear, "Yeah, we're serious."

"I can't believe you wouldn't tell me about having a girl-friend." He's silent for a long moment. I think he may have covered the phone receiver and is talking to Jill. When he returns, his tone is softer; it's Southern Gentleman Dad on the line now.

"Well, son, I was a teenage boy once. I know that I would have done just about anything to not leave my girlfriend for the entire summer. Can't say as I'm happy about it, but it sounds like you've got a good reason not to come visit me. Give my best to Lisa. I'm happy for you."

I fall back on my bed, relaxing for the first time since I'd picked up the phone. I can't believe that worked.

"I'm going to need to talk to your mother. She around?"

I call downstairs for Mom to pick up the phone and wait until I hear her come on the line. Mission accomplished. I feel a little weird about using Lisa to convince my dad to let me stay, especially since Lisa's going to be away at her summer camp all summer, but it's worth it. I'm sure Lisa wouldn't mind. After all, she *is* my girlfriend.

Chapter 2

Ice Cream Orientation starts in less than an hour, but I'm standing on the dock while Lisa drapes her arms around my shoulders. "I'm going to miss you," she whispers, letting one hand creep up the back of my neck where my brown hair is trimmed close. Lisa loves to rub this spot on my neck because she says it feels like velvet.

"It'll go by in no time." I remove my girlfriend's arms and straighten her shirt where it has bunched up while she hugged me. She smiles.

In the morning sun, Lisa's long blond hair is radiant, right out of a shampoo commercial. She's wearing a white T-shirt with a sunflower silk-screened on the front, and pink shorts that only go about halfway to the knees of her long, bronzed legs. She's beautiful in any light, but this light especially.

I've known Lisa since grade school, but we only started dating last November when we were both cast as the leads in *The Music Man.* My Harold Hill to her Marian the Librarian. The whole school was buzzing about how our stage romance extended into real life. I've always been a bit on the fringe in school—drama club, art club, band—but Lisa ran with the popular crowd, so by association I became popular, too. I may not be in love with Lisa, but I am in love with our relationship. I'm not sure I'm ready to give that up. But still, I'm happy that Lisa will be at camp most of the summer. I need the break. Playing the part of the perfect boyfriend becomes exhausting when your heart is just not into it.

Lisa doesn't look like she needs the break at all, not when she throws her arms around me again, but this time her lips go straight for mine. Lisa's not usually too big on PDA, but she's breaking her own rules this morning.

From the motorboat tied up next to us, her father breaks the mood. "C'mon, you two, say good-bye already. We're going to be late." I take the opportunity to end our embrace. I look at her dad and can feel my cheeks flushing with embarrassment. He looks amused though.

"All right, Dad," Lisa says over her shoulder and then turns back to me. She kisses me lightly on the cheek. I help her into the boat.

Looking up at me, Lisa smiles again. "It's only just across the lake." Her father starts the inboard motor, and the boat sputters briefly while he backs out of the slip. He shifts to forward and deftly steers the boat out of the marina. Lisa kneels on the back seat and waves to me.

"Finally," I say to myself. I wave to Lisa and wait patiently for her boat to get beyond the no-wake zone and speed around the point. While I stand there waving, another boat captures my attention, or rather, another boater. Even though my arm doesn't stop waving for Lisa, my eyes follow the new arrival as he rounds the point. His boat is a beautiful blue-and-white twenty-foot Craftsman, but my attention falls on his shirtless—and even from this distance I can sense—well-defined torso. The wind has tousled his hair, and I imagine it is streaked with blond from the same sun that has turned his skin caramel. As the boat drifts into clearer focus, I am surprised to discover that he's not much older than I am. Eighteen or nineteen, at most.

It's not until his boat bumps lightly against the dock that I realize my arm is still waving over my head, even though Lisa's boat is long out of sight. I hope the new arrival hasn't noticed.

"Hey," he calls up to me, a coil of yellow nylon in his right hand, "little help?" He makes as if to toss me the rope.

I nod, and he throws it up to me underhanded.

"Who were you waving to?" he asks while I kneel to secure the rope to a dock cleat.

"Uh, my friend Lisa. She's a counselor at Camp Aweelah."

"That the church camp on Rabbit Island?" He tosses me another rope to tie the stern. I nod. "That must be tough," he says.

"Huh?"

"Church girls."

I look up, not sure if I get his meaning. "She's not my girlfriend." I'm a terrible liar, and I can feel my face turning hot almost immediately.

He grabs a white T-shirt from the passenger seat of the boat and pulls it over his head. The crisp white against his deeply tanned skin is striking, and I suck in a quick breath of appreciation. I'm suddenly all too aware of my own pale complexion, and I make a mental note to be sure to get more sun this summer. He jumps up on the dock and looks down at me tying the cleat. From this angle I have a clear view of the stitching on the inseam of his cargo shorts. The T-shirt doesn't quite meet his waistband, and a thin strip of bronze skin is right at my eye level. Wisps of light brown hair converge in a neat line up to where his belly button should be under his shirt. My eyes are stuck on this inch of skin, and when I realize I'm staring, I look down at the cleat instead.

"You were waving a long time, so I figured, you know." He offers a hand to help me up. "Hey, don't sweat it. I'm Jay."

"Sean," I say as I take his hand. It is dry and smooth, not a boater's hand. I want to hang on, but he lets go once I get to my feet.

"Thanks for the help. Maybe I'll see you around." He smiles

and his teeth match the rest of him, perfect. Then he turns and walks down the dock. At the end he turns around briefly, probably to check his boat. I don't want him to see me staring, so I pretend I need to tie my shoe.

"Nice to meet you, too," I say to the toe of my Reebok.

When I look up from my sneaker, Jay has disappeared. I check my watch. I have Ice Cream Orientation in twenty minutes. A week ago, this seemed like a great idea, but now the thought of scooping mint chocolate chip for complaining senior citizens and whining four-year-olds doesn't necessarily seem better than landscaping in Georgia. But at least I'll stay cool. Sticking my hands in my pockets, I head down the docks toward the narrow white Victorian at the end of Main Street and my new summer job.

When the Fabulous Renée infamously stormed into town ten years back, she made more waves than the lake in a thunderstorm. First, it was the whole deal with the sign. What makes the Pink Cone stand out from all the other Victorian houses that dot the shores of Bell Cove is the enormous pink ice cream cone that sticks out like a clown nose from the front of the building, pointing passersby to the front door. Locals were furious. There was even a petition to have the sign removed. But Renée knew what she was doing, because that pink sign can be seen halfway across the lake, and it attracted a steady stream of boaters and tourists all summer. The increased traffic on Main Street also meant increased sales for other businesses, and by Labor Day the movement to have the sign removed had died. Now the sign is a landmark embraced by everyone; we call it "Bell Cone."

But Renée didn't stop there. She rode her business savvy to a term on the chamber of commerce, where she didn't make many new friends. She may have gotten her way on the sign, but her idea to attract summer business by hosting a Gay Pride festival didn't go over so well with the more conservative members of the chamber. She was forced out of the chamber, but the ice cream shop continued to bring customers to Bell Cove. And Renee's reputation as a crazy lesbian was cemented in the town's consciousness. Eight years later, and here I am, getting ready to work for the "dyke at the ice cream shop," as my dad put it.

There are five of us, and I am the only boy. Two of the girls huddle together, sophomores from Lakes Regional, which is two towns over from Bell Cove. They keep exchanging looks and giggling about everything. I hate them immediately. I know one of the other girls by sight. She's a grade ahead of me at Bell Cove High School, and she's in the band—flute—I think. She gives me a small smile of recognition when I walk in.

The last girl in the shop is hard to miss. First off, she's taller than I am, and outweighs my 155 pounds by a good 25 or 30. And most of that extra weight is right in the middle of her chest, which I can't help but stare at, not because of its ample size, but because she's wearing a bright orange T-shirt with a picture of a rabbi wearing dark sunglasses. The caption beneath the image is "Jew TALKING TO ME?" And I can't help but laugh. She's obviously not a local and I am surprised because usually only the locals take summer jobs. Summer people like this girl are typically on their vacations. The last time I checked, vacation and work were opposites, but maybe this summer girl didn't get the memo.

"Hi, I'm Becky!" she greets me with enthusiasm. "You must be Sean. I saw the orientation sheet, and there was only one boy's name on it, so I figure that must be you. Well, if you count Harleigh, I guess there were two boys' names, sorta, but since Harleigh's not a motorcycle, I pretty much figured it was a girl Harleigh and not a boy Harley."

I'm not sure how to respond to this so I just stand there and raise my eyebrows in what I hope is a friendly way.

"So, are you a local, too?" Becky says, gesturing to the others in the room. "They're all locals. I guess it's pretty unusual for a summer girl like me to get a job." She shrugs. "I get a job every summer if I can, otherwise I'd have to spend time with my family, and OMG, bo-ring!"

"Must be nice. I live down the road on Morgan Beach," I say, and I'm about to add that my family is pretty boring, too, but she cuts me off.

"You live *on* the beach? That must be great, to just go swimming whenever you want. In New York the best chance we have to swim is at the Y, and who really wants to swim at the Y, you know? I mean, for fun anyway. Most of the time the pool is only open for the old people doing water gymnastics or little kids taking lessons, so it's not like there's a lot of chances to swim."

Becky takes a breath but before she can continue, a voice takes us all by surprise.

"All right, kiddos! Prepare for your fabulous Ice Cream Orientation!" We turn to see a woman dressed head to toe in pink come gliding into the room with her arms spread wide. Held above her head, she has several bubble-gum pink T-shirts emblazoned with the store's hot-pink logo of an ice cream cone.

Becky throws me an elbow. "I guess she really likes pink, huh?"

"Shh." I elbow her back and can't help giggling. "That's our new boss."

"I know, the Fab-u-lous Renée," she says, accenting each syllable. "I met her yesterday. I overheard those girls talking before you got here. I guess she's a real bitch."

As if on cue, the Fabulous Renée turns and claps her hands at us. "Enough chitchat, you two! You're on the clock now. You're on Renée time!" She starts tossing us pink T-shirts. "Put these fabulous shirts on. You need to look the part."

One of the two girls from Lakes Regional starts to put the shirt on over the shirt she is already wearing. "You there," Renée whips around. "What's your name?"

"Me?" the girl asks.

"Yes, you. I'm not talking to the freezer."

"Harleigh."

"Well, Harleigh, what are you doing?"

"Putting the shirt on. I thought you said—"

"Not over your clothes. You'll look like a sack of potatoes!"

"Is there a place I can change, then?" Harleigh asks.

"What's wrong with right here?"

Harleigh doesn't say anything, just looks at me.

"You're wearing a bra, aren't you? It's just like wearing a bathing suit." Renée's tone has gone from manic to mean in about 2.4 seconds.

"It makes me uncomfortable."

"Well, maybe it makes me uncomfortable to have you working here," Renée shoots back.

I decide to play hero. "I'll turn my back," I say. Renée whirls around to face me and for half a second I think I am getting her wrath next, but instead she smiles.

"Well, well. What a gentleman."

Harleigh mouths me a silent thank you, and I turn around. We all change, and after about thirty seconds Renée declares, "Fabulous! Now you look the part! Don't you all look fabulous?"

I look down at my pink shirt and almost laugh. Renée may have provided me with a way to take care of my Lisa problem. One look at me in hot pink and Lisa should get the picture.

Renée claps her hands again. "Now let me introduce you to your trainer, ice cream scooper extraordinaire, Jay!"

I turn around and look right into the deep brown eyes of my acquaintance from the dock. Somehow he makes the pink shirt look good. I decide it's the tan.

"Hey, Sean." He smiles at me.

"Uh, hey, Jay." I cringe at the rhyme. I want to crawl under one of the freezers. Jay doesn't seem to notice, though, and walks to the front of our little group next to Renée.

"I'll take it from here, Renée. You've scared 'em enough."

Renée looks up at Jay and gives him a squinty-eyed smile.

Without taking her eyes off him she says, "Listen to Jay here. This is his third summer, and he knows everything there is to know about ice cream at the Pink Cone." Jay turns and smiles down at her, waiting for Renée to leave. When she doesn't take the hint right away, he gives her a little wave with the tips of his fingers. Dismissed.

Chapter 3

"You know him?" Becky whispers to me. "Get out!"

"I don't *know* him, I just *met* him, like, ten minutes ago out on the dock," I say.

"Well, he remembered your name. That's a good sign."

A good sign of what? I'm about to ask Becky, but before I can get the words out, Jay starts our orientation.

"All right everyone, listen up," he says. "Being a good scooper is as much a science as it is an art, but if you just follow my lead you'll be an expert in no time, and hopefully you'll have some fun doing it, too."

"I'd follow him anywhere," Becky says, shoving an elbow in my ribs.

"Ouch!" I say.

"Baby!" Becky elbows me again, even harder.

"Stop that!"

Jay interrupts us. "What's going on back there? Sean, you okay?"

"Uh, I'm fine. I mean, if Becky will stop harassing me."

"Listen, you two, you'll have to work out your problems on your own time." Jay gives us a look that says, *Grow up,* but the corner of his mouth goes up, and I know he is half amused, too.

"Okay," I say.

"Right, boss!" Becky throws Jay a salute and brings herself to attention.

"And, Sean," Jay says, "don't let the girls beat you up." This is, of course, followed by giggles from everyone else in the room. I roll my eyes, but I can't help smiling.

The first thing Jay teaches us is how the ice cream is made. He explains that the Fabulous Renée has a farm on the outskirts of town and all of the ingredients used in the ice cream come directly from the farm. He shows us how the cream is mixed with sugar and chocolate or fruit or whatever and put in this big mixer to churn or "cook" for about ten minutes. Then it's transferred to the deep freezer, which is kept at twenty below zero.

As soon as we walk into the freezer, Becky opens her mouth. "It's so cold I could cut diamonds with my nip . . . ouch!" I give her a quick stomp on the foot.

"You two again?" Jay says to us, smiling, as he takes down an already frozen batch of ice cream and leads us out of the freezer.

Becky and I are the last ones out the door, and she says, "I think he likes you," before turning to leave.

"What?" I say to her back. "What? Did I hear you right?" Becky just shrugs her shoulders and follows the others to where Jay is explaining how the frozen ice cream needs to stay on the warming table for about an hour so it will get to "scooping temperature."

"Why would you say that?" I say under my breath.

"Because he does. Don't you like him? I mean, I'd be all over him if I were you," Becky says to me.

"I'm not gay," I whisper.

"Don't be silly." Becky looks me up and down, letting her

eyes linger on my pink T-shirt. She finally looks up and pats my shoulder. "Of course you are."

Jay heads over to a couple of freezer chests in the rear of the shop. He explains to the others that these chests are the backup freezers, where the ice cream waits until it is needed in the freezers near the front of the store. I hold Becky back.

"Why would you say that?" I give her my most serious look.

"Hon, a Jewish girl from New York can just tell these things."

"You're wrong."

"If you say so." But she doesn't look convinced. Instead she wraps an arm around my shoulder and leads us back to the group.

By this time, Jay is at the front of the store where the scooping takes place. He explains that the ice cream is kept in two-and-a-half-gallon plastic containers, and each container has fifty scoops of ice cream. By the time he rolls up his sleeves to his coffee-ice-cream tanned shoulders so that he can demonstrate proper scooping technique, he has my full attention. Jay, the ice cream professor.

Half an hour later, Jay informs us that we have thirty minutes for lunch, and when we return he'll explain how to make all of the sundaes, milk shakes, and banana splits.

"Make sure you save room for dessert," he says to us on our way out. I'm not sure if I'm imagining things, but I could swear he looks right at me when he says this.

Despite the fact that Becky seems to be able to see right through me, I decide to eat lunch with her anyway. I packed a bag lunch—peanut butter and jelly and a juice box—but Becky leads me down the street to Mr. Mike's, a gas station convenience store.

Becky grabs a bag of Doritos, a Slim Jim, and a bottle of Diet Coke and takes them to the register. I wonder if Jews are allowed to eat Slim Jims.

"I think this might be my best summer job yet," Becky says to me while she pays the old man at the counter. His expressionless face never changes as he plunks down her change and turns back to his sports pages. "You have a nice day, too, now." Becky throws a sarcastic wave over her shoulder as she heads out the door. The man gives a slight nod from behind his paper, but he might have just been falling asleep.

We sit on a bench that looks out at the marina to eat our lunches. "This is going to be way better than dressing up as a taco like I did last summer," Becky says, popping a Dorito in her mouth.

"A taco?" I ask.

"You know, for one of those fast-food joints. I had to wear this ridiculous suit and hand out flyers for a dollar off a combo meal. It wasn't so bad except the suit itched like crazy, especially when it got hot."

"That must have sucked," I say. I'm dying to ask her about her comment earlier, but I don't know how to bring it up without seeming obvious.

"Oh, I can make anything fun, for a while anyway," Becky says to me. "I've had at least one summer job every year since I was twelve. The worst one was cleaning out the stables on my uncle's horse farm. After you spend a summer shoveling shit, you really know how to shovel shit."

Becky crumples her Doritos bag and aims at a trash barrel sitting by the nearest dock. She shoots, and it bounces off the edge before falling in.

"Two points!" Becky throws her arms over her head in mock celebration.

I laugh at her antics, but I'm thinking about how best to bring up the gay thing. I take a bite of PB and J and chew slowly. Becky puts one end of the Slim Jim in her mouth and uses her teeth to peel back the wrapper.

"Becky?" I say through a mouthful of peanut butter. It comes out more like "buggy," but I guess Becky knows peanut butter speak because she stops peeling and looks at me.

"Yeah?" She can tell I'm uncomfortable. She looks down at

the Slim Jim she's about to stuff in her mouth and a look of recognition crosses her face. "Don't worry. I'm not kosher," she says, as if that will make me feel better.

I struggle to swallow my mouthful of peanut butter. "It's not that," I say when I have proper use of my tongue again. "I want to know why you would say what you said. About Jay?"

Becky twists on the bench so she's facing me. "You mean about him liking you?"

I nod.

"Don't you like him?"

"I told you, I'm not gay."

"Proof." It's half question, half statement. When I don't answer right away, she bites off the end of the Slim Jim as if this settles everything.

"So now I have to prove that I'm straight? Is this some kind of witch hunt?" I am thinking about when we read *The Crucible* in English and we learned that in Medieval Europe they tested suspected witches by drowning them or burning them at the stake. The idea was that if the accused was a witch she would use her powers to escape, thus exposing herself as a witch. If she didn't escape, then she probably wasn't a witch. Of course, she was also dead.

"Well, do you have a girlfriend?"

I smile. "Yes." *So there.*

Becky holds up a hand. "Let me guess. She's a good Christian girl, wants to save herself for marriage, really into hugs?"

My mouth goes slack, and all I can do is stare at her. Lisa is a good Christian girl, and she is saving herself for marriage. Becky should be a late-night TV psychic. 1-900-BECKY-TELLS-ALL. Only $3.99 a minute.

It's not like Lisa and I never do anything—I mean, several of our dates have ended on the swing on her front porch with plenty of kissing. She's tried unbuttoning my shirt a few times, too, and I've found my hand inside her blouse on occasion. But no article of clothing has ever been removed, no belts have been undone, zippers have always stayed in place. And that has always been fine with me. It's been a relief to me that Lisa doesn't want more—I'm not sure I could give it to her if she did.

As if reading my mind—again—Becky chimes in with, "I thought so." She repositions herself so she can put her arm around me. "Listen, everyone comes out on their own timeline, so I'm not going to say anything else. But it sounds to me like this girlfriend"—she does finger quotes as she says "girlfriend"—"is just a beard."

"A what?"

"A beard. It's a term for someone who is used as a cover-up, like a disguise. There was a *Seinfeld* about it."

For a minute I don't say anything. I just stare out at the lake and think about what Becky has said. For some reason I trust her.

"What if I were?"

Becky stops eating the Slim Jim and looks over at me. I look back, meeting her gaze for a second before turning away again. She doesn't say anything, but her eyes say, *Go ahead*.

"What if I were . . ." I can't explain why the word *gay* is so hard to say out loud. With somebody listening. I've said it to myself a hundred times before, but I guess if someone else hears, I'm afraid it will make it true. But if it is true, then why can't I say it? Why am I so afraid of what everyone will think? Why is admitting that I'm gay so scary? I take a breath.

"What if I were . . . gay?"

"I wouldn't care," Becky says. I must look skeptical because she continues. "My family lives near Chelsea and my parents have lots of gay friends. I have lots of gay friends. I'm even vice president of my high school's GSA."

"G-S-who?"

"It stands for Gay-Straight Alliance. It's a club that promotes tolerance and diversity. My point is your being gay wouldn't make a difference to me."

I swallow my last bite of sandwich. "I'm not saying I am, just what if, you know?"

"I hear you," Becky says. "It takes a lot of chutzpah to come out, especially in a small town like this. You gotta make that decision for yourself. Listen, I'm sorry I made that joke about Jay earlier. I didn't mean to make you uncomfortable." She squeezes my shoulder. "But for the record, I do think he likes you."

On my bike ride home, I let my mind wander to what Becky said about not caring if I am gay. I actually believe her, but the thing is, I'm not sure everyone else will feel the same way. I mean, if it doesn't matter if you're gay, then why aren't there more gay people in Bell Cove? Renée is the only one I know, and it's not exactly like she's been welcomed with open arms. Sure, the chamber of commerce is happy with the customers she brought to town, but people still say nasty things behind her back. Heck, even my father calls her a dyke.

If that's what he thinks about Renée, what would he think about me? His son the fag? I bet he wouldn't be asking me to come to Georgia for the summer then. Maybe that's what I should have told him last week to get him to let me stay in Bell Cove instead of lying about not wanting to be away from Lisa. At least it would have been closer to the truth.

My mother might be better, but even her I'm not sure about. If I just walk in the door and tell her, "Mom, I'm gay," I have no idea what she'd do. I'm thinking she'd probably regret letting me take the job at the Pink Cone, for starters. There's a decent chance I'd find myself on the next plane to Georgia so my father could straighten me out. I don't think she'd be mad, though. At least not at me.

Becky's talk of GSAs and having gay friends in school is great and all, but it's just talk. Bell Cove is not New York City, and there are no gay people at my school. I'm not about to be the first.

But I'm not in school. It's the summer. And Jay is gorgeous. And Becky thinks he likes me. Is that just talk, too?

Chapter 4

It's Tuesday afternoon, the day after orientation at the Pink Cone, and I look up at the clock above the deep freezer. It's almost four o'clock. My first real shift flew by. It wasn't that busy, but with so much to learn, I felt like I was constantly moving. I slide a freshly made container of strawberry onto a shelf in the freezer and return to the warmth of the shop.

"Becky, you doing anything after this?" I call across to where she stands by one of the service windows.

"Nah. Wanna hang out?" She checks her watch. "I think we're done here."

We say good-bye to Harleigh and Ashley, our evening replacements, and head out into the June warmth.

"So, what's fun to do around here?" Becky says.

"I dunno. You hungry?"

"I am always hungry, but let's not get ice cream." Becky laughs at her joke, but I have to admit I feel the same way. One day of scooping butter pecan, and I am already sick of ice cream. Of course, it may have something to do with the triple-scoop sundae I had on my break.

I grab my bike from behind the shop, and Becky and I walk down the street to the Gold House sub shop. The Gold House's claim to fame is their Greek salad and their onion rings. I think I could go for one of each right now. We arrive at the square brick building. A bell chimes when we open the door and walk into the hideously painted interior.

"I see why they call it the Gold House," Becky says, surveying the yellow walls and gaudy bronze statues of Greek gods.

"The food is great. Don't worry, we'll eat out by the lake," I say.

"Good, then I'll be able to take off my sunglasses. This place is blinding."

Ten minutes later, to-go containers in hand, we head outside to find a place to eat. We stop at a picnic table in a small park next to the marina. As we spread out the food on the table, there's one thought I can't get out of my head.

"Why did you assume I was . . . liked Jay, yesterday?" Why is the word gay so difficult to say?

"Hmm?" Becky is already chewing a piece of pita, and she points to her mouth in the universal sign for, "My mouth is full."

"I mean, you just assumed, and I want to know why. It wasn't just the pink shirt, right?"

Becky swallows. "Hon, it was definitely not the pink shirt. I mean, 'It takes a real man to wear pink.' " Becky makes finger quotes in front of her face. "Whatever that means. It's hard for me to say for sure. It's just a vibe I got, I guess."

"A vibe?"

"Well, I don't know. You were really sweet to Harleigh about the whole shirt-changing thing."

"You thought I was . . . that I liked boys because I was polite?" I say.

"There was also the look you got when Jay walked in."

"Look? I was surprised to see him again."

"I just call 'em how I see 'em. I'm sorry that it bothered you this much. Why do you care so much, anyway?"

I take a deep breath and let it out. Why did I bring this up?

Becky sees my discomfort and tries to break the tension. She holds up two onion rings, one by each ear. "What do you think?" she says, "Are these, like, totally hot, or what?" She turns her head from side to side like a model. "They're the new environmentally conscious accessories. When you're ready for a new look, just eat the old ones!"

I have to admit she's funny, but I just don't feel like laughing. I'm too bothered by Becky's ability to see right through me.

Becky keeps trying. "Look, from hoops to drops with one bite." She takes a bite out of each ring and then lets the remaining onion dangle down. She shakes her head and the onions wiggle like worms. "Why aren't you laughing?"

"Because you're not the first person to assume I'm ... not straight. And I want to know what it is about me that makes people think ..." For some reason the words won't come out.

"You're gay?" Becky adds for me.

I nod. "I mean, I don't prance around lisping and singing show tunes."

"Not being a stereotype is a good thing," Becky says. "Look, being gay isn't about how you talk and what you wear. It's about who you're attracted to. I mean, I like to say I'm a JustinTimberlakeosexual." Becky gives me a grin.

"But if I'm not a stereotype, how can people just ... tell? I mean at school, in the hallways, in the café, at gym. It's constant. If I miss a shot in volleyball, I'm a fag. If I get an A on a test, I'm a queer. Bump into someone in the hallway and I'm a homo. It's everywhere I turn, and I don't know how to stop it. Teachers don't do anything. I can't fight." I feel tears pushing at the backs of my eyes. Why do I feel like crying? Somehow Becky has unlocked a part of me that I have kept locked away for years. God, with emotions as out of control as this, no wonder everyone thinks I'm gay.

"Sean, did it ever occur to you that everyone gets called

those things? Most people probably don't think you're gay; they probably don't think about it at all. That doesn't make it right, but it doesn't mean they know how you feel. Kids are cruel, and they don't think."

I sniff back my tears, but I know Becky has already seen them. "But, Becky . . ."

"Yeah?"

"I *am* gay." It comes out in one quick breath and with it every brick in my carefully constructed wall of defense crumbles.

Becky doesn't say anything, and for a second I think she won't accept me the way I thought she would, the way she said she would. I can't look at her. She seemed like such a safe bet, like no one I'd ever met in New Hampshire.

The silence between us stretches, and the longer it gets the harder it is to break. But then Becky reaches across the table and takes my hands. I look up and I see now it's her eyes that are wet.

"Are you crying?" I say.

"No. I mean, yes." Becky takes back a hand to wipe her eyes. "I'm so proud of you."

"You are?"

"That was the first time, right?"

"Yeah. I've never said that to a real person before."

"It was my first time, too."

I shake my head. "Huh?"

"No one has ever come out to me for the first time before. I know plenty of gay people, but they all came out way before they met me. This is totally different. That's a lot of trust you just put in me, and I'm honored."

"I thought for a minute you were mad."

Becky laughs softly. "Why would I be mad?"

"I don't know, I just, I thought . . . Never mind. Just never mind."

Becky picks up an onion ring and slides it onto my finger. I look at her in confusion.

"It's a promise ring," she says. "I promise to keep your secret until you are ready."

A smile breaks out on my face. "Thanks," I say.

"Well, you better eat it. It's getting cold."

Chapter 5

Becky and I walk down Main Street, heading toward the Methodist church. The sun is still high over the lake, and a cool breeze comes in off the water. Although it's still the tail end of June, July is around the corner and the days have been very warm and humid. Some of the older couples that stopped by the Cone today remarked on the heat, and they were quick to tell me, when I gave them their "baby cones," that it's "goin' to be a scorcha." It's a funny thing about baby cones. The only people who seem to buy them are senior citizens. I guess "senior cone" doesn't sound as appealing, but I do think "baby cone" is a bad name.

"So, what next?" Becky says. We're a block from the church and after that there isn't much Main Street left to walk.

I point to the bike I've been pushing as we walk. "Do you have a bike? We could ride to the top of Mann's Hill and watch the sun set. You can see the whole town from there."

Becky shrugs. "No bike, but it sounds cool."

"I bet my mom would let you borrow hers. It's a little old, but it has two wheels and a seat."

So I lead Becky past the church until Main Street forks. The left fork goes up to the state highway, but the right fork follows the shoreline and leads to a crescent of sand hidden away in a small cove. Morgan Beach is an eclectic mix of aging hippie artists and young families. Many lawns are decorated with strange wood and metal sculptures with meanings known only to the sculptors, while here and there you can see a swing set or a Big Wheel that has replaced the artwork. Most of the houses started as small summer cottages for families from Boston or New York who would spend the whole season trying to stay cool in the lake surf or hiking in the woods. Over time, cottages were winterized, added on to, or torn down and rebuilt, so that now Morgan Beach is a collection of clashing architectures and styles, thrown haphazardly together.

My house is a low rectangular box with a slate roof that slopes up and away from the front door. It is built into the hill so you walk into the second floor, and the first floor is half buried and hidden from the street view. But it's not the wood-shingled front that is the impressive feature of my house; it's the two-story wall of glass overlooking the lake in the back that catches people's attention. In fact, it was the enormous windows that made my mother insist on buying the house in the first place. My father had wanted to live in town, and he didn't like the modern style of the house, but my mother, as usual, got her way. Looking back, it's easy to see why my parents are divorced; they couldn't, and still can't, agree on anything.

I lean my bike against the garage and let Becky in to give her a quick tour of my house. She is definitely impressed by the view, but even more impressed by the artwork hanging in the kitchen. She stands admiring an abstract canvas while I fill a couple of water bottles for us.

"Where did you get this painting? It's beautiful," she says.

"That one, I did."

"No!" Becky wheels on her heel and hits me in the shoulder.

"Ow. Why did you do that?"

"You didn't tell me that you're an artist."

"I'm not. At least, not really. I took art last year, and that was my assignment on Jackson Pollock and action painting." I hand Becky a water bottle. "It was actually a lot of fun. I spent a week dripping paint while standing on a stepladder."

"I love it. You must have been happy when you were painting it. The colors are so bright."

"Yeah, I guess that was a good week. I got the lead in the winter play that week." I pull Becky away from the painting. "C'mon, we're gonna miss the sunset."

"Omigod, another OGT!" Becky follows me to the front door. "So you do drama club and take art and you don't know why people think you're gay? Sean, those are both OGTs!"

"OGT?"

"Obviously Gay Trait. Don't tell me you've never seen *The Broken Hearts Club?*"

We've crossed the driveway to the detached garage, but I stop before opening the garage door.

"Is that a movie?" I say.

"Yes! It's about a bunch of gay guys who live in Los Angeles and try to find boyfriends. It's like *Sex in the City* for gays." Becky looks at me for recognition, but I'm clueless. "We are so watching that movie tonight. It can be your first out-of-the-closet-gay movie."

"I don't think we'll find it at the video store."

"Doesn't matter. It's on Netflix streaming. You are going to love it."

I bend to lift the garage door.

"Okay, so what exactly is an Obviously Gay Trait?"

"It's, like, something that a lot of gay guys have in common. Sort of like a stereotype, but not so negative. You know, like being artistic, or matching your clothes, or liking Lady Gaga."

"I love Lady Gaga!"

"See?"

Becky and I laugh and grab the bikes from against the side of the garage. I lead her out of Morgan Beach and back toward town. There's a small hill heading into town, and I stop pedaling and let gravity do the work. I have to think about this OGT phenomenon. Have I really been doing all these things that make me "obviously gay"? I'm also curious about this movie Becky mentioned. The Bell Cove Cinema only has one screen, and it's safe to say it doesn't play any movies about guys trying to find boyfriends. I'm going fast enough as we approach the church that I don't need to hold on to the handlebars. I throw my hands up in the air and let out a whooping scream. It's going to be a beautiful sunset.

Chapter 6

I'm lying in bed and I can't sleep. Thoughts shoot around the inside of my head like a pinball machine on multi-ball. I can't believe I had the guts to tell someone what I've been feeling. It was scary, and I did cry a little, but Becky was awesome. She somehow knew how to make me feel safe and accepted, even though she said it was the first time anyone's ever come out to her. I wonder if it's always like that. I'm guessing not. I mean, I just don't think my mom will take it as well as Becky did.

But I do think my mother is going to be okay with it.

I think.

After all, my mother is a guidance counselor. She deals with kids' problems all the time, and her job is to be understanding and not judgmental. Of course, it's different when you have to deal with your own child. I'm still not convinced I won't be on the next plane to Georgia.

And what about Lisa? For the past seven months I've reveled in telling anyone who would listen that I was dating the prettiest girl in school, and the smartest girl, and the nicest. Lisa, student council president, lead in the school musical, honor roll, my girlfriend, Lisa. How do you break up with someone like that? Why would anyone break up with someone like that? I mean, how do you tell the perfect girlfriend you're breaking up with her? How do you tell your girlfriend that you're gay?

In my defense, I didn't even know I was gay when I started dating Lisa. I mean, I had my suspicions, but I didn't *know.* Truthfully, I've always had crushes on boys. Boys *and* girls, actually. It just never really occurred to me that I had to choose. I guess maybe it should have, but when you're eight, boys and girls pretty much look the same.

Right about the time that the girls in my class started getting boobs, I started realizing that I was having fewer and fewer crushes on them. At the same time, when Marty Allengari grew three inches before seventh grade, I couldn't help but notice how his formerly pudgy features had become gaunt and, dare I say it, sexy. And who couldn't notice the fine wisps of a mustache that appeared on Kyle Reid's upper lip in eighth grade? I've always just naturally gravitated toward liking the boys ahead of the girls, but it wasn't until the end of middle school, when I realized I didn't have a single crush on a girl, that I started to worry. Could I really be gay? Impossible, I told myself, and set out to find the cure.

And that's where Lisa comes in. I spent my entire freshman year avoiding the subject of sex. I changed clothes in a bathroom stall in gym. I only went to dances with a large group of friends. I daydreamed during health class. I wouldn't even watch romantic comedies at the movies. But I couldn't avoid it. Sex was literally everywhere, and it seemed like everyone around me was pairing up. By sophomore year I had given up avoiding sex and decided that what I really needed was a girlfriend.

I guess part of me thought that if I got a real girlfriend I would stop being attracted to boys. Of course, in order to not be attracted to boys I would need to be attracted to girls, and I have finally concluded that I am not and never will be. And it's not like Lisa isn't a great choice for a girlfriend either; most of the boys in my high school class would give their left nut to date a girl like Lisa. Of course, it's this eagerness that gave me such an advantage in the first place.

Let me explain. Lisa is a girl with what she calls "morals." In other words, she is intending to wait for marriage before having sex, and I think she feels that some horndog who is constantly pressuring her for sex would be too much temptation to handle. So, of course, I'm the perfect match for the chastity-challenged. No pressure here. Sex with Lisa isn't even on my radar. Although I do actually kind of enjoy kissing. It's just that every time she takes my hand and tries to slide it under her shirt, my mind starts to drift somewhere else, somewhere more . . . masculine. I fantasize about the washboard abs and firm pecs of any one of a dozen teen idols or Abercrombie & Fitch models, but never once does my mind land on Lisa. But how do I tell *her* that?

I take some deep breaths. There's plenty of time to figure that out. Lisa is safely away at summer camp. I look at my bedside clock. It's two thirty. My mom gave Becky a ride to her family's cottage almost three hours ago, but I just can't get these thoughts out of my head. I have to work again tomorrow at ten thirty, so I really need to get to sleep. I close my eyes and try to force myself to relax.

"I did it," I say to the dark room. "I did it. I'm gay. I'm gay. I'm gay."

There's power in those words. They're comforting. They put me to sleep.

Chapter 7

"That's the last one!" Becky shouts over her shoulder, sliding the little pass-through window closed with a cracking thunk, an exclamation point to end the shift. It has been an incredibly busy night, and we all smile with relief that it's over. It's still unseasonably warm, and it seemed like everyone had the same idea for how to cool off. We must have served cones to three-quarters of Bell Cove. We went through almost fifty gallons of ice cream.

After about twenty-five gallons, I started scooping ice cream with my left hand. It was hard at first, but after a little practice I declared myself an ambidextrous scooper.

When I was in fourth grade, we did this project where we had to read a book about a famous athlete and do a book report on it. I got some famous tennis player who I guess my teacher, Mr. Hanson, really liked. I had never heard of Roy Emerson. Anyway, the only thing I remember about the book I had to read was this picture that showed Roy's arms, and in the picture, Roy's left arm, his tennis arm, was twice as big around as his right arm. It was freakish. It was like he was some kind of Frankenstein's monster and he had been put together with arms from two different corpses: one from a bodybuilder and one from some Joe Schmo. I couldn't get that picture out of my head. I was terrified I would wake up at the end of the summer, look in the mirror, and realize I had turned into Roy Emerson. That I would have to go back to school and everyone would start calling me Frankenstein or something. So I learned to scoop with my left hand.

But seriously, scooping is way harder work than I thought it would be. Not only does your arm ache at the end of a shift, but you are sticky up to your elbows, and you can barely feel your fingers from the cold. I asked Jay how he can stand it, and he told me that eventually you get used to it. He said that your arm muscles strengthen and once you get the technique down the sticky part goes away, too. Of course, Jay never scoops anymore. He's always the helper, making sure that the main freezers are stocked and that the right kind of ice cream gets made and the soft-serve machine doesn't run out. The advantages of being the manager apparently include avoiding frostbite. I'll remember that for next summer.

I snap the lid tightly onto the last plastic container of ice cream and shut the door on the freezer. Jay walks out of the deep freezer and latches it carefully behind him.

"All right. Call it a night. Good work, you two. I'll tell Renée she's going to have to start scheduling an extra person if it stays warm like this. It's a little early for the summer rush, but apparently the tourists don't know that yet."

"I'm wiped," Becky says, pushing her hair behind her ears. "I swear, if I had to scoop one more cone, someone would have been walking home funny!"

"Becky!" I scold her, but I can't help laughing at the same time.

"Well, as far as I'm concerned the night is just getting started," Jay says. "It's only ten o'clock. You guys want to hang out?"

Becky and I give each other a sideways glance. We're both thinking the same thing: why would Jay want to hang out with us?

"I was supposed to go to a club in Manchester with a couple

of buddies of mine, but I got a text earlier, and they all bailed. I don't really feel like going alone," Jay offers in response to our skeptical looks. "You guys are cool. We could pick up a pizza at Porfido's Market and hang out on my boat."

"I'm in." I try not to sound too eager. I can't believe Jay wants to hang out with me.

"It sounds like fun to me," Becky says, "but I think I have to pass. A girl needs her beauty sleep. You two have fun."

"Becky! You have to come!" I give her a look that I hope says, *Don't leave me alone with him.* When it was going to be the three of us, it seemed safe and a little bit exciting. Without Becky, I'm afraid of making a fool of myself. I'm afraid I'll have nothing to talk about, or worse, that I might try to talk and prove my loser status in front of Jay.

Becky tilts her head and lets her eyes do all the talking. She's telling me that I shouldn't worry so much.

"It is kind of late," I say.

Jay has a half smile on his face. He shakes his head just a little, and turns to go to the back room to grab his stuff.

"It's just an idea," he says over his shoulder. "Don't sweat it." He leaves the room and immediately Becky shoves an elbow in my ribs.

"Ow! What's that for?"

"Stop being a baby. Go with him."

"Not without you."

"Sean, this is the chance you've been waiting for."

"No, this is the chance *you've* been waiting for." I can feel the heat rush to my face.

"He obviously likes you, otherwise he wouldn't have invited you. You like him, don't you?"

"You don't even know if he likes guys. And anyway, he invited us."

"He was being polite."

"Becky, I can't. I mean, I like him and all, but I'm scared to be alone with him. I mean, I've been—" I feel the word catch in my throat for just a moment. I'm still getting used to the sound of it. "—*gay*—for less than two weeks."

"Sean, you've been gay your whole life. It only seems scary because you've never allowed yourself to feel what you're feeling right now. What do you think is gonna happen anyway?"

Her question catches me off guard. What am I so scared of? Is it that a small part of me still thinks I can go back to pretending, that if I fall for a guy there'll be no turning back? The only person I've come out to is Becky, and she'll be gone at the end of the summer. She's safe. I'm not sure I'm ready for the next step or even the possibility of the next step. I open my mouth to tell Becky this when Jay returns. He's changed out of his gaudy Pink Cone T-shirt, and the tight black one he's put on shows off his muscled shoulders and toned chest. I swallow to keep my jaw from dropping.

"I brought this along because I thought I was going out tonight," he says. "Have you guys decided what you're doing? Porfido's weekly special is Hawaiian."

I can't speak, but fortunately Becky is never at a loss for words. "Oh, I can't do Hawaiian. Not kosher."

I look over at her. Not kosher? As if.

"But you two go. I'll tag along next time."

She gives me a push, and before I can turn around to stop her, she's out the door, leaving me alone. With Jay.

"Just you and me, then?" He walks past me and I can smell the cologne he must have put on when he was changing. He hits the light switch by the door. I stand there in the dark, frozen. "You coming?"

"Huh? Oh, yeah." I turn around and follow him out the door.

Chapter 8

"Hold this."

I'm standing in Jay's boat as he hands me the pizza box and the bag with the sodas we picked up at Porfido's. I can feel the warmth of the pizza seeping through the thin cardboard. It smells of melted cheese and warm bread, and I realize exactly how hungry I am. Scooping ice cream can really make you work up an appetite.

Jay runs around to the front of the boat and unties the bowline. He runs back and jumps down beside me in one practiced motion. I'm impressed with his agility. I've been in boats plenty of times, heck, I grew up on the lake, but Jay moves with a confidence that eludes me.

"You just gonna stand there all night?" Jay asks with gentle sarcasm. He is reaching over the back of the boat and untying the aft line. His loose-fitting cargo shorts have slipped down a few inches, and I can see he is wearing a pair of blue-and-black plaid boxer shorts. Thank goodness I have the pizza to distract me.

"What? Oh. The pizza." I turn in circles looking for a place to put the pizza, but every surface of this boat seems to be curved and futuristic. I feel so helpless.

"Here." Jay turns and pulls out a collapsible table from some mysterious hidden panel. He takes the pizza from me, and his hand brushes mine. Was it my imagination or was it on purpose? I let my hands drop to my side and turn away, embarrassed. They're shaking, and I stick them into the pockets of my shorts. Why is this so nerve-racking? It was never like this with Lisa. With her, I knew she liked me, and I knew what to do.

"You gonna eat? Sean, you still with me?"

I turn around to look at Jay. He's holding a piece of pizza in his hand, carefully folding it so the sauce doesn't drip. He smiles at me. My stomach does a somersault, but his smile puts me a little more at ease.

"Yeah." I take a piece out of the box. The cheese has cooled enough so it breaks away easily from the others. I can smell the salty Canadian bacon slices and spicy tomato sauce. Porfido's Hawaiian is the best in town because they use real Canadian bacon instead of regular ham. It makes all the difference.

Jay pats me on the back before heading to the controls. My skin tingles through my shirt where he touches me. It's only a pat on the back, I tell myself, but somehow it feels, I don't know, deliberate, like he went out of his way to do it. I still don't know why Becky is so sure that Jay is into guys, but with every brush of a hand, pat of the back, I wish harder that she's right. Jay turns the ignition and the inboard motor sputters to life with a low gurgle.

"You might want to take a seat," Jays says. He waits for me to find a perch on the leatherette-covered bench at the back of the boat and then guns the throttle. The motor behind me roars, the bow lifts out of the water, and we are off. Suddenly, the lights of the marina are a hundred yards behind us, and the darkness is only broken by the boat's running lights. It's a quiet night, and the lake surface is glassy. The night air is warm, but a fine mist floats up from where the boat's hull breaks the water. The mist cools my face, and the breeze created as we speed around the point pulls my hair back off my forehead with dozens of invisible fingers. I look behind us and watch the wake spread out in a frothy fan, marking how far we've gone. I turn back and catch Jay looking at me over his shoulder. His face is pink in the glow from the running lights, and I can see he is smiling. But he turns away after a second, and I'm not sure if he was smiling at me, or what.

I take a bite of my pizza and look up at the stars above me. It's funny, because as fast as we are moving in the boat, the stars are fixed points, stationary. There are no clouds to block the view, and the moon is only a crescent off to the east, not bright enough to outshine the stars. They look like tiny grains of salt spilled across a black tablecloth.

Jay pulls back the throttle, and the boat slows. He kills the motor, and suddenly it's quiet, peaceful. The boat lurches slightly as our own wake overtakes us, but then we settle in the calm waters that splash against the hull in whispered gurgles. Jay comes to take another slice of pizza. He takes a bite and stands over me, chewing. I look up, smile slightly, timidly, without showing any teeth. The white running light on the back of the boat illuminates his face. He is looking at me.

"Beautiful," he says.

Is he talking to me? "What?"

"The stars. I like to come out here at night. The lake is the best place to see the stars. There's no trees or streetlights, and if the moon's not too bright, you can see everything."

I adjust my gaze upward from his face to the sky. He's right; growing up in New Hampshire, I'm used to starlit nights, but out here on the lake is incredible. I wish I had my star chart, or even my telescope, a birthday gift from my father, who also sent me to astronomy camp last summer.

The leatherette squeaks with Jay's weight. I'm aware that he's suddenly right beside me. Close. I get a whiff of his cologne again, sweet and spicy like sandalwood.

Having Jay so close to me is exhilarating but scary. Certainly he wouldn't be so close if he wasn't interested in me, a little voice inside me whispers. But a much louder voice screams in my ears, *Don't assume anything!*

Jay throws his crust out into the lake. The splash shatters the placid surface. "Look, it's Orion." He points off to the right to the telltale stars of Orion's belt hanging just above the trees.

"Still pretty low in the sky," I say. "It'll be higher up in August."

"You've done this before," Jay says, turning to face me.

"Yeah. I mean no, I haven't been out . . . I mean, well, my dad sent me to astronomy camp last summer."

Jay chuckles. "Well then, Galileo, where's the North Star?"

"Over there." I point to a star almost directly above the boat. Suddenly, I feel Jay's head on my shoulder. He's using my arm as a sight, and his ear is right on top of the rounded part of my shoulder. His soft, sun-streaked hair tickles my neck. I can't control myself, I jerk away.

"Sorry," I say, embarrassed. "You surprised me."

"It's okay." Jay smiles. He seems unfazed by my dorkiness. "Show me." He drapes his left arm around my shoulders and with his right he gently takes my hand in his. I can feel the muscles in his arms, the warmth of his body against mine.

He raises my arm toward the sky, and I point out the North Star for him again. This time I don't panic at his touch. "It's not that bright," he says.

"No, it's not important because of its intensity. Sailors used it because its relative position is always the same so they could navigate with it. It's like a natural compass. The other stars change position as the seasons change, but Polaris, I mean the North Star, doesn't—"

Jay's hand leaves mine and lands on my lips. "Shh."

I freeze. Was I talking too much?

"Shh," Jay says again, but this time he lowers my hand and turns me to face him. The leatherette squeaks. What a stupid thing to notice when a gorgeous boy is staring directly into your eyes. And he is. Staring. "I'm going to kiss you," he says.

I swallow. Did I hear him right? I croak out a weak, "Okay." And before I know it Jay leans in and his lips are against mine. They are soft but firm like a ripe plum, warm and dry. They carry with them some mysterious power that fills me from the head down. I'm reminded of Rogue from the X-Men, how she drains the life from anyone she touches. This is the opposite. He keeps his mouth closed, but he holds his lips against mine, pressing slightly, and I'm aware of his hand on my neck, his fingers creeping through the short hair on the back of my head.

Then he parts his lips just slightly. It feels natural for me to match his movement. I feel his tongue slide between my lips and run along my teeth. The electricity surges through my body, down through my chest, my stomach, and suddenly to my legs. The reaction is almost instant, and I feel myself pressing against my shorts. I open my eyes, which I didn't even realize were closed. I pull back. Jay doesn't fight me.

"What's wrong?" he asks with genuine concern.

I stare back with an open mouth. I can still feel his heat pulsing on my lips. I can't say anything, but somehow he reads my mind.

"Have you ever kissed a boy before?"

I shake my head.

He smiles and covers his mouth with his hand. I think he is laughing at me, and it hurts. I try to turn away, but there isn't very far to go. Jay reaches out and puts his hand on my shoulder. When he speaks he is close to my ear.

"Sean, I like you, but I didn't know you hadn't . . . I mean, I should have guessed, what with your girlfriend and all, but . . . "

"I'm sorry." I don't know what else to say.

"Don't be sorry. It's not your fault. If anything it's mine." His arms fold around me; it feels warm and reassuring like my grandmother's quilt. "We'll take it slow."

"You're not . . . "

"No. I don't want to make you do something you're not

ready for, but I do like you, and I think you like me, too. So maybe we can continue this another night. When you're ready."

His words warm me almost as much as his touch. I can say only one thing.

"Yes." *Yes. Yes. Yes. Yes. Yes.*

I can hear the smile in Jay's voice. "Do you want me to take you home now?" He starts to get up, but I grab his hand on my shoulder.

"No. Can we just look at the stars a little more? Like this?"

He whispers, "Of course," and I can feel his breath on my cheek. He leans back on the banquette and pulls me against him. His body is somehow familiar and contoured to fit mine. My head lands just above his shoulder, and I tilt my head so it rests in the crook of his neck. He wraps his arms around me. His hands find mine, and our fingers slide together. Out on the lake, the night has turned cool, but his embrace is warm, comfortable.

We lie like that on the banquette for an hour until I finally think to look at my watch. In the dim glow of the running lights I realize it's after midnight. I don't have a curfew, but if I am going to be out past eleven thirty, my mother expects me to call. Shit.

"Jay?" He doesn't answer, and I realize that he's fallen asleep. "Jay?" I say louder.

"Hmm?"

"I think I need to get home. It's kind of late, and my mom doesn't know where I am."

"What time is it?"

"A little after twelve thirty."

"I guess I fell asleep. You're pretty comfortable."

I stand up and look down at Jay. He smiles and sits up, his palms on his knees as he gathers his strength to get up and drive me back to Bell Cove.

"Yeah. You too," I say.

Minutes later we are rushing back toward shore, the lights of Bell Cove directly ahead of us. I'm sitting in the back again while Jay steers the boat. I relax and realize I haven't stopped smiling. This whole night seems too good to be true. I close my eyes and let the memory of Jay's arms wrap around me, shutting out the chill of the lake breeze as we speed toward the marina.

Chapter 9

By the time Jay drops me off at the dock, and I ride my bike all the way back to Morgan Beach, it's almost two A.M. I lean my bike by the garage door, not even bothering to put it away. My mom is asleep when I get home, and I'm a little disappointed. I'm never out late and I've earned the trust my mother puts in me, but part of me wishes she'd be like TV sitcom moms and be waiting to catch me trying to sneak in. I know I should be grateful for the freedom, but coming home to a quiet house feels too surreal, like maybe this whole night didn't really happen.

By the time I'm climbing the stairs to my room, I'm stripping off my shirt. I head straight for my bed, skipping the bathroom and my toothbrush. I barely manage to kick off my cargo shorts before I collapse among my blankets. Right before I pass out, I run my tongue over my teeth and it occurs to me that I didn't brush. But then I think about Jay and how he tasted against my lips. The thought fills me with warmth and sleep takes over.

The phone wakes me up.

Why is someone calling me before eleven? This is a clear violation of my new no phone calls rule. I wait, and my mother answers after three rings. Good. I let my mind drift back to Jay and hopefully back to the dream that I was having just a few minutes ago.

"Sean?" my mother calls from downstairs. "Are you awake yet?"

I crack open my eyes for the first time.

"No."

"It's Becky." Now I'm confused. Becky knows my rule about early morning phone calls. We agreed on it the first day we met. I roll over and look at my alarm clock. 1:02. I blink, not sure my eyes are seeing clearly. Where's the other number? It can't be after one.

"Sean? You want me to take a message?"

"No." I prop myself up and reach for the phone by my bed. "I got it!" I wait until I hear my mother hang up before I speak into the phone. "Hello?"

"Omigosh, don't tell me you were still sleeping?! What did you do last night that you're that tired? Sean! Don't tell me you—"

"No. Slow down. We didn't. No."

"Well, tell me, then! I waited all morning. I couldn't wait any longer. When did you get home?"

"Uh, about two, I guess."

"Two! What did you do for four hours? Did you go out on his boat? Tell me!"

"Becky, slow down. Take a breath. I'll tell you everything, but I just woke up. I need to clear my brain." I swing my feet over the edge of the bed and stand up. I try to wedge the phone between my ear and my shoulder while I stretch. I slept a lot longer than I meant to, but I feel great.

"You hungry? Wanna meet for lunch downtown? Gold House?" she says. I can tell Becky is trying hard not to reach through the phone, grab me by my T-shirt, and drag me there immediately.

"Sounds good. I'll meet you in half an hour."

Becky almost sounds disappointed. "Half an hour? Skip the

shower and make it twenty. I'm dying to find out what happened."

"Half an hour. See you in a bit." I hit the button on the phone to hang it up, and I realize I've been smiling the whole time. I walk over to the window behind my desk and spread the curtains apart. The sunlight makes me squint, but I can tell it's a beautiful day. Heck, it could be pouring down rain and I would think that.

I take a quick shower, using the shampoo like body wash to lather and rinse in one step. No need to repeat. When I step out, the cool air on my damp skin tingles. Jay. I look at myself in the bathroom mirror; I wasn't in the shower long enough for it to steam up. I don't look any different. Still the same Sean—on the outside, at least. I find myself trying to figure out what someone with Abercrombie looks like Jay would find attractive about me. I mean, I'm not too bad, I guess. Not having a car means I have to ride my bike everywhere, so I'm pretty fit. I *do* have nice legs, if I say so myself. But my short, spiky hair is just brown, not dirty blond or sun streaked. I think my ears are slightly too big. I guess my hazel green eyes are okay, though; they're unusual at least. I'm no Abercrombie model, that's for sure, but I guess I'm not that bad. I do a couple poses in the mirror, give it my best "sexy face." Yeah, not that bad.

My modeling session is rudely cut short when a sudden, insistent beep cuts through the bathroom door. I recognize my computer's way of telling me I have a new IM. I wrap a towel around my waist and head back to my room.

In the middle of my computer screen a dialogue box flashes, begging for my attention.

LuvBug922:   HEY BABE!! {{{{HUGZ}}}}

LuvBug922:   u there???

LuvBug922:   Helllllooooooo?

Why is Lisa IM'ing me? Isn't she off counseling campers or whatever it is camp counselors do? I could ignore it. Pretend I'm not around.

LuvBug922:   Guess ur not there. ☹

She won't know if I don't say anything. There's a gnawing at the back of my throat. I swallow.

LuvBug922:   Well, I wanted to let u know that they have a computer here and I get to use it twice a week for 30 mins. I'll try u again on Friday.

I know Lisa, and I know that ignoring her will not make her go away. I stand over the keyboard and type.

NHBeachBoi: Hey! Was in the shower.

LuvBug922:   UR THERE!! {{{{HUGZ}}}}

NHBeachBoi: {{{HUGZ}}}

I grab a pair of cargo shorts off the floor and hold them up to check for stains. They seem safe.

LuvBug922:   What's up? Camp is so much fun! But I miss you!

NHBeachBoi: Getting ready to go to lunch.

LuvBug922:   That's cool. Who with?

NHBeachBoi: Girl from work. Her name's Becky.

LuvBug922:   Oh

NHBeachBoi: She's a summer girl. Her family's staying at the lake cabins.

LuvBug922:   That's cool

I find a balled-up T-shirt in the top drawer of my dresser and pull it over my head. I decide a change of subject is in order.

NHBeachBoi: How's camp?

LuvBug922:   It's AWESOME! I have 6 little girls and they're all
                    so cute. ☺

NHBeachBoi: How old?

LuvBug922:   7 and 8 yr olds

NHBeachBoi: 6 of them in one cabin? Yikes!

LuvBug922:   u should see them at bedtime

NHBeachBoi: Bad?

LuvBug922:   Let's just say Cabin 6 is *always* the last one to
                    fall asleep. ☺

LuvBug922:   I have my first day off on Monday. Want 2 meet
                    up? I miss u!

This could be my chance to tell Lisa face-to-face about being gay. I'll probably leave out the part about me and Jay on his boat, though.

NHBeachBoi: Yeah OK. What time?

LuvBug922:   I'll catch a ride with Brad, so . . . the marina about
                    11?

NHBeachBoi: Sounds good

I find my sneakers under the bed where I kicked them last night, and take a quick glance in the mirror. My hair's still damp, but it will dry on the bike ride into town. Time to end this conversation.

NHBeachBoi: Well, I gotta run. TTYL!

LuvBug922:   Monday! Love you! {{{{HUGZ}}}} ttyl!

I sign off quickly to make it look like I had to leave in a hurry. And then I leave in a hurry.

I try to avoid my mom, who is reading a book out on the deck. My hand is on the front door when I hear her voice behind me.

"Good morning. Or rather, good afternoon."

I turn around. She is standing in the kitchen doorway, her arms folded across her chest. She is not smiling.

"Uh, good afternoon," I say.

"You were out late last night."

"Yeah, I uh, I lost track of time. I should have called. I didn't realize what time it was until too late and then there wasn't a phone nearby."

"Where were you that had no phone?"

"On a boat."

My mother's eyes widen just a little, but she's trying hard not to show any strong emotions. It's a guidance counselor technique.

"Whose boat? Not your little boat?"

"No, Mom. A friend from work. Jay."

She squints. "Is Jay a girl?"

I hold back a laugh. "No."

"I thought you only worked with girls."

"All girls and Jay."

"And what does Jay's mother think about him being out so late?"

"Jay doesn't have a curfew. He's eighteen."

My mother's head snaps up, shaking her dirty-blond hair into her face. She pushes it back behind her ears. "Eighteen? Who else was with you? No drinking? Drugs?"

"No, Mom, Jay's not like that. Honestly, he's just a friend from work."

"I was worried about you."

"I know, Mom." I give her a sheepish grin and look her in the eyes. "I'm sorry."

"Apology accepted. Don't let it happen again. And next time you're out late, I'm not letting you sleep past noon, just so you know." She uncrosses her arms and places her hands on the hips of her Levi's.

"Okay." Somehow by not getting angry my mother makes me feel much worse than if she had yelled.

"Oh, and I want to meet this Jay. When does he work?"

"Uh, I don't know." Of course I know: he works tomorrow night. Same shift as me. "I'll find out for you," I say. I slink out the door to meet Becky. I can feel my mother's eyes follow me out.

Chapter 10

I meet Becky in front of the Gold House. Today she is wearing a bright yellow shirt with a picture of a braided loaf of bread. Underneath it says CHALLAH BACK, a Jewish reference, I guess. I'm starting to think Becky only chose to work at the Pink Cone for the brightly colored T-shirt.

"Tell me, tell me, tell me!" Becky practically squeals when she sees me. I give her a coy smile and head inside to place my lunch order. "Omigosh, Sean, you can't do this to me!"

I turn around with my hands palm to palm and give her my best Japanese bow. "Patience, Daniel-san. All will be revealed."

"Okay, okay. I'll be patient. But seriously, can we hurry it up?"

We take our food outside to the picnic tables by the marina again. Becky doesn't even touch her food but gives me an expectant look. I have fun slowly chewing on a french fry. Becky's eyebrows shoot to the top of her forehead and her eyes double in size. She starts squeezing a ketchup packet between her fingers, forcing the liquid inside to slide from one end to the other. She doesn't say a word. Finally, when I'm afraid she might squeeze my head like she's squeezing the ketchup packet, I give in and tell her everything.

When I get to the end and the bit about my mother putting me on a guilt trip, I grab a cold fry and pop it in my mouth while I wait for Becky's reaction. When it comes, it's not what I was expecting.

"Sean, that's awesome, but I want you to promise me something," she says.

"Okay."

"Promise me you won't move too fast with this guy."

"What do you mean?" I say.

"Well, right now he seems perfect, but you see these shoulders?" She puts her hands on her shoulders as if she was doing some sort of stretch before playing sports.

"Yeah."

"Well, these shoulders were made for crying. I'm used to playing the sympathetic best friend, the girl who watches and encourages while everyone around her gets their man, but what I've never gotten used to is playing the shoulder to cry on when everyone around me comes back with a broken heart."

"You're saying Jay will break my heart?"

"I'm not saying that. I'm saying that first love is called *first* love for a reason. There's usually a second . . . and a third."

I can feel warmth rush to my cheeks. I don't want to get mad at Becky, but this isn't what I want to hear.

Becky sees that I'm upset and tries to fix the damage. "Sean, I'm sorry. Look, I'm excited for you, really excited. It sounds like a great night. Jay was obviously sweet—a perfect gentleman—and I'm excited that he likes you, that *he said* he likes you. I just don't want you to get hurt."

"Well, maybe you should let me take care of myself. I've been dying to tell you what happened, and you said you wanted to hear it. Heck, you practically threw us together by refusing to come last night, and now you're being a total tool and trying to ruin the best night of my life."

"I'm just trying to put it into perspective."

"I don't need perspective." I grab our lunch trash and smash it into a tight ball.

"Look, Sean, I'm sorry. I shouldn't have said anything." Becky reaches for my arm, but I swivel away off the bench seat of the picnic table.

"Not if what you have to say is to stay away from Jay." I shoot the ball of trash with perfect form toward the black barrel that sits ten feet away. It falls a good two feet short.

"Hey, another OGT," Becky says, trying to break the tension. "Bad at sports."

"That's not an Obviously Gay Trait," I say. "It's just a stereotype." I march over to the ball of trash and throw it in the barrel. I stand there with my back turned to Becky. Somewhere in the back of my head, there's at least one brain cell that knows she's right, that understands she doesn't want to see me get hurt. Somewhere in the back of my head, I know I should proceed with caution.

Becky doesn't say anything, and I figure out that I'm not the only one with hurt feelings.

"I'm sorry," I say, turning back to the picnic table. "I shouldn't be so mad."

"It's okay. I'm sorry, too. You put a lot of trust in me, and you wanted me to share in your biggest secret, and instead I told you it was a bad idea. I'd be mad if I were you, too."

I cross back to the picnic table and hold out my hand for her to shake it. "Still friends?"

She grabs my hand, then pulls me onto the picnic bench beside her, wrapping me in a bear hug. "Still friends." After a long moment, I untangle myself from her arms. We get up together and start to walk down Main Street toward the Cone.

"You want to get some ice cream?"

"Are you serious?"

"Maybe a little."

"Okay. Let's go." We start to walk in silence, but then Becky says, "You know how if you eat ice cream too quickly, it gives you a headache?"

"Yeah?"

"Well, ice cream's not the only thing that works that way. That's all I'm saying."

I nod. After all, Becky hasn't been wrong yet.

After we get our ice cream, we continue walking and licking down Main Street.

"Becky," I say, "how is it you know so much about OGTs and GSAs and LGBT stuff?"

"What do you mean?"

"Well, you're not gay."

Becky laughs at me. "No, but I guess it's different living in the city. My school has had a GSA for ten years. There's enough gay kids that they buy their own table at prom. The Pride parade passes blocks from my apartment. It's just something I grew up with."

I think about this for a minute, licking my ice cream cone.

Becky turns to me. "So, are you saying you know nothing about gay culture? How is that possible? New Hampshire has gay marriage!"

"I'm not totally clueless. I mean, I've seen the political ads about gay marriage. I watch *Degrassi*. I know about the Don't ask, don't tell repeal. But those things don't really apply to me, or to Bell Cove."

"How so?"

"Well, *Degrassi* takes place in Toronto. It's not even the United States! And other shows with gay characters . . . they're all in the city. Bell Cove isn't exactly a thriving metropolis, if you haven't noticed. Even our brochure calls us 'quaint'!"

Becky puts a hand on my shoulder to calm me. I didn't realize I was getting so worked up. I lower my voice. "I mean, besides Renée, is there even another gay person in Bell Cove?"

Becky is laughing at me again. "Of course there is! Renée's girlfriend, for one."

"What?"

"I'm sure you've seen Hannah, the woman who restocks the supply room every Tuesday?"

"What?" I've met Hannah a couple times. She's really friendly, about forty, pretty, with long hair she usually wears in a ponytail that reaches almost all the way down her back. She looks like one of the artists who live up in the hills and come to town to sell their sculptures to tourists in the Main Street shops. I assumed she helped out Renée for some extra cash.

"Sean Jackson, there are gay people everywhere. You just need to open your eyes!"

I finish my ice cream cone while I digest this. Is Becky right? I mean, at the Pink Cone alone, there's me, Jay, Renée, and now Hannah. That's like almost half the people who work there. But then why aren't there more gay people in other parts of Bell Cove? Why not at school? I once read in one of my mom's guidance counselor books that one in ten people may be gay. I didn't really think much of it at the time, but if that's true, there's a lot of people in Bell Cove who are gay but just aren't saying it. But then why not? Why would they have to hide? Then I think about my dad. And Renée and the chamber of commerce. And I start to figure it out.

"C'mon," I say, licking my fingers from the last of my ice cream. "Let's go back to my place and watch another gay movie."

"Okay, how about *Beautiful Thing*? Or *Get Real*? Have you seen those?"

I give Becky a look.

"What am I saying, of course you haven't. Let's go."

By the end of the night I've seen two more gay movies, and Becky's made me a list of about fifteen more I have to watch.

Some I've heard of, like *The Birdcage* and *Brokeback Mountain,* but others like *Trick* and *Latter Days* are new to me. She says we'll have time to watch most of them over the course of the summer. Becky also makes me go to the Advocate.com, a Web site exclusively about gay-related issues. She says it's not smutty like a lot of gay sites, and that I should start reading articles to get up to speed on "my people." I laugh at that. To think that I have people now.

Somehow, I feel like by the end of this summer, I might just have people. Even people right here in Bell Cove.

Chapter 11

I'm sitting on a bench by the marina waiting for Lisa's boat to arrive. I stopped at the Dunkin' Donuts on the edge of town on my way in for a bagel, and now I'm feeding half of it to a family of ducks splashing in the water a few feet away.

It's been two weeks since my Ice Cream Orientation, the Fourth of July is this weekend, and soon Bell Cove will be swarmed with tourists. And just like Bell Cove is about to transform from a sleepy lakeside town into a bustling summer resort, I feel like I am a completely different person.

In just two short weeks, I've gotten my first summer job, made a new best friend, stood up to my father, and oh, yeah . . . kissed a boy. I look around at the couples walking along the water's edge and realize every single one of them is heterosexual. Becky assured me that gay people do exist in Bell Cove, but they sure hide well. I look down at my khaki cargo shorts, black V-neck T-shirt, and beat-up Nikes. How many of those couples would look over at me and see me as gay? I'm not exactly waving a rainbow flag. I didn't think I was hiding, but I'm starting to realize what Becky meant when she said I "need to open my eyes."

"Sean!" I look up to see a delapidated outboard ski boat

coasting into the marina. The thing must be thirty years old. It's a wonder it floats. Lisa is standing, leaning on the windshield, which is cloudy with age and use. She's waving to me.

She's obviously been spending a lot of time outside because her already blond hair is nearly white from the sun, and her arms have turned a nutty golden brown. She looks like she should be on the cover of an outdoor magazine.

And despite this, my eyes are focused on the beautiful man standing next to her. He's standing in order to see over the clouded windshield, and I can see his entire body as he maneuvers the boat into a slip. He's a good five or six inches taller than Lisa, so about six two with curly brown hair and broad shoulders that have obviously seen a workout or two. He looks to be about twenty, and as my eyes drift down his body, I see that his Hawaiian shirt is unbuttoned, revealing a six-pack worthy of a Calvin Klein ad. The sun glints off a pendant around his neck.

I walk over to the boat and help Lisa out. While we tie the boat off, the curly-haired Adonis jumps up on the dock.

"Sean, this is Brad," Lisa says as an introduction. "Brad, meet Sean, my boyfriend." She wraps herself around my arm as if she's afraid Brad might try to steal me from her.

Brad holds out his hand to shake, and I take it with my free hand. His grip is very strong. I can tell he works outside a lot by the rough texture of his palm. I also see that the pendant I noticed earlier is a silver cross.

"Nice to meet you," I say, letting go of his hand. "Thanks for giving Lisa a ride."

"No problem," Brad says. He turns to Lisa. "I've got to grab some stuff at the hardware store and Pastor Ben asked me to pick up some donuts for a treat for the counselors tonight. You want to meet back here at"—he looks at an old black chronograph on his wrist—"say, four o'clock?"

"Sounds good," Lisa says. "We'll be here."

We both watch Brad take off down the dock toward Main

Street, and then we're alone. Lisa looks at me expectantly, and I know what she wants. And I'm not ready to say no, so I lower my head and kiss her. I try to make it a quick peck, but apparently she's really missed me at camp, because she won't let me pull back.

I've never really minded kissing Lisa before. Even when I knew I wasn't in love with her, the kissing was still pretty fun, but now that I know what it's like to kiss Jay, kissing Lisa feels completely foreign. Her lips are too soft, her skin too smooth. The heat I feel when Jay presses his body up close to mine is completely nonexistent with Lisa. But she doesn't seem to feel the same way, because this kiss doesn't end. I have to push her away, just to get some air.

"Somebody will see," I say by way of explanation.

"I don't care. I missed you."

"I missed you, too, but I don't get to go off to an island after the day is over."

"Fine. Take me to get some ice cream."

I do a mental calculation of the day's schedule. Jay won't be there until the evening, but Becky's on the afternoon shift. If we rush now, we might be able to get ice cream without being seen. I really don't feel like having to introduce Lisa to Becky, who has a tendency to say what she's thinking without actually thinking. I grab Lisa's hand and we walk up the dock. I set a brisk pace, and cross the fingers of my other hand that we don't run into Becky.

We're almost to the Pink Cone when I hear my name being called. I don't need to turn around to know it's Becky.

"Sean! Wait up!"

I put on a smile and Lisa and I turn to face Becky, who's half jogging to catch up to us. She's already wearing her Pink Cone T-shirt, and the sight of her big boobs bouncing up and down in bright pink is something to see. She's out of breath when she reaches us, so I take the lead on introductions.

"Lisa, this is Becky. I told you about her on IM. And Becky, this is Lisa, my girlfriend." I try to stress the girlfriend part in hopes that Becky will pick up on it and be tactful.

I've caught her off guard, and she almost blurts out something, which I am sure we both would have regretted, but manages to cover it by bending over in a coughing fit. After a few moments, she straightens up again.

"I hate running," she says with a half grin and a quick look at me. To Lisa she says, "So you're the Lisa that Sean told me about. You're a counselor at the Christian camp across the lake?"

"That's me. I hope Sean's only said good things."

"Of course." Becky punches my shoulder, hard enough that I wince. "What are you doing here?"

"I have the afternoon off, and I got a ride in with another counselor. Sean was going to take me to get an ice cream."

"It will be my pleasure to serve," Becky says with a deep bow. "Meet me around front."

We've reached the Pink Cone and Becky heads toward the back employee entrance while Lisa and I head to the front. After a minute or two, Becky shows up at one of the windows to take our order. I tell Lisa to find us a bench over by the water while I wait for our cones. When Becky comes back with our cones, Lisa is out of earshot.

"You're going to tell her, right?"

"I don't know." I puff out my cheeks in frustration. "I know I should. I know I need to, but I don't know if I'm ready. I don't want to hurt her."

"Trust me, she'll hurt a lot more if she thinks you lied to her. Even more if she thinks you cheated on her."

I know Becky's right, but it doesn't make it any easier. I'm still deciding what to do as I take the cones over to Lisa.

"Here you go." I hand her a small cone of strawberry and sit down on the bench beside her.

"Thanks."

We sit in silence eating our ice cream. Lisa keeps giving me mischievous sideways looks while licking her ice cream cone in obscene ways. Sometimes I forget that Lisa is a "church girl," as Jay called her.

I smile back at her and do my best to respond to her flirtation, but my mind is somewhere else. No matter how I feel about Lisa romantically, I do think of her as a close friend. She's easy to talk to, we share lots in common, and we have the same sense of humor. I'm as afraid of hurting Lisa as I am of losing her friendship. Before the silence gets to that awkward point, I decide to break it.

"So, how's camp?"

"It's amazing! The little kids are so cute. The counselors are awesome. They're from all over New England." She slips her hand into mine. "How's your summer been? Do you like your job?"

"It's cool. Becky's fun. She's from New York City."

"Really? Has she seen all the Broadway shows?"

"Yeah. She says her favorite is *Avenue Q,* but *Wicked* is a close second." We listened to the soundtrack from both shows one afternoon when we were hanging out. When Becky found out I already knew all the words from *Wicked,* she said it was another OGT. This thought reminds me what I need to say to Lisa.

"Lisa," I start, "I need to tell you something."

She turns her body so that it's facing mine on the bench and her knees are pressing into my thigh. Her eyes have this Bambi look to them, innocent and open for anything I have to tell her. *Except one thing I could tell her.* This thought flows through my head and pushes the words I'm about to say to the back of my throat. Instead of *I'm gay,* I say, "I love you."

Even though we've said the "three magic words" to each other plenty of times on IM, or have written notes to each other that end with little hearts, I've never said it to her in person. Even on the dock when she was leaving for the whole summer, we didn't say it. So right now, the words land on her ears like an entire Hallelujah Chorus. *What have I done?*

"I love you, too!" Lisa throws her arms around my shoulders, and she squeezes me so tight I can feel her necklace, a small gold chain with a cross—not that different from the one Brad wears; now why am I thinking about Brad?—pressing into my chest. "You've seemed so distant the last few times we've talked, I was worried."

"I've had a lot of stuff to think about."

"You know I'm always here to talk."

Not about the things I want to talk about. "I know."

She finally lets me go, and it's like I've changed out her batteries for a new set. The next thing I know, I am being dragged off the bench and we are again walking hand in hand down Main Street, but at a pace that's hard for me to keep up. Lisa swings my arm like a manic pendulum. I'm sure this is what it must look like to be in love. It's too bad I don't feel the way I look.

After my colossal mistake, it's impossible to say anything to Lisa now, so instead I try to enjoy the afternoon with her, which isn't that hard. Like I said, Lisa really is a good friend, so we have fun playing the pinball machine in the back of the Gold House, feeding the ducks with the leftover crust from our pizza, and then I introduce her to the soundtrack from *Avenue Q*, which I downloaded on to my iPod from Becky. She loves "There's a Fine, Fine Line," but thinks that "The Internet Is for Porn" is obscene. I think it's hilarious.

What we don't do is head over to my house, because I'm afraid that Lisa will want to make out, and now that I'm dating Jay, that would feel like cheating. The irony of this is not lost on me.

Eventually, we meet back up with Brad at the marina as he's loading some lumber and tools into the boat. The muscles in his arms ripple under the heavy load of wood; I have to stop myself from staring. Lisa kisses me on the cheek before hopping down into the boat where Brad catches her from falling. As he maneuvers the boat out of the marina, I have a crazy thought: maybe I can convince Lisa to go after Brad. Then she would forget about me, and I'll be off the hook without ever having to tell her I'm gay.

Chapter 12

Jay walks out of the deep freezer and looks at his watch. "Ten o'clock. Hit the lights."

"I thought you would never ask," Becky says, flipping the switch for the exterior lights that include the OPEN sign and the gigantic pink ice cream cone that protrudes from the third story.

It's two days after my failure with Lisa, the first day of July, and as if Mother Nature is playing a joke, it's unseasonably cool instead of warm, so it was pretty slow all night. We only had two customers after nine o'clock: an older couple out for their evening "constitution," as they called it, and a car full of teenagers on their way home from seeing a movie at the Odeon. We've been ready to close for a good half an hour.

"Let's get out of here, guys," Jay says.

"You don't have to tell me twice," I say, grabbing my sweat-shirt from a peg in the back. I follow Becky through the open door that Jay is holding for us.

I push Jay's hands away when he musses my hair as I walk past. "Hey!"

He follows us down the back steps. "You don't like to have your hair touched? Well, what about here?" He pushes his fingertips just below my rib cage and tickles me. He's gentle, but his fingers send electric currents up and down my body.

"Stop! That tickles! Stop!"

"That's the point, silly."

"Yeah, well, how do you like it?" I try to tickle him back, but he dodges out of the way and hops gracefully on top of the stone wall that runs in front of the Cone. "Hey, not fair!" I whine, looking up to where he is perched. My head is at his knees. I hear a high-pitched beep, and Jay pulls his cell phone from his jeans pocket.

"Boys, boys," Becky says from behind me.

I had almost forgotten that Becky was still with us, so strong is the Jay potion.

"Quiet down. It's past Bell Cove's bedtime, and we don't want to wake the neighbors," she says.

"Okay, Mom," I whisper. "Whatever you say."

Jay looks down at us from his perch. "Hey, my friend just texted me. We were supposed to head to Manchester, but he had to cancel. You guys want to do something? It's not past my bedtime." He's wearing a zip-up hoodie and from one of the pockets, he produces a pack of cigarettes and a lighter.

"I didn't know you smoked." I try not to sound too shocked.

"Filthy habit," he says. He pulls a cigarette out of the pack with his teeth, then cups his hands around the end. When he removes his hands, the tip of the cigarette glows orange. He exhales a stream of smoke. "You smoke?" He holds the pack out to me.

"No." He offers the pack to Becky, but she shakes her head.

"I don't smoke much, like a pack a week. Picked it up from a guy I dated once. A couple of years ago."

Whoa. This admission almost knocks me over. On the one hand, I'm totally thrown off by this smoking thing. My father smokes a pipe, and I always told myself growing up that I would never become a smoker like him. I hated how it made his clothes smell and his teeth all yellow. Although somehow Jay makes it look sexy, grown-up. I wonder if it feels grown-up, too. But even more significant is the way Jay casually mentions his ex-boyfriend.

Becky must be reading my mind, because suddenly her hand is on my shoulder. "People do a lot of things when they're in love. Hey, I'm starving. You guys want to get some food?"

Jay jumps down from the wall. "Great idea. Porfido's is still open; that's about it for Bell Cove."

"Pizza's delish," Becky says. "Lead the way."

We pick up our pizza and head down to the marina. Jay suggests we eat on his boat, and Becky and I agree. We sit in the bow of the boat, with the pizza on the floor. Jay makes a point of sitting next to me, and keeps one hand on my thigh even while he uses his other hand to eat his pizza. It feels weird, but in a good way, to be part of such an obvious public display of affection. Lisa and I barely ever touched in public, so this is new for me.

After several minutes, Jay finally breaks the silence. "All right, what's the plan? You two want to go out on the lake?"

"Sounds good to me," I say. I look over at Becky, wondering if she'll duck out like she did last time. But Becky seems against leaving me alone with Jay tonight.

"Why not? But let's have an adventure. We need something with a little danger to it," she says.

"You've come to the wrong state if you want adventure," Jay says.

"Oh, come on, there has to be something that could get us into trouble."

"What about Camp Aweelah?" Jay says.

"What's that?"

Even in the darkness, there's a gleam in Jay's eyes. "It's a Christian summer camp across the lake. We could sneak in and—"

"And what?" Becky gets the same mischievous glint in her eyes. "We could scare a few little kid campers?"

"That's mean," I say.

"Sounds like fun," Becky says.

"Let's go." Jay jumps around to the steering wheel and starts the motor. "Sean, you wanna untie us?"

I hesitate. I don't really want to go to Camp Aweelah. I don't know if it's because that's where Lisa is, and I am afraid to see her right now, afraid that she'll see me with Jay, or just because I'm afraid of getting into trouble. I try to think of an alternative, something that will keep me from going along on an adventure that I don't want to go on. But my brain is quickly approaching overload, and nothing comes to me. I shrug, give a quick smile to Becky, and lean over and untie the bowline.

Within seconds we are speeding out of Bell Cove and beyond the point to Camp Aweelah. It finally occurs to me that I could have just said I didn't want to go, back out like Becky did the other night. But it's too late now. We're headed across the lake, and we're not turning around.

So I sit in the stern and look at the lights of Bell Cove scattered along the shoreline and up into the hillside. There's only a few houses lit up at this hour, and as the distance grows, they start to twinkle, as if the sky has extended down and swallowed the town, absorbed it and turned it into just another corner of the universe.

"Sean," Jay calls to me. I turn to face him. "Come here. Show me some more of your constellations."

Like an obedient dog, I cross and stand beside him. Becky is still sitting in the bow seats, the wind whipping her hair into a tangle of frizzy black wire. She smiles at me. Jay puts his arm around my shoulders. He's warm. I didn't realize how cold I was. I stand closer and lean into him, letting his heat warm me.

Chapter 13

There's only a quarter moon tonight, but it's bright and reflects off the pale sand of Camp Aweelah's beach so that we can
see it from several hundred yards off. A handful of lights dot
the shore, probably marking the paths to the bathrooms for
campers who have to get up in the middle of the night. Jay
heads toward one of the lights hanging on the end of the dock,
and cuts the motor to half throttle.

"Is that it?" Becky asks.

"Yes." Jay holds a finger to his lips to signal quiet and kills the
throttle altogether. We drift toward the dock, the only sound
the gentle splashing against the hull. Jay grabs a paddle from a
storage bin underneath the rear banquette and inserts it into
the dark water. There's no sound as he steers us to the dock.

I feel more than hear the dull thud as the boat hits the rubber tires hanging along the dock edge. Jay wastes no time tying
the stern line and signals for me to do the same in the bow.
Within a few seconds we're tied up.

Jay leads the three of us into the camp. We keep to the shadows as we cross the beach up to the cabins nestled among the
trees. Jay has grabbed a flashlight from the boat's emergency

kit, and between its narrow beam and the moonlight we can make out the paths through the trees.

There's a large green space with a flagpole in the center as we approach the main grouping of buildings. This must be where they hold the big camp gatherings each day. There's a volleyball net off to one side, and I can see the trampled lines in the grass where they must have had a softball diamond set up. The camp is eerily quiet, and it feels like we're committing some deadly sin just being awake right now.

"They go to bed early at church camp," Becky whispers. "I would never make it as a counselor."

The first building we go to is the mess hall. It's a big screened-in building with rows of tables set up in the middle. Once I see there's no one here, I think we'll move on, but Jay motions to Becky and me to follow him, and he leads us around the back of the building to a screen door.

Jay swings the flashlight along the ground and seems to be looking for something, but I don't know what. Suddenly, he stops and bends over and comes up with a stick about a foot long. I look at Becky for an explanation, but she only shrugs her shoulders. We both watch as Jay goes back to the screen door and pulls the handle. The door only opens an inch, and when Jay shines the flashlight I can see why. An old-fashioned hook-and-eye lock holds it shut. Jay hands me the flashlight, and I train it on the lock while he slides the slender stick underneath the hook. After a second of jiggling, he has it. He stands back, holding the door wide, and ushers us in like a doorman at a fancy city hotel.

"This way, *monsieur, mademoiselle,*" he whispers.

Jay seems to know where he's going and leads us to a small room off the side of the kitchen. When he shines the flashlight inside I can see that it's a pantry. This early in the summer it's well stocked, and every shelf is full of camp staples like maple syrup, pancake mix, mustard and ketchup, pasta, and bags of potatoes. I feel guilty thinking we are going to steal food from camp kids, but that doesn't seem to be what Jay has in mind. He is clearly looking for something specific. He pulls out a box of trash bags and takes the strip of twist ties and shoves them in his pocket. But he's not done looking. After several more seconds he clicks his tongue in recognition. He bends, then hands me a gallon-sized plastic tub: vegetable shortening. I have no idea what it's for, but Becky claps her hands in delight. Jay is on the move again. We follow him back outside. Now Becky seems to know where we're going, too.

"You've done this before, haven't you?" I say into the darkness. Becky giggles in reply.

Jay turns and puts the flashlight underneath his chin, casting sharp shadows that give him a sinister appearance. He turns his voice to a demonic whisper. "Whatever gives you that idea?" He lets out a low, evil laugh that makes Becky giggle even more.

We head across the grounds toward a couple of low, windowless buildings. As we get closer I realize they are the bathrooms, one for the boys and one for the girls. Jay goes in the boys' bathroom first and waves for us to follow. Becky doesn't even hesitate.

"What are we doing in here?" I ask.

"Shh," Becky says. "I did this last summer when I worked at a fat camp in New York."

"Fat camp?"

"I know, a lot of good it did, huh?" She squeezes her middle and sticks out her tongue in disgust. "Anyway, I worked in the kitchen cooking egg whites and turkey bacon for the campers. Once a week we were allowed to cook them dessert, so one week we made brownies. I snuck some laxative in the batter."

"You didn't!"

"Just imagine a camp full of overweight twelve-year-olds who haven't had chocolate in a week. The brownies were gone in about three seconds."

"What happened?"

"It's funny. 'Cause all week these kids are eating nothing but fruit and salad. High-fiber stuff, so their systems were already primed. So anyway, like twenty minutes later, suddenly all that roughage has got to come out. There's this mad rush for the bathrooms. I swear to you, a stampede. These kids were running faster than they had in their entire lives."

"Sounds kind of cruel to me." But also very funny.

"It is, but trust me, every summer camp has pranks. It's part of the experience."

"I guess. But where does this come in?" I ask, holding up the tub.

"Well, we didn't actually have any vegetable shortening at that camp, so we had to use Vaseline, but the effect is the same. Watch."

Becky points to where Jay has gone into the first stall, and we both squeeze in behind him. Taking the tub from me, he pries off the lid and scoops out a small handful of shortening. I watch him spread it around the toilet seat, like frosting a cake. It's a thin layer, not so much you'll notice if you're not looking, but enough that you'll feel it when you sit down. I can just imagine the sensation of sitting on vegetable shortening when you are expecting hard plastic. I shudder at the thought. But suddenly I realize I'm having fun, too.

It only takes a few minutes to "frost" the toilet seats in both bathrooms. I do feel slightly guilty, but the thought of screaming eight-year-olds is too funny to make me stop. I wish I could be there to see the faces that go along with the screams.

After we finish with the bathrooms, I figure it's time to head back to the boat. I don't have a watch, but the moon is high enough in the sky that I know it must be near midnight—and my curfew.

Before this summer, I've never broken curfew before. In fact, before this summer, I was such a good son, I had never had a curfew to break. My mother's never been seriously mad at me

before, and I have no desire to see what it's like. I start to head
back toward the dock, but Jay and Becky go in another direction.

"Where are you going?" I whisper. "The dock is this way."

"We're not finished yet," Jay says over his shoulder, as he
heads across the center green toward the cabins. I notice he
hasn't put the lid back on the shortening.

"Becky?"

But Becky just puts her finger on her lips and follows Jay. Curiosity gets the better of me, and the next thing I know I'm running behind them, trying to keep up.

Jay slows down when we get close to the cabins, and I realize
he's trying not to make any noise. He waves his arm toward us,
his palm pointing to the ground to indicate we should follow
his lead. I'm suddenly aware of my feet crunching on the gravel
pathway that connects the cabins. It's like trying to open a bag
of candy at the movie theater; no matter how careful I am, the
sound echoes in my ears.

The cabins are dark brown boxes in a wide arc around one
side of the center green. In the front of each box, there's a
screen door and a wooden plaque with a number on it. There's
one window in the center of each of the other three walls. I
count twelve cabins.

We approach the first cabin, and Jay sneaks right up to a window and looks in. He gives his eyes a few moments to adjust and
then turns away from the screened opening.

He shakes his head at us. "Boys."

"What's wrong with boys?" I say.

"Not as fun as girls."

I look at Becky. She smirks, but nods in agreement. We head
to the next cabin. It's boys again.

"The girls must be at the other end," he says.

He leads us down the row of cabins, skirting the edge of the
woods. We stay off the gravel pathway and stick to the soft bed
of pine needles that muffles our footfalls. About halfway up the

row, Jay holds up his hand for us to stop. He crosses over to the cabin and looks in the window. The moon is directly overhead now, and I can make out the plaque over the door: 6.

"This is Lisa's cabin," I say to Becky.

"Lisa, your 'girlfriend'?" Becky asks, using more of her finger quotes.

Jay turns away from the window with a broad smile. My stomach jumps a little. Even in the dark his smile is magical. "Bingo," he says.

He sweeps the flashlight across the pine needles at our feet until he finds what he's looking for: pinecones. He grabs three and heads back to the cabin. First he smears each cone with the shortening. Then, I watch as he pulls the twist ties from his pocket and begins to tie the pinecones together. He uses the twist ties to attach the pinecones to the door handle. Finally, Jay pulls out his cigarette lighter and lights the bottom of the cones. Suddenly, I see what he's done.

If you've ever been camping, then you know that pinecones are nature's firecrackers. Throw a couple of pinecones into the campfire and sit back and enjoy the show. A large dry cone will pop and crack for several minutes as the pockets of dried sap ignite and cause the pine nuts to act like popcorn kernels. Jay has made a makeshift Roman candle.

"It won't be long," he says. "C'mon." Jay leads us back into the woods, where we crouch out of sight behind some low bushes and wait for the excitement.

We only have to wait about thirty seconds. Once the flame hits the shortening, the reaction is instantaneous. And loud. It sounds like a hundred popguns firing all at once, but even louder are the screams that come right after. The air is filled with the shrill screeching of six little girls. Within seconds the door flies open, and they're running out into the open grass. They finally stop screaming and huddle in a small group. They're all wearing oversized T-shirts and I can see the white skin of their bare feet in the moonlight.

Next I see Lisa come running down the path. The counselors' cabin must be at the end of the row. She stops to comfort the girls while a male counselor investigates the pinecone firecracker, which has by now burned itself out. The doors of other cabins are opening as the other campers get up to investigate. I want to stay and watch as the soap opera unfolds, but I feel Jay put his hand on my shoulder.

"We gotta get going. Too many people awake now."

I nod and reluctantly follow him through the woods back to the dock with Becky right behind. I can't believe I almost missed this.

Jay rushes us through the trees toward the dock and his boat, no longer caring about staying silent. Our footsteps sound like thunder as we crash through the underbrush. No one seems to be following us, so I guess the commotion is enough to cover our tracks. I can hear Becky making little snorting sounds behind me, barely holding in hysterical laughter. I feel bad for Lisa after what she told me about how difficult it is to get her campers to sleep, but I have to admit it was funny.

"Shut up, they'll hear you," I hiss over my shoulder.

"If they were going to hear us, they would have by now," Becky says with a small gasp of laughter. She is losing her battle.

"C'mon!" There's an edge to Jay's voice.

"What's wrong?" But then I see. We break through the trees and onto the camp beach, a swath of light-colored sand separating us from the lake.

Becky catches up to us, breathing heavily. "Where's the dock?"

For a moment no one speaks. My mind races with questions. Does the camp have two beaches? How did we get turned around? How are we going to get out of here?

"There," Jay says, pointing. "Shit."

Becky and I follow his finger. The dock is a hundred yards down the beach, the boat tied up at the end, drifting silently. And between us and the dock, the beach is in full view of the cabins. A wide section of trees has been removed to provide easier access and a view to the lake. There is no way to get to the dock without being seen. The adrenaline that had been pumping through me freezes in my veins. I feel like I just swallowed lead.

"How are we going to get back?"

"Over here." Jay leads us away from the dock toward the other end of the beach. There are ten or fifteen canoes here, pulled up into the sand like dark stitches sealing a cut. Jay grabs the closest one and starts pushing it toward the water. "A little help?" he says, his voice pinched in exertion.

Becky and I grab the other end and pull the canoe into the lake. The water soaks through my sneakers as I splash into the shallows with deafening eruptions of water. I'm sure they must be able to hear us up at the cabins. Compared to the chilled night air, the water actually feels warm against the skin of my legs. I'm in up to my knees before I realize the canoe is floating.

"Get in," Jay whisper-yells at us. He is holding the other end of the canoe to stabilize it. I swing one leg into the canoe. I feel it wobble beneath me, but I keep my balance and push up with my other foot. I crouch in the bow of the canoe, trying to keep my center of gravity as low as possible.

Becky watches me, but doesn't move.

"C'mon," I say.

"Jews and canoes don't mix," she whimpers.

"Just get in." I shrug and put my hands out in a gesture of helplessness. What does she want me to do?

She takes a deep breath and manages to get one leg over the side of the canoe and then sort of bellyflops into the bottom. The canoe tips wildly, but Jay holds us steady. Becky starts to get up. The shift in weight sends us tilting again.

"Don't move," I say. "Just stay where you are."

Becky lays spread-eagled in the bottom of the canoe, one

foot still hooked over the edge. Jay gives us a push and then gracefully lifts himself into the back. Within seconds we are cutting through the shallow water away from the shore.

Luckily, there are two paddles in the bottom of the canoe, and soon Jay and I have us taking a wide arc around the beach toward the dock. Becky, still too afraid to shift her weight, looks up at me from her contorted position.

"Won't they see us anyway?"

"They won't be looking this far out into the water," Jay says.

We guide the canoe toward the dock, approaching from the other side to stay out of sight of the cabins.

"Okay, Becky, we're almost there," I say.

"You want me to move?" Becky says as if I'm asking her to have my baby.

"Slowly." Jay and I have guided the canoe up beside his boat at the end of the dock. I put my hand on a cleat by the engine housing to steady us and watch as Becky tries to maneuver. She manages to get herself on her hands and knees and slowly rotates so she is facing the boat. Her movements are slow and deliberate like a drunk looking for the toilet. "You can do it," I prod.

She pulls herself up to the edge of the canoe and then places her hands on the side of Jay's boat. She hoists herself to an almost standing position and gets ready to jump. I realize what she's about to do, but it's too late. Becky thrusts herself from the canoe, pushing down hard on the side. It rocks steeply, threatening to dump Jay and me into the water. We lean back to counterbalance, but we overcompensate. As soon as Becky's weight is shifted to Jay's boat, the canoe rockets back the other way, and there is nothing we can do to stop it.

"Oh, shit," Jay lets out, but then I'm underwater. It's dark and the roaring gurgle of bubbles past my ears is disorienting. I kick out trying to break the surface, and my outstretched arm hits sand and rock. Light doesn't seem to be penetrating into the water; my eyes are open but I can't see and I can't find up. I think I can hear someone yelling my name, but it's distorted through the murky water. I can't tell where it's coming from.

I try to kick myself around, but I can't move my right leg. It's stuck. I kick harder and my sneaker hits something solid that gives way, and I'm free again, kicking, stretching my arms for the surface of the water. My lungs have started to ache for air, and I thrash harder for the surface. I can feel my heart beat in panic. I need air. And then I am lifted out of the water. I'm still holding my breath and kicking for several seconds before I realize I'm upright.

"Sean! Sean! I've got you." Jay is holding me to his chest and stroking my hair out of my eyes. My vision is blurry with lake water, but I see the overturned canoe floating beside us.

"Are you okay?" Becky is hovering over us in Jay's boat. She unlatches a ladder from the back of the boat, and it unfolds into the water. Jay pushes me toward the ladder, and I suddenly realize I can stand. We're only in a few feet of water. I try to speak, but I end up coughing up lake water. "C'mon," Becky says, "I think I hear someone coming."

We don't waste any more time. Jay pushes me up and into the boat and then pulls himself up in one fluid movement. The engine starts right away, and Jay expertly backs us away from the dock and out into the lake. Becky and I watch behind us and see flashlights bobbing down from the cabins, but by the time they reach the beach, we are too far away to be seen.

I spend the ride back to Bell Cove standing next to Jay at the wheel, trying to let the breeze created by the boat dry me out. Jay and I take off our T-shirts, and I lay them across the bow seats. The cool night air causes goose bumps to form across Jay's smooth chest, and when I return to stand next to him he pulls me in with his free hand and wraps me in a one-armed embrace. I can feel his skin against mine, and it's warm and electric. I almost forget that Becky is with us, which I think is what she wants. It's like she's trying to hide in the back of the boat out of embarrassment.

By the time we get back to Bell Cove I'm still wet, but I pull my T-shirt on anyway. After Jay's warm body, it feels like putting on a piece of lunch meat, cold and clingy. I cross over to Becky, but she won't look at me. As we enter the marina I sit down next to her.

"I'm sorry," she murmurs, just loud enough for me to hear over the engine.

"You were right. I did have fun."

"You're not mad?"

"Of course not. You didn't do it on purpose. And besides, you got Jay to take off his shirt." I stick my tongue out.

"Pretty tasty," she says with a smirk. "You know, you're not too bad yourself."

I shake my head at her, but I can't stop the smile that spreads across my face. I jump up and offer her my hand. "C'mon. We're home. Try not to tip this boat over, okay?"

She takes my hand, and I pull her up, but don't let go, forcing her into a bear hug.

"Sean! You're still wet!"

"That's the idea." I hug her tighter, trapping her in the embrace of my sodden clothes. Jay kills the engines and comes up behind Becky. He's holding his damp T-shirt and drapes it across her shoulders before wrapping his arms around her, too. Becky starts to squeal as the damp starts to soak through her clothes.

"This is sooo not fair!" Becky tries to wriggle free, but she's trapped. "I can feel it soaking through my shirt! I'm going to cry rape."

"Like anyone would believe that," I say, loosening my grip. "We're gay, remember?" I realize as it comes out of my mouth that it's the first time I've called myself gay without choking on the words. No one else seems to notice, but I feel a small rush of adrenaline flood my veins.

"Aww, did we make you wet? Isn't that usually a good thing?" Jay taunts Becky, and she pushes him hard enough to knock him onto the banquette seat.

"It figures my fantasy of being sandwiched between two beautiful men would come true, and they're both gay." Becky crosses to the side of the boat and jumps up onto the dock, displaying much more grace than she did at the camp. "I've had enough excitement, boys."

"Good night!" I call after her as she walks down the dock. She waves her hand over her shoulder, and then turns to blow me a kiss. And then Becky is out of sight in the darkness. And I'm alone with Jay.

He comes up behind me and puts his arms around my shoulders. "So that was fun," he whispers in my ear.

"Right up until we were underwater."

"I liked rescuing you."

"I liked it, too." And I did. The moment Jay pulled me out of the water, he became my knight in shining armor. Even though I wasn't really in danger of drowning, it felt like I was, and then I was in Jay's arms, and I was safe again. I knew he wouldn't hurt me, that he was there for me. I felt closer to him in that moment than I have with anyone else. In that moment, I knew what it feels like to be in love.

Jay turns me around in his arms so I am facing him. He's still shirtless, and I lay my head on his warm shoulder, my hands pressed in close against his chest. Then his hand is pushing my head up; our lips are nearly touching.

"I'll be your lifeguard anytime." And then his lips are on mine and the fire is flowing through me again. Jay pulls me in tight against him; I slide my arms around him, let my fingers caress the muscles in his back. His hands find the bottom of my shirt and creep underneath it, inspecting every inch of my stomach and up to my chest.

One hand finds my left nipple and gives it a gentle squeeze. It's like he's found a switch that makes my knees weak. An involuntary gasp escapes my lips. He pinches my nipple again, but a little harder, and it feels like he's plucking a guitar string that connects my head and my crotch. The vibration thrums through my body, and I feel myself start to get hard. I have to come up for air. I pull myself away from Jay.

"Wow."

"You okay?" Jay asks, a sly grin on his lips, his hands still exploring under my shirt.

"Very." I dive back into him, pressing my lips against his and letting my hands start to explore more than just his back. They work their way down to the waistline of his underwear, where it clings to his skin and sits above his shorts, which have sagged from the weight of being wet. I let one finger lift up the elastic waistband, and then let it snap back into place.

Jay stops kissing me. "Nice," he whispers. "Do it again."

I'm about to follow his command when the clock on the Methodist church begins to chime the hour. It always does Westminster chimes followed by single bongs to indicate the hour. I figure it must be one A.M., which means I'm late, but not enough to be in real trouble with my mom. But there are two bongs. That can't be right. I grab Jay's arm and pull his hand from under my shirt to look at his watch.

"Shit!"

"What's wrong?"

"It's already two! My mom will be pissed." More than pissed. I have to go. *Now.*

I start scrambling to find my wet shoes and put them on my feet. I shove the socks into my pocket. I can bike home in ten minutes; I just hope my mom isn't waiting up. She didn't last time, and if she doesn't this time, I might be able to convince her that I got in at a more reasonable hour.

I get the shoes tied and start to jump up on the dock, but Jay catches my hand.

"Sean, wait."

"I can't wait, I—"

"I know, but I want you to know how much fun I had with you tonight. You're really special." There's a tender note in his voice as he says this, and he brings my hand to his lips and kisses my fingers. Then he lets me go, and I am off to find my bike chained at the end of the dock. And even though I'm rushing, I have time to let Jay's gentle touch sink in. Something in my chest flutters at the thought of it. It flutters all the way back to my house.

Chapter 14

There is a blanket over my knees and chest. I pull it up to my chin and feel the worn cotton fabric, almost silky to the touch: my grandmother's quilt. I'm suddenly aware that my knees ache, and there's a dull pain at the back of my neck, like I've been holding it in an awkward position for too long. I pry my eyes open; they feel like they have a layer of rubber cement keeping them closed, but finally I manage it. The room is dim; the window by my bed is a pale gray with predawn sunlight. I look up at it for several seconds before I understand that I'm on the floor, propped next to my bed. Did I fall out? Did I...

I inhale sharply. The night before rushes back and would have knocked me over if I wasn't already on the floor. Jay and Becky at the camp. Jay and me on the boat. Rushing back to the house. My mother waiting for me. Me telling my mother I'm in love with Jay. There are no tears this time, but I can feel my heartbeat quicken, and a jolt of electricity radiates from my chest to my fingers and toes. Did I really just come out to my mother? I could have been dreaming. It feels like a dream. At least, it doesn't feel real. But my damp sneakers feel real. I kick them off into the far corner of my room, as if distance can undo last night.

I'm on my feet. My grandmother's quilt falls to the floor. I have just enough time to realize that my mother must have put the blanket over me during the night before I have to sit down on the bed because my head has started to spin, black dots floating across my vision from the head rush of standing so quickly. I wait for my vision to return, breathing slowly to calm my heart. The clock by my bed reads 5:09.

There is nothing to do. My mother was here, but she left. It's too early to call Becky. And I'm still tired. I reach down for the blanket on the floor, then lie back on my bed. There's an immediate feeling of warmth as my circulation returns to my feet, stretched out for the first time in hours. I let my head sink into the pillow. Crunch.

There's something stiff and crinkly on my pillow. I reach up and find a single sheet of white computer paper. I recognize my mother's precise, distinctive cursive.

I love you, Sean. When you're ready, let's talk. When you're ready. Will I ever be ready? But the paper is reassuring. I pull my grandmother's quilt up to my chin and close my eyes.

When I finally wake up for real, the sun is streaming into my room, and I can tell the day is well under way. I roll over in bed and see the paper my mom left me. When you're ready. I know she means it, but something tells me that I'd better be ready pretty soon, because I don't think she'll be able to wait very long.

I force myself out of bed and make my way to the bathroom. I'm still wearing my clothes from the night before, and my shirt is stiff from the lake water. I can feel it scratch against my skin when I pull it off to take a shower. The water makes a loud static hiss in my ears, drowning out the outside world. I enjoy this isolation for as long as I can, until I start to feel the water begin to run tepid. I quickly lather and rinse before it turns cold, and I almost make it. I'm leaning into the freezing stream of water trying to get the last of the shampoo out of my hair without let-

ting the water hit the rest of my body. The cold water makes my
scalp tingle, and it's not entirely unpleasant. I take a deep
breath and put my entire body underneath the frigid stream of
water. I can only stand it for about four seconds and then I twist
the shower control, stopping the water. The sudden cold is in-
vigorating. I briefly relive last night's plunge in the canoe, only
this time Jay isn't there to pick me up. But the thought gives me
strength.

She's sitting on the deck when I get downstairs. A cup of coffee is on the table beside her, and she has a book in her hand.
But she's not reading. The book rests in her lap with a finger
holding the page. She's staring off over the lake, which is very
blue today, reflecting the cloudless sky.

There's still half a pot of coffee in the coffeemaker, and I
pour myself a cup, or rather half a cup, which I then fill the rest
of the way with milk and four or five or six spoonfuls of sugar. I
stir only enough to turn the mixture a uniform caramel color. I
don't want the sugar to dissolve entirely; I look forward to the
granulated sludge that will be left at the end. I taste the coffee
and it's sweet, like melted coffee ice cream. Perfect. I take another sip. My mother hasn't moved. I can't stall any longer.

She looks up when I slide the glass door open. She doesn't
say anything when she sees me, but her mouth stretches into a
tight-lipped smile. Her eyes shine in the bright sun. She's not
wearing any makeup, and I can see the wrinkles around her
mouth and eyes. I've never really thought of my mother as old
before, and I guess she isn't really. I'm just suddenly aware of
her age. Did those wrinkles appear overnight?

I sit down in the Adirondack chair next to her and sip my
coffee. She picks up her own mug, and I see that it's one I
made for her in art class in elementary school. We took pre-
made white coffee mugs and painted them with our own designs and then gave them to our moms for Mother's Day. Mine
has a big red heart and says, *I love you, Mom* on it. I didn't even

know she still had that. Neither one of us says anything for a long time. We just drink coffee and watch the lake. A small sailboat enters the cove and heads toward the dock, the sail a gash of red and yellow against the dark blue water. Finally, my mother breaks the silence.

"When did you start drinking coffee?"

"A while ago."

"I never noticed." She takes a sip from her mug and studies its design carefully. She rubs her thumb across the heart, following the brush strokes in a curved line. "I guess I haven't noticed a lot of things."

I turn my head, and I see that she's looking at me. She reaches out a hand, and I let her run her fingers through my hair. It feels good, actually. I can't remember the last time she did that. She stops.

"Can we talk about this?" She's asking my permission, giving me the power in the conversation. I have the option of saying no.

I lick my lips slightly, but I have no words. I nod.

"Good," she says.

But I don't know where to begin. The words are stuck in my throat again, and I don't know why. She knows my secret, so what am I afraid of?

"Sean, I have to ask." She waits for me to look at her. "Are you gay?"

I thought that I had made that clear last night. I open my mouth, but again there are no words. Why does she have to ask if she already knows the answer?

"If you are, it's okay. I think that's what you were trying to tell me last night. I just . . ." She stops and turns away. She pinches the bridge of her nose like she's trying to stave off a headache. "I just need to know for sure."

I'm replaying the previous night in my head, and I realize I told her I'm in love with Jay, but I never used the word *gay*.

"I need you to say it," she says.

And I need to say it. It's like with Becky all over again. It doesn't have meaning until the word comes out of your mouth. It's not real. You can still turn back. Take it back. Until . . .

"Mom." She turns back to me, and her eyes hold mine.

She nods slightly. "It's okay."

"I'm gay."

My mother's face crinkles. Her mouth moves up in a smile while her eyes squint together and tears shine in the deep creases. She puts down the coffee mug and reaches with both arms to give me a hug. She's sobbing, but she's not deflated. Her embrace is strong and warm. I hug her back.

"Oh, Sean, I know how hard that was." And now I'm crying, too. "Thank you. Thank you. Thank you," she says in my ear. "You're my son. I love you."

The phone rings, shattering the moment between us. My mother pulls back, wiping her eyes with the backs of her hands.

"Shit," she says. She smiles at me with this ironic grin that says, "Always at the worst moments," and gets up. She goes through the slider, leaving it open behind her and crosses to the phone. "Hello?"

I've had enough emotion for one morning. I tilt my coffee mug toward the sky and let the thick coffee-flavored syrup make its way to my mouth. I wipe the residue on the bottom with a finger and take my mug into the kitchen. My mother is looking very serious on her end of the phone, but she gives me a crooked smile when she sees me. I don't ask who it is, and instead give her a little wave as I head out the door.

She waves back and mouths, "We'll talk more later."

I'm sure we will, but in the meantime, it's a perfect day for a bike ride.

Chapter 15

I ride my bike to Mann's Hill. On a day like this, you can see clear across the lake from the top. Right at the highest point there's a small clearing with a grouping of rocks that overlooks the lake. It's a favorite spot for picnickers. One of the rocks is almost flat on top, and it makes a perfect "table." Today, I climb up on this rock and lie flat on my back, looking up into wide-open space. It's getting near lunchtime, and the sun is almost directly overhead. I shade my eyes with one arm and breathe in. A breeze is blowing off the lake, and I take in the sharp tinge of pine trees, and the moist, clean scent of the lake that reminds me of towels and bathing suits drying in the sun.

My mother didn't say much, but she said enough. I realize how heavy the secret I had been keeping from her had become. With it lifted, there's nothing to stop me from simply drifting away on the lake breeze. It was easier than I thought, telling my mother. I should have known she'd be cool, given her position as a school counselor, but there's always a chance.

But really, my mom and I have always been close. Even before my parents divorced, it was just the two of us a lot because my dad was so busy with work. My dad worked as a school principal in a neighboring town, and it seemed like he had meetings nearly every night. Even on weekends or during the summers, he would make excuses to be at work. Looking back now, it's easy to see why my parents divorced.

So my mom and I would make the most of the time we had. We'd go hiking or swimming in the summer, skiing or sledding in the winter. Some weekends, if my dad said he was busy at work, she would pack me up in the car, and we'd head to my gram's house in Vermont. My mom and I were best friends. We didn't have secrets.

So I don't know why I felt the need to keep this part of me a secret. I guess, as I've gotten older, I haven't been as close to my mom. We haven't grown apart exactly; I just don't tell her every detail of my life. But I should have trusted her on this. I should have known she'd be cool.

The thoughts drift through my mind like the clouds in the sky above. It's almost like I'm drifting with them on the lake breeze. A new smell rides up on the wind, and my nose is filled with pizza from the Gold House and fried clams from the Clam Hut. My stomach clenches, reminding me that all I have had to eat is a cup of coffee. Reluctantly, I climb down from the table rock and find my bike. I don't use my brakes all the way down the hill. By the time I reach Main Street, I'm flying.

I don't stop until I get to the Lakeside Cottages. I ride to number 8 and park my bike by a tree. The Lakeside Cottages are a series of small log cabins with screened porches that overlook the lake on the east side of Bell Cove. Each cabin has a corny, tree-themed name to distinguish it from the others, like "The Pines," "The Willows," or "The Elms." Number 8 is "The Spruces."

I knock on the screen door and call inside, "Hello! Becky?"

"I'm on the porch!" I follow the sound of her voice through the cabin. There's a small kitchen with a two-burner stove and an ancient-looking refrigerator, the kind where the freezer is an aluminum box inside the refrigerator instead of a separate compartment. The kitchen is connected to the combo living/ dining room. There's a table and four chairs, a sagging sofa in a green burlap material straight from 1967, and an Adirondack chair just like the ones on our deck except for a floral print cushion. Two doors off the living room lead to a bathroom and to the main bedroom. I also see the ladder that goes to the loft where Becky sleeps. Lofts are a really cool idea, except for the total lack of privacy and the fact that you have to go up and down a ladder every time you need to use the bathroom.

I find Becky lying in a hammock on the back porch reading a book. "So this is what the Lakeview Cottages look like. I always wondered."

Becky hates spending time at the cottage so much that I never come here with her. She always meets me in town or at my house.

"So you gave yourself the grand tour? Saves me the trouble," she says without looking up. "And what brings you here? Why didn't you call me?" Becky keeps reading her book.

"My mom was on the phone and then I was on my bike. Where are your parents?"

"My dad took my mom fishing," she says.

"Fishing?"

"Yeah, actually my mom loves it, as long as she doesn't have to touch any bait or any fish." Becky finally puts her book down and looks at me. "What's up, Chuck?"

"I told my mom."

It takes a moment for her to register my meaning. "You told your . . . ?" Then she's out of the hammock so fast she almost flips and lands smack on her butt. I have flashbacks to the canoe. "Sean Jackson, get out!"

"Apparently, I am."

"Oh—my—God! I am so proud of you! You're smiling, so it went well?"

"Yeah. There was a rough moment or two, but it was hugs and tears by the end."

"This calls for a celebration. Let's go shopping and get you some new clothes!" Becky is on her feet and already pushing me toward the door.

"But..."

"No buts! Move it!" she orders.

"Can we at least stop for lunch first?"

Chapter 16

Becky and I eat our Gold House sandwiches on the same bench we had lunch the day we met. It hasn't even been a month, but I feel like I've known Becky forever.

"So, where are the best places to shop around here?" Becky asks between mouthfuls of meatball sub.

"Well, there's a Walmart a couple exits down the highway."

Becky practically chokes on a meatball. "Sean Jackson, please tell me you are not serious!"

"Well, not totally serious." Truth is, I do own a few articles of clothing from Walmart, but I keep this fact to myself. "The nearest mall is in Concord. Probably thirty miles away or so," I offer instead.

"Nothing *in* town?"

"Not unless you want to buy a magnet shaped like New Hampshire or a sun catcher made by a local artist."

"Country living." Becky throws her hands in the air like she's offering herself up for sacrifice. "Gotta love it."

"Hey, this is my hometown!"

"And a sweet hometown it is. A little sleepy, though."

"I'm sorry we disappoint the New York princess!" I roll my eyes at Becky. "But at least our streets are clean, you can breathe the air, and you don't have to keep a pocket full of change for the homeless guy on every corner."

"Well, of course you don't have any homeless people. They'd have to spend their quarters at Walmart. In New York, our homeless have style. It's Dolce & Gabbana and Ralph Lauren for them. Nothing else will do."

"You like New York, don't you?"

"I love it. You're right about some of the drawbacks, but it makes up for it in culture, and food, and especially shopping. There's seriously nowhere to get you some new duds?"

Becky's joke about the homeless actually did give me an idea. "Well, there is one place."

After lunch, I take Becky to Sew Much More, the local thrift and consignment shop. The mother of one of my classmates at school owns the store, and it features a wide selection of "gently used" clothes. Also, the owner is a seamstress, and there are many original designs as well. I've never been in, but then again, I've never been much for shopping, especially for clothes.

"What do you mean, you don't like shopping?" Becky asks me as we enter the store. "Are you gay or aren't you?"

"Not so loud." Just because I came out to my mother does not mean I am ready for the whole town to know. Sometimes I think Becky does it on purpose.

"It's just a stereotype. Just because you're Jewish doesn't mean I think you like bagels," I say.

"But I love bagels!" Becky puts an arm around my shoulder and pushes me toward the racks of clothes. "You just need to see what's out there. I've only ever seen you wear cargo shorts and T-shirts."

"What's wrong with what I wear?"

"Nothing. But change is good. A new outfit can make you feel like a new person." Becky has pulled me to the back of the store where there are several racks of men's clothes. She's quickly shuffling the hangers, which make high-pitched squeaks as they slide across the metal rack.

She pulls out a pair of dark blue Levi's and holds them out toward me. "What size are you? I think these might fit." She tosses the jeans at me and turns back to the rack. She's already on to the shirts before I can answer.

"Omigod, look at this!" She has pulled out a white shirt with a ruffled front. The ruffles are tipped with light blue. It's hideous.

"What is it?" She can't possibly expect me to wear it.

"It's a vintage tuxedo shirt with baby-blue piping! It's fabulous!"

"You sound like Renée."

"You'll look great in it."

"I will?" She spins me around and has the shirt up to my back. She measures the sleeves against my arms and hums an approving sound.

"Go try these on," she says. Before I know it I'm in the changing room at the back of the store. How can I say no? With a deep sigh, I pull off my trusty cargos and put on the jeans. Becky must have magic clothes powers or something because the jeans fit perfectly. When I go shopping with my mother I usually have to try on six or seven pairs before I can find a pair that's acceptable, so I'm shocked at Becky's instant success. I'm still skeptical about the tuxedo shirt and I stare at it for several seconds, trying to decide how hurt Becky would be if I refuse. I'm surprised by a knock on the door.

"Are you decent?" Becky doesn't wait for me to respond and pulls open the dressing room door.

"Becky!"

She shoves another hanger at me and closes the door again. This time I use the little metal hook to lock it.

"What do you want me to do with this?"

"Don't you love it?" "It" is a bright yellow T-shirt with diagrams of the sign language alphabet across the front. Over the pictures in blue letters it says, LET'S HEAR IT FOR SIGN LANGUAGE! I have to admit, it's pretty funny.

"But what about the ruffles?"

"Wear them both, silly. You'll need something under the tuxedo shirt anyway," Becky says through the door.

I look at the two shirts with skepticism, but there's only one way out of this store, and that's through Becky. I put them on.

"What do you think?" I step out of the dressing room and do a spin for Becky.

"You look so cute!" Becky says. "If you weren't gay, I'd eat you up right here."

"Shh! Becky, please! This is a small town." I look toward the front of the store where the owner is absorbed in a sewing project. She doesn't seem to notice. But Becky's right, I have to admit, I do kind of look like I belong on the cover of a magazine.

"Oh, and look what else I found." Becky holds up a worn leather jacket. "It's perfect."

I slip the jacket on, completing the look.

"Do you really think it's me?"

"The new you," Becky says.

We go to the front of the store to pay for the new clothes, and the owner gives me smile.

"You look great!" she says. She puts my cargo shorts and old T-shirt in a bag for me. "Let's see, thirty-seven dollars."

I open my wallet, but I only have a twenty and three ones.

"Um, Becky, do you have any money?"

"Just a ten." I give Becky a helpless look.

"I don't really need the tuxedo shirt."

"Forget it, hon." The owner reaches across the counter and pats my hand. "Thirty-three will be fine."

"Really?"

"You look too good to make you put anything back." She hits a button and the cash register opens. "Do me a favor? Make sure you tell everyone where you got the clothes, and we'll call it even."

Outside the store, the sun is still bright, but everything looks different. Becky was right: a new outfit does make you feel like a new person, and with it comes new perspective.

"I can't wait to show Jay my new look."

"I think he's working tonight; maybe we can stop by after dinner."

"Is it weird that I feel so much better about myself?"

"No. For the first time in your life you're being honest with your feelings and with the important people in your life."

"I guess you're right."

"Of course I'm right. Look at you, this is the happiest I've seen you. You're like a walking commercial for honesty." Becky stands in front of me and puts her hands up, making a "frame" with her thumbs and index fingers. She looks at me as if she was directing the commercial. "Thrift-store jeans, six dollars. Graphic T-shirt, two dollars. Vintage tuxedo shirt, four dollars. Vintage leather jacket, twenty-five dollars. Coming out of the closet—"

We both shout together, "Priceless!"

"Hey, let's head back to my cabin. If my parents are back from fishing, I can bum some more cash from them and we can take your mother out to dinner, my treat."

I think about my empty wallet and give Becky a skeptical look. She points a finger at me to stop me from arguing.

"I told you we were going to celebrate. Besides, you're all dressed up; now you need someplace to go."

Chapter 17

It's incredible how a new outfit can completely change you. I'm practically strutting as we walk down Main Street away from the thrift store. It's like being on stage. When I'm in a stage production at school, as soon as I put on that costume, I have a part to play. I'm expecting all eyes to be on me, so I act the part.

With my new outfit, that part is Sean Jackson, who just came out to his mom. I'm proud of myself; I've started a new life for myself. I'm the kind of guy who doesn't mind if he gets noticed.

It also happens to be two days before the Fourth of July, and Main Street is crowded. Independence Day is one of the biggest holidays in Bell Cove. Not only is it the height of summer, but the lake always draws people from all over for the fireworks. A lot of the lakeside towns have fireworks displays, so if you have a boat it can be fun to go out onto the lake where you can see several displays at once. The towns all try to coordinate as well, so no two towns are going off at the same time. If Bell Cove is at seven thirty, then maybe Eastford will be at seven forty-five, and Bolton will be at eight. I'm hoping Jay will invite me out on his boat to watch.

Becky and I dodge through the crowds walking along the lake as we make our way toward her cabin. We're just passing the post office when I spot them.

"Shit," I say under my breath but loud enough for Becky to hear.

"What's up?"

"Dan Sweeney and friends." I jerk my chin in the direction of three teenage boys walking toward us on the other side of the street.

"The no-necks at ten o'clock?"

I nod. "Let's just say we don't travel in the same circles."

Dan is tossing a football in the air as he walks, and with his attention on that, I'm hoping Becky and I might sneak by unnoticed. No such luck.

Morgan Watson, the tallest of the three, wearing a Tom Brady Patriots jersey, spots me and shouts, "Jackson!" Next thing I know, all three are heading across the street.

There aren't many kids at school that I have a real problem with. Bell Cove is a small place, and most of us have known each other since at least first grade. So even if I'm not friends with someone, we know each other well enough to stay out of each other's way. Dan Sweeney is the exception.

Dan and his ubiquitous buddies, Morgan Watson and Tom Michaud, are the stereotypical jocks who run the school. Dan is the captain of the football team, the popular kid who throws keggers on the weekends and gets away with it because he led the team to the championship for the first time in twenty years last year. They're not really bullies; they just feel the need to remind some of us who's in charge on occasion. As one of the "artsy" kids, I'm one of their more frequent targets.

"Who's the girl, Jackson?" Dan stops tossing his football long enough to look Becky up and down. "She's got nice tits."

"Excuse me?" Becky takes a step forward. She's not intimidated by anyone. I really admire that.

"It's a compliment." Dan shows his teeth in a leering grin at Becky. "What are you doing with Jackson, anyway? I didn't think he was into tits."

"Judging from that shirt, I don't think that's changed," Tom chimes in from behind Dan. "Nice outfit, Jackson."

And just like that, the Sean Jackson of two minutes ago, the one excited to show off his new look and ready to celebrate his coming out has been thrown back in the closet. I don't say anything; I can't figure out what I could say that Dan wouldn't just twist into some cruel gay joke. Instead, I just stand there, feeling like a deflated balloon.

"I think he looks hot," Becky says, latching herself on to my arm. "C'mon, Sean, we need to get going." Becky starts to walk off, pulling me with her.

Dan's smile shrinks just a little bit, as if he's confused that Becky won't defer to his superior physical presence. He takes a step forward to block me from passing. But Becky doesn't stop, and I just keep following. Dan's shoulder crashes into mine, with a force that surprises me since I didn't even see him move to make it happen, but I don't slow down. I can feel Becky's energy start to flow into me. Dan Sweeney can kiss my ass. A smile comes to my lips as I pass the trio of jocks.

"Fag," Dan says, so he can have the last word, but he doesn't try to come after us. I take a deep breath and let it out in a slow stream.

"Wasn't he a charmer," Becky says as we get out of earshot.

"How do you do that?"

"Do what?" Becky stops for a moment and looks me in the eye. "Guys like that have nowhere to go but down. They've already reached their peak. Honestly, it's pretty sad. If you remember that, they just don't seem so scary anymore."

All I can do is shake my head. The logic of Becky strikes again. But I can't stop to think about it for too long because Becky is already off and heading toward the cabins. I've got to run to catch up.

* * *

We return to the cabin just as Becky's parents are pulling a small fishing boat up to the dock. Becky's parents look surprisingly normal. They're both about forty, dressed in standard "vacation wear": khaki shorts and short-sleeved polo shirts. Somehow I expected something more. I find it hard to believe that two people so normal looking could have Becky for a daughter.

"Did you catch anything?" Becky shouts from the porch.

Her dad holds up a stringer with four bass on it. They're each about a pound. Not bad for a guy from the city. Becky's mom ties up the front of the boat and climbs onto the dock, then takes the stringer of fish from her husband. She holds them out away from her body as if they were radioactive. One of the fish still has some life and flips its tail in a futile attempt to escape. Becky's mom squeals and drops the stringer on the dock. The fish continues to flop and manages to make it over the edge of the dock.

"Hon, watch out!" Becky's father says.

"Oh, Frank, they're getting away!"

"The stringer, Judy!"

Becky and I watch her mom do a stomping dance on the dock as she tries to get her foot on the end of the stringer before the fish makes it into open water. Her father almost tips the boat over trying to grab the stringer himself. Becky smacks a palm to her forehead, but she's laughing.

"Leave it to my parents."

There's a yelp from her dad when her mom misses the stringer with her foot and hits his hand instead.

"Ow, that's my hand!"

"Sorry."

From the porch, we watch the bright blue stringer disappear over the side of the dock.

"Well, there goes dinner," Becky's dad says. He's chuckling to himself, and he puts an arm around his wife's waist. He guides her down the dock. When they reach the path to the cabin, he stops and gives her a kiss.

"PDA! PDA!" Becky sticks out her tongue beside me.

"I think they're cute."

"You would. You don't have to live with them."

Her parents make their way to the cabin, and Becky introduces them to me.

"So you're the famous Sean," Frank says.

"I don't know about famous," I say.

"The way Becky talks about you, you're famous to us," he says.

"I'm so glad we finally got to meet you," Judy adds.

I feel my cheeks turn warm, and I shuffle my feet. But the embarrassment has only just begun.

"Guess what? Sean finally came out to his mom." Becky practically shouts it to the entire lake.

"Becky!"

"You did?" her mom says. "Honey, that's great!" She comes forward and gives me a hug. I let her hug me, as I'm paralyzed by Becky's announcement. "I'm sure you being honest with her has lifted a load off her mind."

I glare daggers at Becky over her mom's shoulder, but Becky's oblivious.

"I took him shopping to celebrate. What do you think of his outfit?"

"Let's have a look." Judy releases me from the hug and holds me at arm's length.

"I had a shirt just like that," Frank says, poking me in the chest. "In fact, I think I got married in that shirt. Where'd you find it?"

"Sew Much More on Main Street," Becky says.

"I might have to check it out."

"Frank, the shirt is making a comeback, not you," Judy says.

"I want to take Sean and his mom out to dinner to celebrate

his big news. Would it be okay if I borrowed some money?" Becky gives her dad her best puppy dog eyes.

"Why don't we all go out?" Frank says. "Seeing as your mother let dinner swim away." Judy swats playfully at Frank. He rolls his eyes.

Judy adds, "Why don't we meet you at the Depot at six? We need time to change out of these fishy clothes. You and Sean can go and get his mother."

"Sounds great," Becky says. "We'll see you then."

Chapter 18

Becky has been keeping my mother's bike at her cabin, so we ride together back to my house. When we get there, a vehicle I've never seen before is parked in the driveway.

"Whose car?" Becky asks me.

I shrug and enter the house.

"Mom?"

"In here, sweetie," she calls from the kitchen.

"Who's here? There's a new car parked—" I stop short when I get to the kitchen. Becky runs right into me.

"Hey there, son."

My dad is sitting at the kitchen table beside my mother. There's a plate of cheese and crackers between them and glasses of iced tea. My jaw drops. My father is getting up and crossing to me. His arms are spread wide, but I don't move. He hugs me, and I don't resist. But I don't hug him back.

"Your dad surprised me, too, hon," my mom says.

"Flew in this morning. I cashed in that ticket you didn't want to use and bought one for myself. Figured if my son wasn't coming down to see me, I would come up to see him." He lets go of me.

I still say nothing.

My mom breaks the silence. "That's a nice jacket."

"We found it at the thrift shop downtown," Becky tells her.

"You must be Lisa," my father says over my shoulder to Becky. "The reason Sean didn't want to leave Bell Cove." He turns his attention back to me. "She's quite a catch, son."

My mother and Becky both talk at once.

"I'm not Lisa."

"This is Becky. She works with Sean at the Pink Cone."

"Oh," my father half grunts. He gives me a slap on the shoulder. "Well, she's still quite a catch."

"Mr. Jackson," Becky starts, "you don't understand. Sean—"

I whirl around and give Becky my best *You'll shut up now if you know what's good for you* look. Now is not the time for another outing. She takes in my set jaw and narrowed eyes.

"Sean and I have only been on one date. We're not a couple."

I mouth a "thank you" to Becky.

I feel my father's hand on my shoulder. "Give it time," he says.

Finally, I find my voice. "Dad, what are you doing here?"

"I already told you, I—"

"Don't you have a job? I mean, what about Georgia?"

"Turns out I have some vacation time. And your uncle Steve is letting me use his hunting cabin."

"Don't expect me to stay with you out there." Uncle Steve's cabin is a one-room box on the north side of the lake. No electricity, no indoor plumbing, and only accessible by boat. You take a shower by jumping into the lake.

My dad laughs. "You won't have to. It's only for this week. After that I've got a reservation at the Lakeside Cottages."

"That's where I'm staying," Becky says. "Mrs. Jackson, Sean and I came to invite you to dinner with my parents."

"How nice. Where?"

"The Depot."

My dad chimes in. "Very nice. Will I be imposing if I join you?"

I could have guessed he would invite himself.

"I don't think so," Becky says. "We're meeting them at six."

"Great. Jeanne, would it be okay if I used your bathroom to change into something nicer?"

"Sure, it's up the—"

"I remember."

"Right." My mother smiles. My father leaves to go get his suitcase.

As soon as I hear the door close, I wheel on Becky. "I can't believe you invited him!"

"I didn't invite him," Becky says. "He invited himself. I can't believe you made me lie for you."

"This was supposed to be a celebration dinner. How am I supposed to celebrate with him there?"

"You could tell him you're gay."

"Trust me, that wouldn't give anyone a reason to celebrate."

"It's better than lying."

My mom steps between us. She pulls me close to her and gives me a hug. "It's going to be okay. We can still celebrate. We'll tell your dad it's because you got a job." She lets go of me with one arm and pulls Becky into our hug. "And you," she says to Becky, "thank you for everything you've done for Sean. But this is one obstacle he's going to have to get over on his own."

My father reappears in the kitchen, rolling a suitcase behind him. My mother lets us go, and fusses over my new outfit.

"You really do look great. Did Becky help you pick this out?"

I notice she has tears in her eyes. There's been a lot of crying today.

"Well," she says taking a deep breath and pulling herself together, "I'm going to need to change myself, if we're going to the Depot." She heads upstairs, followed by my father and his wheelie bag.

While we wait, Becky and I head out to the deck where we can talk in private.

"So," Becky says, "that's your dad." It's a statement, not a question.

"The one and only."

"What's his deal? He lives in Georgia?"

"He moved down there a year ago with his girlfriend."

"You been down to visit him?"

"No." I'm leaning on the railing and looking out over the lake. Becky rests her elbows on the railing beside me.

"You don't have to talk about him if you don't want to."

"No, it's okay. We're just not that close. He wasn't around much when my parents were married, and after they got divorced it was even less. You'd think I'd be upset that he lives so far away, but it's actually easier. I don't have to worry about spending weekends with him anymore, and screwing up my plans."

Becky doesn't say anything.

"I mean, I love him. He's my dad. But I don't how he'll take it when he finds out his only son is gay."

"You think he'll be upset?"

"I know he will."

We're both silent for several minutes.

"But I need to tell him, don't I?"

Becky puts her hand on mine. "You know I can't tell you the answer to that. You also know what I think."

Chapter 19

The Depot is one of the nicest restaurants in Bell Cove. It occupies an old train station a few blocks away from Main Street. After the interstate went in, the passenger rail quickly died. The train station remained empty for years, but it was built solidly from brick and native timber, so it weathered the years relatively intact. When the new owners took it over with plans for an upscale restaurant, they didn't have to do much to the existing structure at all.

They did knock out large parts of the front wall and replace it with floor-to-ceiling windows. The Depot is far enough up the hill that the windows provide a stunning view of the lake. In the summer, reservations for a table by the windows are hard to come by.

Becky's parents must have connections, because when we arrive at the Depot, we're ushered to a table with a view. We're too early for sunset, but the expanse of dark blue water below us is still breathtaking. We take our seats around the table, and I pick up the menu. My father starts right in on Becky's parents.

"So, Frank, Judy, how long have you been coming to Bell Cove?"

"This is our first year, but I don't think it will be our last," Judy says.

"It's a beautiful location. I don't know if Sean mentioned that I live in Georgia. During the hot months, like now, I really miss this place."

"I bet," Frank says.

As long as the conversation stays on the weather, I might make it through this dinner alive. Do I want the stuffed pork chop or the shrimp scampi?"

"Becky, why is it that you decided to get a job on your vacation?"

"To get away from these two"—Becky throws a thumb toward her parents—"and to meet people my age to hang out with."

"Looks like you hit the jackpot with Sean."

I shoot my father daggers with my eyes.

"Oh, definitely, Sean's a real catch."

Becky's parents look up from their menus startled, but Becky says to them, "Sean's dad doesn't know about his problem."

"What problem, son?"

"Uh," I manage. I kick Becky under the table.

"How he's one of only two guys that work at the Pink Cone. And how *all* the girls are all over him."

"Really?" My dad seems impressed. I decide to run with the ball.

"Well, not really, but there are a couple of girls."

"Tell me."

The waiter approaches the table and asks if we are ready to order.

My father smiles at him, "Why don't you give us a few—"

"I'll have the stuffed pork chop," I say.

"And I'll have the rosemary chicken," Becky says. While the table is briefly distracted by the waiter, I whisper to Becky behind the menu.

"What are you doing?"

"Your dad thinks you're straight. I'm making you straight."

"I'll take those for you," the waiter interrupts us, taking the menus out of our hands and leaving us exposed. We turn sheepishly to the rest of the table.

"Sean," my father says, "we're at dinner."

I'm speechless. He actually thinks we were kissing.

"Oh, Mr. Jackson, you know how it is at the beginning of a relationship."

"Becky?" Her mother is looking very confused.

I change the subject. "Where'd you catch your fish today, Frank?"

I know my father can't resist sharing his expertise on the best fishing holes on the lake. By the end of the meal, my father and Frank are making a date to go fishing tomorrow. My father guarantees that Frank will come home with a lunker.

Chapter 20

We are leaving the Depot, and I think I've made it through the evening without any major catastrophes, when my father does it again.

"What do y'all say to some after-dinner ice cream?"

I freeze as solid as a tub of vanilla in the walk-in. There's only one ice cream place in Bell Cove.

"Why would you want to spoil such a great meal?" I ask.

"I want to see where you work."

I look at Becky, who's reading my mind. Jay is working tonight.

"Sean and I eat so much ice cream," she says.

My mom is slow to catch on. "I thought you said you could eat ice cream every day."

"Um, well, yeah, but my manager is working tonight, and—" Oops. That was the wrong thing to say, because now my mother is back in "mother mode."

"You mean your manager, Jay? I'd love to meet him."

"It's decided then," my father says. And it is. We pile into our respective vehicles and head downtown.

* * *

When we pull in to the Pink Cone, I'm relieved to see that it's crowded, a line forming almost to the sidewalk. Hopefully, that will mean Jay is too busy in the back to even notice we're here.

"Grape-Nut?" Frank asks as we get close enough to the board to read the available flavors. "What's that?"

"It's made with Grape-Nuts cereal," Becky explains. "It's really popular with older customers."

"Oh, I'll skip that one then." Frank chuckles. "Maybe you should try it, Judy."

Judy hits Frank playfully.

"Remember when we used to come here, Jeanne?" my father says.

"I do. That was a long time ago," my mother says.

The line moves quickly. I'm looking around to see where Jay is when Becky sends an elbow into my ribs.

"Ouch, what's that for?" But I already know. I see why I haven't been able to see Jay in the back. *Jay is working the window.*

"Why is he on the window? He never works the window."

Becky shrugs. "Maybe he knew you were coming."

We're steadily moving toward the front of the line and the moment when Jay will meet my parents. I'm trying to figure out some way to warn him, when he spots me in the line. His face lights up in a smile, and I melt, just a little. *Stay focused,* I tell myself.

"Hey, boy," he calls to me. "You want to watch the fireworks with me on my boat?"

I step around the customers in front of us and stand to one side. "I'm with my parents," I say in a quick breath. "And yes, I want to watch fireworks with you, but let's see if we can avoid them tonight?"

Jay turns his head sharply toward me and almost dumps the waffle cone he's holding on the woman at the window. He sees I'm not joking.

He turns back to the customer to hand her the rest of her order and speaks to me without turning his head.

"Gotcha. Best behavior."

The woman leaves, and my parents approach the window.

"Hello, Mrs. Jackson," Jay says. "What can I get for you?"

My mom takes her time and looks Jay straight in the eye. "Nice to meet you, Jay. I think I'll have a small scoop of Rocky Road in a sugar cone, please."

"Coming right up." Jay turns to scoop my mother's order, but she reaches out and grabs his wrist. He turns back, startled.

"Jay," my mother says quietly, "Sean told me about the canoe."

"The canoe," Jay repeats. It's half question, half statement.

"Yes. And I made it clear to him that I am concerned about how he is choosing to spend his time."

Jay glances at me. I'm as confused as he is; I thought she was cool.

"Because if his late nights continue, he may have to give up his job."

"Mom." I can't believe what I'm hearing.

"But," and my mom's voice becomes hard and heavy, "Sean has told me how important this—job—and the people here, are to him." My mom takes a breath. She doesn't want her meaning to be mistaken. "And I want you to know that I support Sean completely. I'm just concerned for his safety. So, Jay, can you promise me that you will make sure Sean doesn't get hurt?"

There's a moment of silence as my mother's words hang in the air. Jay blinks a couple times. The message was received loud and clear.

"Yes, Mrs. Jackson. I promise." Jay looks at me and raises his eyebrows slightly. I shake my head. I had no idea. "Will there be anything else tonight?"

"No, I think that will do it for me."

Jay leaves the window to get my mother's order.

"Jeanne?" my father says. "Is everything all right?"

"Everything's great." She reaches out and puts a hand on my shoulder and gives it a gentle squeeze. Jay returns to the window.

"It's on the house, Mrs. Jackson."

Two days later, Bell Cove is absolutely overrun. Tourists and locals alike stake out their spots hours in advance. Every inch of beach, every square foot of grass, every bench, every picnic table has been claimed by a blanket, or a towel, or a picnic basket.

The Fourth of July is the biggest holiday on the lake. People plan their barbecues for months in advance. For many it doubles as a family reunion, and it's not unusual to see cars from several states away cruising down Main Street looking for parking that probably doesn't exist. But the real place to be on the Fourth of July is out on a boat. All day long, the lake is dotted with multicolored sails and the white froth of speedboats cutting back and forth across the dark blue water.

When the sun starts to set, people toss anchors overboard and turn on their running lights, staking out the spots with the best view of the ring of villages along the shoreline. Soon the glittering jewels of fireworks will erupt all around the lake, proceeding in order as if rotating around a clock face. A well-placed boat will be able to see five or six different displays over the course of an hour and a half. A few of the more adventurous will even set off their own fireworks from the back of their boats.

The air is filled with the aroma of charcoal and grilled meat from hibachi grills set up by the families with pontoon party boats or the larger cabin cruisers. Later, the smell will be replaced by sulfur and the bitter smoke from handheld sparklers and Roman candles.

From Jay's boat, I can see all of this. He stops the boat a little ways away from the main group of boats so we can have some privacy. We might not have the best view on the lake, but it's still way better than the people back on shore. My mom and dad are out with Becky and her parents, camped along one of the beaches along the shore. I feel a little bad for Becky, trapped with the adults for the evening, but I wouldn't trade places for anything.

I'm standing in the bow seats of Jay's boat and he's just thrown the anchor overboard, a long yellow rope snaking down into the water after the metal weight. He comes up behind me and places his arms around my shoulders. I feel his lips tickle my ear and then he kisses my neck. Once, twice, three times before I give in and turn to face him. Then we are kissing, his tongue sliding between my lips, his hand at the back of my neck. We stand in this embrace for a long minute before we both need air.

"I've never been out on the lake for the Fourth before," I say when we break apart. "My mom's not a fan of boats, so we always watch from shore."

"You're going to love it from here then."

"I'm already loving it, and it's not even dark yet."

"Just wait." Jay turns away and opens a compartment beneath one of the bow seats. It's a cooler and he's stashed several sodas in ice. He tosses one to me. He opens another compartment and pulls out a small picnic basket. "Here, I brought us dinner."

Jay leads me to the back of the boat where he opens a fold-down table and begins setting up a spread of cheese, meats, crackers, and olives. He pulls out a small candlestick in a holder, and lights it with his lighter. There's also a plate of sliced veggies and hummus. It looks like something out of a fancy catering magazine.

"Did you make this?" No one besides my mom has ever made me dinner before, and even though this is simple, it's also very romantic.

"I wouldn't exactly say I made anything," Jay says with a grin. "But I hope you like it."

"I love it." And I find myself kissing Jay again, the food nearly forgotten for the moment.

Eventually, we do eat the food while we wait for the sun to finish its descent. As darkness falls, the boats surrounding us turn on their red and green running lights. Soon, the lake is alive with twinkling lights. It's so different from the last time on Jay's boat when we were the only boat for what seemed like miles.

And then it starts. Off to the left, the fireworks begin. There's a whistle and then a bang that rolls across the water, and a bloom of white appears in the sky. Similar explosions of red and blue and green follow it. The display goes on for several minutes, and I watch in fascination as each rocket is also reflected in the water, creating mirrored displays.

Jay slips my hand in his and squeezes. "Do you like?" he says into my ear.

In response, I turn and kiss him on the cheek. "It's beautiful," I say.

Almost as soon as the first display has finished in a grand finale of multicolored pinwheels and sparkling chandeliers, the next one starts. And then the next. It's a never-ending pyrotechnic display. By the time the third and fourth towns have started their fireworks, Jay and I have moved to the front of the boat, but we're no longer watching the show. Instead, we are making our own fireworks, my lips on his, his hand on my back, my hand in his hair. I don't think this is what they mean in the movies when they say you see fireworks when you kiss the right person, but it sure feels like a scene from a movie.

On this night, everything is perfect: the lake, the boat, Jay. I never want to leave this moment. And even though the fireworks do end, the vibrations don't stop inside of me. They're exploding long after the smoke has floated away on the night breeze and Jay has guided his boat back toward the Bell Cove marina. It's a feeling I've never felt with anyone before, and I wonder, Could this be what it feels like to be falling in love?

Chapter 21

After a month of working at the Pink Cone, the job starts to settle into a routine. I work three nights during the week and Saturday afternoon and evening. Becky works the same schedule as me, so even a slow shift is fun. The best part is that Jay works all of my shifts, too. I'm not sure if he arranged it that way, but I'm not complaining.

It does mean we can spend lots of time together before and after work. Most of that is spent on his boat. Jay puts up the collapsible sunshade for privacy, and we make out on the rear banquette. Sometimes we'll get a pizza and Becky will join us, though we don't plan any more trips out to Camp Aweelah.

Of course, not every day at the Pink Cone is cherry vanilla.

"Thank goodness you're here," Ashley says to me as I walk in for my shift on a Saturday afternoon at the end of July.

"That bad?"

"Harleigh called in sick so it's just been Jay and me for the past four hours. Harleigh's new boyfriend just got a motorcycle."

"Is it a Harley?" I smile.

Ashley practically throws her ice cream scoop at me. "Jay said when you got here I could take a break." Amanda marches past me and out the back door. I watch her go, wondering what could have usually quiet Amanda so worked up. I'm about to find out.

First of all, Becky's late, which wouldn't be a big deal except that I've barely pulled my bright pink T-shirt over my head when a parade of six-year-olds bounds up the porch steps to the window. There's about ten of them, all shouting their desired flavors at the top of their lungs. I'm thankful for the clapboard wall saving me from a stampede and it's sure-to-be-bloody aftermath.

"Chocolate chip!"

"Cookie dough!"

"Do they have Mooth Trackth?" shouts one little girl who is missing her front teeth.

"Jay!" I shout over my shoulder, calling for reinforcements.

A blond woman in her early thirties splits the sea of children and approaches the window. She lets out a deep sigh before telling me, "Ten kiddie cones." She turns back to the kids. "Tell the nice man what flavor you want," she says, prying a boy with red cheeks off her leg.

I am bombarded by ten shrieking voices simultaneously.

"Chocobanacookiepepperminillabutter!"

"One at a time," I say.

"Quiet!" The woman's sudden volume makes me jump, and I hit my head on the top of the window. I briefly see stars. "Line up! Jimmy is the birthday boy; let him go first." The mother directs the children as they push their way into a single-file line.

I look over my shoulder. Where's Jay? Where's Becky? I grab a pencil and a pad of paper that we keep by the window to keep track of big orders.

"Chocolate chip," the red-cheeked boy says and then buries his face in his mother's jeans.

"Laci, what would you like?" the mother says to the girl next in line.

It's the girl with no teeth. "Mooth Trackth."

"We don't have Moose Tracks," I say. "How about something else?"

The girl stares at me. After a moment the mother bends down. "They don't have it. What would you like instead?"

"Mooth Trackth!" the girl yells, as if being louder will change my mind. I look at the mother and try to give her a smile, but already I can see tears forming in the girl's eyes.

The mother kneels in front of Laci. "Shh," she says quietly and then turns to look up at me with an apologetic smile. She turns back to the child.

I take the opportunity to figure out what happened to Jay. Surely he can hear all of this racket and realize I'm in over my head.

"Jay?" I call toward the freezer. No answer. I suddenly realize that I'm the only one in the store. I feel my face grow warm and my heart rate increase just a touch as I turn back to the small army of children in front of me. I am outnumbered and out-gunned. I take a breath.

"We have peanut butter cup," I offer. "It's like Moose Tracks."

"It's not the same!" The girl bursts into tears. I'm left hold-ing the pad and pencil, helpless.

"Maybe I can get everyone else's order?" I ask the mom, but she is too focused on the crying girl to hear me. So I turn away and start to scoop chocolate chip. Leaning over the freezer, I imagine myself crawling inside and away from the crying chil-dren behind me. I lean a little farther over; the frozen air feels good on my face.

I feel a shooting cold at the base of my spine, and my body involuntarily reacts. I raise my head too quickly and hit it on the freezer lid.

"Ow! What the—"

"Hey, Sean." Jay is standing behind me with a five-gallon con-tainer of rum raisin in his arms. He smiles at me and lets his hand brush along my back as he bends forward to put the ice cream away. I don't have to ask him where he's been; this close, I can smell the cigarette he was smoking out back.

"I really need your help. Becky's late, and the girl wants Moose Tracks, and—"

Jay holds up a hand to quiet me. "Watch and learn, young grasshopper," he says in an exaggerated Japanese accent. He turns around to the window where the little girl's wails have slowed to staggered sobs. "Hey, there," Jay says. "It's your lucky day. I found a container of Moose Tracks in the back. It's the last one." The girl's face immediately relaxes into a smile, and the mother looks up gratefully.

"But, Jay," I whisper behind him, "we don't—"

He turns around and says so the girl can't hear, "Just give her a scoop of peanut butter cup. One thing you should learn now, six-year-olds can't tell the difference."

And he's right. I scoop the peanut butter cup into a cone and hand it to the girl. Jay helps me finish the rest of the order, and the army of six-year-olds retreats to a pair of picnic tables on the side lawn, devouring their ice cream with sticky-fingered gusto.

When the children have all left the porch, I turn on Jay.

"Where were you?"

"I was out back. I thought you'd have everything under control."

"Well, I didn't." I turn away from him.

"Hey, babe, I'm sorry." Jay puts his hands on my shoulders from behind and squeezes. I shrug him off.

"You should be. You're the manager."

I can hear Jay's mouth open to say something, but just at that moment a voice interrupts us.

"Not so close, you two! This is a place of business."

I wheel around. "Becky! Where have you been?"

"Sorry I'm late. Did I miss anything?"

"Only Sean getting beat up by a six-year-old."

"Beat up?" Becky says.

"Oh, yeah." Jay smiles. "Lots of tears. It wasn't pretty."

"Shut up." I give Jay a shove into the freezer. He's about to retaliate, but Becky jumps between us.

"Okay. I get the picture. I see that I can't leave the two of you alone." She turns to Jay. "Don't you have some ice cream to make or something?"

He bows deeply. "Your wish is my command, my queen."

"Are you talking to me or Sean?" Becky gives me a wink.

I feel my face turning red as heat rushes to my cheeks. I think about jumping in the freezer again.

"I was talking to you, sweetheart. Sean is my prince." Jay blows me a kiss, but I am too embarrassed to respond. He just laughs at me and leaves to finish the night's ice cream batches.

"He really is sweet on you," Becky says. "I'm so glad I got you together!"

"*You* got us together? As I recall—" I am cut off as an older couple walks through the front door. The man holds the door for the woman and gestures grandly with his free arm in a sweeping motion to usher her in. They're in their eighties, and it's cute to see two people still in love after so many years. "What can I get for you?" I ask.

"What's wrong with you kids? None of you has any patience. Give us a minute to look at the menu," the man says. The smile he had been giving his wife has turned into a frown for me. I'm too surprised at his rudeness to respond, but Becky saves me.

"Take your time," she says.

"Of course I'll take my time. I don't like to be rushed."

Becky only smiles and adds, "Just let us know when you're ready." She turns away from the window.

"How do you do that?" I say.

"What?"

"Smile."

"If you had grandparents like mine, you'd understand," she

says. "When you spend every Saturday with an eighty-year-old Jewish couple, complaints just go through one ear and out the other."

The man calls through the window. "Can we get some service over here!"

"Yes, sir," Becky says. "What can I get for you?"

"Why don't you have jimmies on your menu?"

"We do, but we call them chocolate sprinkles," Becky explains.

"Why don't you call them jimmies?"

"Some people think it's a racist term," Becky says.

"That's ridiculous! It's the damn liberals at it again!" The man's eyes grow wide, and he starts to spit as he talks. "How can something you put on ice cream be racist? When I was a boy we could call people whatever we wanted, and no one took offense. You wanted to call a woman a broad or a doxy, you did! If a guy was a queer, you called him a queer, and no one made you feel bad about it."

I completely freeze up. I have no good reason, but I can't move. Living in a small town, you get used to hearing bigoted language, but it's not usually quite so in-your-face. Luckily, Becky has no such fear.

"Well, sir," she says, her words polite but her voice hard-edged like a knife, "you're not a boy, and times have changed, and people are more respectful and open-minded."

"Times have changed. You young people don't respect your elders anymore."

"I respect you," Becky says softly. "I just don't respect your opinions." She turns away from the window and grabs a paper bowl. She scoops vanilla ice cream, slamming the scoops into the cup. Finally, she grabs the chocolate sprinkles. When the vanilla is completely covered in brown flecks, she returns to the window.

"On the house," she says.

The old man grunts, grabs two spoons from the container by

the window, and guides his wife out the door. Just before the door shuts behind them, Becky shouts, "You're welcome!"

She turns around and lets out a throaty scream without opening her mouth. "People like that make me so angry!"

I just look at Becky for a moment. Then I throw my arms around her in a bear hug.

"You're choking me."

"You're my hero. I can't believe you did that."

"I'm not a hero."

"You are to me. You stood up for something when I couldn't." I continue to hug Becky until I realize we are being watched. A guy about my age is standing at the window. I realize he's not alone. Another boy of about eight is next to him, his wispy blond hair just sticking up above the counter. He raises himself up on his tiptoes, and I can see his freckled nose.

"Uh, hi. Can I help you?" I say, releasing Becky. She stifles a giggle.

"Yeah, can I get a kiddie-size strawberry in a . . . Sean? I didn't know you worked here."

It takes me a second to recognize Matt Maguire, a classmate at school. He used to have long shaggy hair, but now it's cut short and styled in messy spikes. I knew that eventually some-one would recognize me working here, but this still catches me off guard.

"Matt. You got your hair cut."

He smiles and looks at his feet. "Yeah. My mom was on me about it for months." He runs a hand through the hair above his ear. "Nice shirt."

I roll my eyes. "This was the only job left by the time I got around to getting one."

"That sucks, man."

"It's not that bad. It's fun sometimes. Becky's fun."

Becky, who had been helping another customer at the other window, perks up when she hears her name.

"Nice of you to introduce me to your hot friend." She shoves me to the side, and before I can say anything, she sticks her hand through the window opening. "I'm Becky, and you are?"

"Matt. And this is my cousin Andrew. I'm babysitting."

"That's sweet. Seeing as Sean's been totally ignoring you, what can I get you?" she says.

I tap Becky on the shoulder and hand her the strawberry cone. "Who said I was ignoring anybody?"

"I stand corrected. Here you go." She hands the cone to Andrew, who takes it happily. She turns back to Matt. "And what about you, cutie? Did Sean bother to ask what you'd like?"

Matt blushes and shakes his head. "I'm good," he says.

"Oh, come on, it'll be on the house," Becky says, "for Sean's friend."

"Maybe a small scoop of"—he looks over the menu—"Purple Cow?"

"Coming right up!"

Becky scoops out the ice cream and collects the money for the strawberry cone. Matt thanks her and leaves the porch with his cousin. He smiles at us and raises his cone in thank you before heading out the door.

"Why didn't you tell me you had such cute friends?" Becky bites a fingertip in a gesture of repressed lust.

I roll my eyes. "Matt's not a close friend. We're in drama together, but that's it. I think we had algebra together freshman year. He's much cuter now that he cut his hair. I never really noticed him before. I hope he doesn't go and tell everyone at school where I work."

"What are you so worried about? Even if he does, so what?"

"People will think I'm gay!"

"Newsflash—people already think that." Becky folds her arms and gives me a knowing look. Her words are prickly and sting.

"How would you know that?" I say. "Just because you assume every guy you meet is gay doesn't mean everyone does. I happen to like my straight life."

"That's only because you're hiding your gay one."

"Shh! I don't want anyone to—"

"To what? Hear? C'mon, Sean, I thought you were over this."

"Well, I guess I'm not, okay?" I can feel tears forming, and I don't know why. Becky has hurt my feelings, but even I think I'm being dumb. Maybe it's just not that easy to come out after all. "I need a bathroom break."

Before Becky can see how she's affected me, I'm out of there. I rush through the back room, where Jay is standing at the mixer, and directly to the bathroom. I don't want Jay to see me, either.

I stare at myself in the bathroom mirror for several minutes, leaning hard on the porcelain sink attached to the wall. The day has been one bad thing after another. I take a deep breath and run water into the sink, letting it warm up a little. After a few seconds I feel the temperature change, and I cup my hands under the stream and splash my face. I do this a few times until the tears have been washed away. I no longer want to cry, which is good, but I still feel awful. There's a knock on the door.

"Sean?" It's Jay. "Are you okay?"

"I just need a minute."

"Okay. Just checking. You've been in there a while."

"I'll be right out."

I pull out several paper towels from the dispenser mounted on the wall above the sink, and dry my face and hands. I take a last look in the mirror and turn to leave. There's still two more hours until my shift is over.

I open the bathroom door, and I am surprised to find Jay waiting for me.

"Jay?"

"Hi, boy. Are you okay? Becky said you were pretty upset."

"I'm okay now. It's just been a bad day so far."

"Some days are like that. Listen, I'm sorry I stranded you

with all of those little kids earlier. I should have been there to help."

"It's okay. I need to learn how to handle tough situations."

"Let me make it up to you. We're off in a couple hours. Let's take my boat over to Clearlake and catch a movie. You, me, a bucket of popcorn, and a dark room. What do you say?"

I don't say anything. I just let myself fall into Jay's chest and feel his arms wrap around me. Finally, I whisper in his ear, "Can we get gummy bears?"

Jay is my hero for the rest of the afternoon, and fortunately no more bad customers show up to ruin my salvaged mood. I can't wait for our shift to end so that I can be alone with Jay. I even make Becky buy a newspaper on her break so that I can look at the movie listings.

"I don't see why it matters what's playing," she says to me when she returns with the paper. "It's not like you're going to watch the movie."

"Shut up. You're just jealous." I'm not angry with her anymore. I know she doesn't mean to hurt me, even when she does.

Finally, it's nearly six, and our replacements arrive. I head to the back to change out of my pink shirt. I just get my shirt over my head when there's a knock on the break room door.

"Just a minute."

"Sean," Becky says from the other side of the door, "your dad's here."

"My dad?"

"Yeah."

"I'll be right out."

I throw my fresh shirt over my head and don't bother with my hair. I race to the front of the store. Why would my dad come to visit me at work?

He's standing on the porch with a coffee ice cream cone, looking out at the lake.

"Dad?"

He turns when I say his name. "Sean. Your mother told me you got off at six. I'm glad I caught you."

"What are you doing here?" But all I have to do is look down the walk to where his rental is parked at the curb. I can see them sticking out of the rear window from here. Fishing poles.

"I thought maybe we could go fishing. I just drove over from the tackle shop in Mason, and I can tell you the fish are rising all over the lake."

"I kind of had plans." My father looks hurt. "Besides, what are you going to use for a boat?"

"You don't need a boat to go fishing, Sean, but since you asked, there's a couple of boats down at the cottages for guests to use. The little outboard motor won't take us too far, but I know some good spots near Bell Cove. Whaddya say?"

I'm still trying to decide what I want to say when Jay walks out on the porch. "There you are. Are you ready to go? Oh, hi, Mr. Jackson." Jay's body goes rigid as he puts on his "best behavior" act for my father.

"I'm impressed you remember who I am. You're Sean's manager, right?"

"Jay." Jay holds out his hand. My father takes it and gives it a vigorous shake. "Sean and I were about to go see a movie. Did you have other plans?"

"I was going to take my son out fishing. Do you think you guys could do the movies later?"

I give Jay a look that I hope says, *No! Please save me from having to go fishing with my father!* but I can see that Jay has no good reason for coming between a man and his son.

"I'm sure there's a late show. Maybe we can go tonight," Jay says, giving me a hopeful look. This compromise is hardly acceptable, but I shouldn't be surprised, considering how everything else has gone today.

"Great," my father says. "C'mon, Sean, we've still got a good two hours before it starts to get dark."

I watch him go down the porch steps. "I'll be right there." I turn back to Jay. "I'm sorry."

"It's not your fault."

"Tonight?"

"Yeah. Call me when you get back. Catch a big one for me." I give Jay a fake laugh, and reluctantly follow my dad to his car.

Chapter 22

With one foot in the bow of the boat, I push us off from the dock with the other foot. I swing my leg over the side and sit on the bow seat while my father starts the motor. It's just a little eight horsepower, but it is surprisingly noisy. It's too loud for conversation as my father guides the boat along the shoreline to one of his favorite local fishing spots.

There are two poles and a small tackle box that he must have bought that afternoon because the price tag is still stuck on the side. I stare at the fluorescent orange "$9.99" and try to forget that I could be racing across the lake with my arms around Jay, lake breeze and spray on our faces.

My father reaches into his back pocket and pulls out a gold cellophane pouch. I recognize his Captain Black pipe tobacco. I have been with my father many times when others have complimented him on the smell of his pipe, but I find it repulsive. The sickeningly sweet scent fills my nose almost as soon he opens the pouch. I wish the boat were going faster so that the breeze might help blow away the smell. He hooks the tiller under one arm while he fills his pipe with a wad of tobacco from the pouch. He holds the black strings between his thumb and index finger and then in a practiced movement tamps it down in the bowl of the pipe with his thumb. He pulls a lighter from his shirt pocket and lights it. He does this with one hand, cupping the bowl of the pipe and lighting the lighter all at the same time. I'm impressed with his dexterity even as I am nauseated by the smell.

Once the pipe is lit, my father looks off across the lake, puffing silently. The sun has started to drop toward the horizon and an orange glint comes into my father's eyes. I realize he is a handsome man. I've never thought of him as anything but my father, but looking at him now, when I haven't seen him for almost a year since he moved to Georgia, I can see him differently. He's a big man, over six feet, with salt-and-pepper hair that makes him look a little older than he really is. "Distinguished," my mother would say. He has an impressive, but neatly trimmed, mustache that gives him a scholarly look. I notice that he has taken to wearing glasses all the time now. The last time I saw him, he was still insisting he only needed them for reading. He's chosen a stylish pair of wire-rimmed glasses, and I wonder if his new girlfriend helped him pick them out.

He continues to stare off to the distant shore, and I wonder what is on his mind. I haven't been fishing with him in years; there must be something important to talk about.

And then a scary thought enters my head. He knows. My mother must have told him. Becky thought I was weak because I was afraid someone at school might figure out that I'm gay, but I am terrified that my father will find out. Telling my mother was bad enough, and I pretty much knew she'd take it all right, but I am not ready for this discussion with my father. I look around. We are only a hundred feet from shore. I could swim it easily, but then what? We've reached a swampy arm of the lake where there are no houses or roads.

I am stuck. Captive. Trapped. A prisoner. There is nothing I can do but sit. And fish.

Finally, my father cuts in toward a bank of lily pads and cattails where a couple of ancient trees have long ago fallen over into the water. The weathered trunks are silvery gray in the evening light. My father hands me a fishing pole.

"This is the spot," he says. "This is where we catch the ten-pounder." He double-checks his lure, a green-and-orange tiny torpedo, meant to look like a frog. He flicks his wrist and the lure sails through the air and lands with a tiny splash just off the end of one of the trees. He lets the lure sit for a few seconds before retrieving it. Then, slowly, he begins to reel it in. Every few seconds he jerks his wrist and the lure does a little splashy "jump." Then he lets it sit again a few seconds, and the whole cycle repeats. He does this until the lure is only a few feet from the boat.

"Had one following it. A big one." My father is always saying things like this while fishing. When I was little I would practically fall overboard craning to see the "monster fish" that was constantly threatening his tiny lure. I'm a more skeptical audience now.

Fishing with my dad when I was little was one of the few times we'd have to ourselves. I used to complain when my dad would wake me up to go fishing when I was little. The sun wouldn't have risen and you could still see your breath, and Dad would drag me out on the water in search of the "big one." But in reality, most of my best memories of my dad are with a fishing pole in my hands. It was the one time all of his attention would be on me and I didn't have to compete with a job or any other adults. Even now, it's peaceful out on the lake. The dusk has brought a stillness to everything, and as angry as I've been with my father the past few days, I feel closer to him than I have in years. Close enough maybe to share the new me. Maybe.

"See if you can hit that lily pad over there, with the flower." He points to a white water lily about forty feet to my right.

I flick the fishing rod in the direction of the flower. I'm pleased to see it go in the right direction. Even without practice, I get the lure to hit its target. My father doesn't say anything. I turn to look at him, but he is concentrating on his own lure. I'm disappointed that he wasn't watching. When I was little he would have given me an "All right," or "Nice cast."

I go about the business of retrieving the lure, following the same rhythm my father used. No luck. I try again, aiming for a water lily about ten feet to the left of the first one. For several minutes the only sounds are the whine of the reels as line is let out and the soft splashing as the lures hit the water.

"Sean." My father breaks the silence. "I brought you out here because there's something I need to talk to you about."

I knew it.

"I talked with your mother the other night after we had dinner, and she said that I needed to talk to you."

I don't say anything.

"Becky's a really nice girl, Sean."

He seems to be waiting for me to respond, so I say, "Yeah."

"I hope she wasn't offended when I called her quite a catch."

"I doubt it." I cast out my lure again. Waiting for my father to get to the point is like waiting for a fish to bite.

"Finding someone to share your life with is tricky. It takes time. I know you've only met Jill a few times."

Jill is his girlfriend in Georgia. She seems nice enough. She moved with him to Georgia, and before they moved she would sometimes be around when I would visit on weekends. She always treated me well; she never tried to monopolize my time with my dad or anything like that. And since he met her, Dad's been much less of a workaholic, so there's that.

"She and I took some time before things got"—he pauses to check something on the fishing reel—"romantic."

This is killing me. I decide to force the issue. "Becky's not my girlfriend."

He seems surprised, like I've broken his train of thought. "What about Lisa?"

"Lisa's a counselor at Camp Aweelah."

"So, you two are on a break for the summer then?"

"We're on a break." I've reeled my lure right up to the boat.

I let it trail in the water. The little propeller on the end makes a mini wake as I move my rod back and forth.

"Your mother said you weren't seeing anybody."

"She did?"

"Was she wrong?"

I pause before answering. "No."

The pause gives me away. When I was five years old, my mother left me with my father for the day while she went to visit my aunt Maureen who had just had a baby. Normally, when my father was left to take care of me, he threw a life jacket over my head, plopped me in the boat, and we went fishing. But this day it was raining; fishing was out. So instead my father produced a deck of cards and proceeded to teach me how to play poker. He started with the basics: seven-card stud and five-card draw. He introduced wild cards. He taught me "Fours, Whores, and Mustache Growers," and his personal favorite, "Aces and Jacks and the Man with the Axe, and a Pair of Natural Sevens Wins." Eventually, I had emptied my piggy bank onto the living room floor, and we played penny ante all afternoon.

That first day he let me win. I took all of his pocket change, which seemed like a fortune to a five-year-old. But it was a long time before I won any money from my father again. Not until he taught me about "reads" and bluffing did I understand how he always seemed to know what I had in my hand. My father is a good poker player. He never misses a "tell," the little facial expressions or gestures or verbal tics that give a person away. And my pause was an obvious tell.

"Sean, what doesn't your mother know?"

I stay silent, watching the lure in the water.

"You can trust me, Sean. You can talk to me about anything. Your mother doesn't need to know."

"I'm not seeing anybody, Dad." I don't look up, but I can feel his eyes on me. He knows I'm lying. He's silent for a long time, and then I hear the whine of his fishing reel as he casts his lure again.

"If you decide you want to tell me, I'm here."

The funny thing is, a part of me does want to tell him. A part of me wants to stop lying, lying to my own father, and to stand up in the bow of the boat and scream, "I'm gay! I'm in love with Jay! You met my boyfriend at the Pink Cone today and I'm in love with him!" I'm starting to realize how much energy it takes to hide all the time, to always be looking over my shoulder and wonder who might be watching, listening, suspecting. And hiding from my own father is especially tiring. I'm finally starting to understand why Becky has been pushing me so hard.

With a sigh, I cast out my lure again. Start to reel it in.

After about forty-five minutes, the sun has started to drop below the trees, and we need to head back before we get caught on the lake in the dark. My father pulls the starter on the motor, and we are heading home.

The entire ride back I try to play out the conversation in my head. "Dad, I'm gay." But I can't get any farther. The truth of the matter is I have no idea how my father will react. Will he be hurt? Maybe. Disappointed? Almost surely. Angry? I hope not. But I don't know.

It is full-on dusk when we finally spot the lights of Lakeside Cottages. My father steers us toward the dock in the failing light, and I prepare to jump out and tie us up.

"Sorry we didn't catch anything," my father says while I hook the bowline to the cleat on the dock. "I thought for sure they'd be biting."

"That's okay."

I start to walk toward the cottages, but my father catches me by the shoulder. He holds his fishing poles in one hand, but with the other he pulls me to him and gives me a one-armed hug.

"When you want to talk, I'll be here."

I nod. He smells of Old Spice and Captain Black, but I wrap

my arm around him and hug him back. Then with a squeeze on my shoulder he lets me go.

As soon as my father drops me off at home, I run inside to call Jay. It's not too late to go to the movie, I think. I dial the numbers and the phone rings. And rings. And rings.

No answer. Where is he? He knew I'd be calling, and now he's not answering. Great. A great finish to a great day.

Chapter 23

"So your dad took you fishing?" my mother asks me when I wake up the next morning.

"Yeah." I've been awake for about ten minutes, and this is not how I want to start my day.

"That must have given you some time to talk."

"Yeah."

"What did you talk about?"

"Wow, Mom."

"You don't have to tell me if you don't want to. I just thought—"

"You and Dad have been doing a lot of thinking recently, haven't you? I should be the one asking you what you talked about with Dad."

"He told you we talked after dinner the other night?"

"It came up."

"I didn't tell him."

"I know. Thanks."

"It's up to you to tell him when you're ready."

"Yeah. He knows something's up. But I'm not ready yet."

"Okay. By the way, Becky called for you last night before you got back from fishing."

"Oh?"

"Wanted to know about a date with Jay?" My mother looks curious herself.

"The one that never happened?"

"No?"

"Yeah, I called him after I got home, but he didn't pick up his cell. It's no biggie. We were going to go to a movie, and it was probably too late by then, anyway."

"Well, there'll be other movies. Don't be afraid to keep me posted."

"I know, Mom. I will. I'm going to go call Becky, okay?"

She smiles at me and turns around to refill her coffee mug. I have been dismissed.

Becky picks up on the second ring.

"Sean?"

"Yeah. You weren't waiting by the phone or anything were you?"

"Only a little. Sean, we have to talk."

"Okaaay." I can't help but wonder why Becky is using the dreaded four-word phrase. "Are you breaking up with me?"

"No." Silence.

"Becky?"

"I'm not breaking up with you, but I think Jay might be."

"What?" My stomach clenches and churns like I ate some bad sushi.

"I probably shouldn't be telling you this, but after you left with your dad yesterday, I overheard Jay calling another friend to go out to a club. He was out back and didn't know I could hear him. I was in the bathroom."

"What?"

"Sean, what was I supposed to do? If Jay has another boyfriend, you want to know, don't you?"

"I . . . don't . . . know. Wait. What exactly did he say?"

"I didn't catch all of it. I heard the end. He said he was free and that he'd meet the person on the phone at ten."

"Well, that doesn't mean it was a date." But it sure sounds like one. And he wasn't free. He had made plans with me.

"Sean, I don't want to hurt you, but I don't want you to get hurt."

I take a deep breath. "You're right. You shouldn't have told me."

"Sean."

"No. You say you don't want me to get hurt, but that's exactly what you're doing. You make it sound like you want to protect me at the same time you shove a knife in my back. I can take care of myself."

"Sean. Please."

"You've done enough. I have to go." I hang up the phone, but the conversation continues in my head. Jay has other friends. The first night we went out he had made plans with his other friends to go to a club. It means nothing.

But he said he was free. He was not free. He had plans with you. You were supposed to go to the movies.

But I got home late. He got tired of waiting.

He made the plans before he knew you'd be late.

He can have other friends.

He should have told you.

He should have told you.

I decide to take a shower to drown out my thoughts.

I spend the rest of the day shut in my room. Twice I pick up the phone to call Jay. Once I even dial. But I hang up before the phone starts to ring.

The problem is I don't know what to say. Do I ask about his night? What if he lies? Worse, what if he tells the truth and breaks up with me? What if I come right out and ask if he went out with someone else? If it's not true, he'll think I don't trust him. And what if it is true?

I kick the phone under my bed.

* * *

I decide to sign online. I find a familiar screen name in my buddy list. I open up a chat.

NHBeachBoi: Are you really there?

I only have to wait a few seconds.

LuvBug922:   I'm here!!! SEAN!!!!!! {{{{{HUGS}}}}}

NHBeachBoi: {{{HUGS}}} What are you doing online?

LuvBug922:   OMG, I totally twisted my ankle riding horses
                 yesterday. I got my foot caught in the stirrup! ☹

NHBeachBoi: OUCH! You ok?

LuvBug922:   I'm fine but I'm not allowed to walk on it for 24 hrs.
                 I'm stuck in the office all day today. At least I get
                 to use the internet. ☺

NHBeachBoi: That's cool.

LuvBug922:   how r u? How's the pink cone?

NHBeachBoi: ok

LuvBug922:   only ok?

NHBeachBoi: yeah. I'm fighting with everyone there right now.

LuvBug922:   about what

NHBeachBoi: OMG, everything.

At first chatting with Lisa seemed like a great idea. Even if I was never really interested in Lisa as a girlfriend, she was still my best friend. We talked about everything.

But how can I talk to her about Jay?

LuvBug922:	Tell me

I stare at the computer screen for a long time without typing anything.

LuvBug922:	Sean?
LuvBug922:	u there?
NHBeachBoi:	I'm here. Sry.
LuvBug922:	it's ok. Can u talk about it?
NHBeachBoi:	idk
NHBeachBoi:	I want to
NHBeachBoi:	but it's hard.
LuvBug922:	Try me.

I don't know where to begin. I wish Lisa could read my mind.

LuvBug922:	Sean? Did u meet someone else?

Did I mention that Lisa and I were best friends because we could read each other's minds?

NHBeachBoi:	yes
NHBeachBoi:	OMG I'm sooooooo sorry!
LuvBug922:	I knew it
NHBeachBoi:	I'm soooo sorry! I'm the worst human being on earth

While I'm typing more apologies and cursing at myself for being the kind of guy who will break up with someone over IM, Lisa's screen name disappears from my buddy list.

LuvBug922 has left the chat

No! I pick up my computer mouse and throw it off my desk. It hits the wall and then dangles by its cord off the back of the computer. I am so stupid. What did I think I was doing? I throw myself facedown on my bed and pull a pillow over my head.

I want to cry, but I can't. I'm so used to tears coming when I don't want them to, it's a weird feeling when it happens the other way around. I slam a fist into the pillow on my head.

And then I hear the familiar creaking door sound telling me someone has signed online. And almost immediately, my computer beeps with an incoming message. I look up.

LuvBug922:	SEAN? R U STILL THERE?
LuvBug922:	I'M NOT MAD
LuvBug922:	THE INTERNET HERE IS REALLY BAD

I rush to the computer, but I can't find the mouse. I have to crawl all the way under my desk to reach it.

LuvBug922:	SEAN?
LuvBug922:	Well, hopefully I'll catch you soon.
LuvBug922:	I want to talk about this

I scramble to type as fast as possible.

NHBeachBoi:	OIM HEER
LuvBug922:	Sean!
NHBeachBoi:	I'm Here!
NHBeachBoi:	UR really not mad?

LuvBug922:   No. I was actually thinking about breaking up with
              you.

Ouch. She was going to break up with me?

LuvBug922:   some of the other counselors and I were talking
              about relationships, and the more we talked the
              more I realized that we're really just friends.

LuvBug922:   Do u agree?

NHBeachBoi: yes. U read my mind. So ur really not mad?

LuvBug922:   nope. ☺ Actually wanna hear something funny? I
              was telling my friend Therese about u, and u no
              what she said?

LuvBug922:   She said u sounded gay!! LOL

LuvBug922:   Isn't that hilarious?

If people who have never met me can figure this out, why is it
so hard for me?

NHBeachBoi: lol

I realize that Lisa has just kicked a door wide open for me.

NHBeachBoi: What if it's true?

LuvBug922:   ??

NHBeachBoi: What if I am gay?

LuvBug922:   OMG

LuvBug922:   R U?

NHBeachBoi: Yes.

LuvBug922:	Did you meet a guy?
NHBeachBoi:	Yes.
NHBeachBoi:	RU mad now?
LuvBug922:	Actually, no. I'm not sure how I feel, but I'm not mad.
LuvBug922:	I think I might have always known.
NHBeachBoi:	really?
LuvBug922:	yeah, it's not like ur like the other guys at school
NHBeachBoi:	u don't want to have God save me now?
LuvBug922:	LOL NO!
LuvBug922:	actually one of the other counselors here is gay
NHBeachBoi:	at a Christian camp!??
LuvBug922:	yeah, he told us right away at orientation and said if we had any questions that we should just ask.
NHBeachBoi:	really!??
LuvBug922:	Yeah, you remember Brad? He gave me a ride on his boat?

Of course I remember Brad. How could I forget? I wanted to set Lisa up with Brad!

| NHBeachBoi: | Brad is gay!??? |
| LuvBug922: | I know, right? So beautiful. Such a loss. |

This is almost too much for me to process. First Jay and now Brad. Is every beautiful man with a boat who sails into Bell Cove gay? Becky talks about gaydar, but I clearly don't have it.

NHBeachBoi:	How old is he?
LuvBug922:	19 this is his third summer here. Wanna know sumthing funny?
NHBeachBoi:	what?
LuvBug922:	he thinks you're cute!! ☺

We go back and forth for a while after that, me pumping her for information about Brad, her teasing me about my sexuality as if nothing's changed and I've been her gay best friend forever. I'm not sure why I was so nervous to tell Lisa. Becky, Mom, now Lisa. Coming out isn't as bad as I thought it would be, but that doesn't mean I'm ready to tell my dad yet.

I think some more about Brad. I wonder if I'd ever have the guts to stand up in front of a bunch of Christian camp counselors and tell them I'm gay. I wonder how Brad told his parents. His dad. I've only met him once and he's sort of become my role model. I kind of want to talk to gay Christian camp counselor Brad. Maybe he can give me some advice.

Chapter 24

Despite renewing my friendship with Lisa, I am not in a mood to go back to work the next day, so I take a detour to the top of Mann's Hill with my bike. It's finally August and the days have been getting hotter and hotter, and I am sweating by the time I make it to the top. To make matters worse, my favorite rock is too hot to sit on. I find a grassy spot nearby and lie down and watch the clouds. It's not what I came here to look at, but it's still peaceful and helps me start to forget about my fight with Becky, and Jay standing me up. The grass is cool on my skin, and the soft ends tickle the backs of my knees. I feel like I am almost floating with the clouds myself.

I watch them drift by. A puffy one looks like a bunny nibbling some clover, but then the wind stretches the nose and it looks more like a dog with floppy ears. One of the ears detaches from the body. It's long and pointy on one end and rounded on the other. It looks like a giant white *ice cream cone*. Oh, shit. How long have I been here? I grab my bike and pedal all the way to the Pink Cone without stopping.

By the time I'm parking my bike behind the Pink Cone, I'm calm. After all, both Jay and Becky left me to fend for myself last time, so they deserve it if I'm a little late. I put on my best "I couldn't care less" face and walk up to the door. In my head I'm practicing snappy retorts as I pull it open.

"Nice of you to join us. It's the hottest day of the summer. Do you know what that means? Customers!" The smirk disappears from my face. This is not Jay's voice. Or Becky's.

"Renée," I stammer. "I didn't know you'd be here. I didn't mean to—"

"Can it. I don't care about excuses. Poor Becky's got frostbite out there serving everyone herself. I'd help, but we're almost out of chocolate. Harleigh apparently forgot to make it last night. Chocolate! Who forgets to make chocolate? I mean, pistachio, I'd understand, but chocolate . . ."

Renée continues to complain while she dumps ingredients into the mixer. It takes a few seconds before I realize she's not talking to me anymore, but I don't wait around to get her attention again. Cursing my luck, I pull on my bright pink work shirt and go to relieve Becky.

Becky doesn't say anything when she sees me, just raises her eyebrows before turning to fill a sugar cone with chocolate chip. If that's how she wants to play it, fine. I don't say anything either, and instead go straight to the window to ask for the next customer's order.

We work side by side like that for an hour without speaking. A couple of times we need the same flavor, and one or the other of us stands impatiently, scoop on hip, waiting for the tub to be free. Normally, Becky would throw in a jab, like "leave some for the cows," but not today.

Eventually, Renée comes out from the back with a couple of replacement flavors. She narrows her eyes. "You two look like you're having fun," she says. "What's up? I thought you guys were, like, BFFs?"

"Sean is mad at me because I tried to warn him that his boyfriend is cheating on him."

I stop in mid-scoop. I feel my face go warm despite the

freezer-cooled air. I clench my jaw, determined not to react to Becky's overstep.

Renée doesn't miss a beat. "Sometimes people don't like to hear what's good for them, especially not from people they care about."

I'm still leaning over the ice cream, and Renée slaps my butt. "Sean, get your head out of the freezer; these are heavy."

I stand up, and Renée drops the tubs in place.

"Now, Becky, apologize to Sean."

"What? But I didn't—"

"I know your heart was in the right place, honey, but sometimes we gotta just keep our mouths shut."

I'm pretty sure Becky has never apologized to anyone in her life, and I doubt Renée is going to make her start now.

Becky raises her chin and purses her lips. But then she says, "Sorry."

Never underestimate the power of Renée.

"Now, Sean, forgive Becky for caring about you too much."

My mouth opens to protest, but I shut it again, and the corners of my mouth go up involuntarily. "I guess it is kind of dumb to be mad at you."

Renée makes a low gurgling laugh and shakes her head at us. "Fabulous! And now that we've all kissed and made up, can we please get back to serving my customers?" She hands us each a clean ice cream scoop and pushes us toward the windows where a line of customers is growing out the door. "I'm going to run out for a bit. Don't burn the place down, okay?"

Now that Becky and I are talking again, it occurs to me to ask why Jay isn't working. It's not that I don't like Renée, it's just that I had only seen her a handful of times since she hired me.

"I don't know. Renée said he asked her if he could work tonight's shift instead."

"But I'm off at four."

Becky just shrugs.

"Okay, I get it," I say.

"Forget about Jay for now. Let's play a little game," Becky says with a mischievous smile.

"We are not putting laxatives in the chocolate ice cream."

I swear I see a glint in her eye, but it might just be a reflection off her ice cream scoop.

"No. We need to liven this up a bit," she says.

"So?"

"Let's make a new flavor."

"But Renée—"

"If it sells, Renée won't care."

"And if it doesn't sell?" I say.

"What do you think? Chocolate Grape-Nut?"

"Becky!"

"No? How about Almond Joy fudge brownie?"

I cover my eyes.

"Pistachio maple walnut?"

"Gross! At least do something people will eat."

Becky puts her hands on her hips. "Then you suggest something, genius."

"I don't know. Coffee and black raspberry?"

Before I can stop her, Becky has the half-empty tub of black raspberry tilted over the coffee container and she starts to scoop. My mouth opens, but I have no words.

"Don't just stand there, grab a scoop and start mixing." Becky has emptied the black raspberry and is already writing *Raspberry Latte* on the whiteboard we use to list flavors. She grabs a red marker and writes *Today's Special* next to it and then stands back to admire her handiwork. "Let's see who can sell the most," she says to me.

I shake my head. "You win. You could sell eggs to a chicken."

"C'mon, it'll be fun."

For the next two hours we suggest raspberry latte to every customer who comes to the window, and we even get several takers. None of them seem disappointed with their choice, although a few do a double-take when they see the garish color combination. I decide that the next time, we should mix the flavors in advance, so it has a more uniform look.

As predicted, Becky is crushing me in sales of raspberry latte, but I try hard to keep up. I talk two old women who my mother would call "blue hairs" into trying it, although they insist on a small cup with two spoons.

"That only counts as one!" Becky says.

I turn away from the window. "C'mon!"

I'm getting ready to plead my case when a voice behind me says, "Hi, Sean." I turn around. It's Matt.

I try to keep the surprise out of my voice. "What's up?"

"Came for an ice cream—without my cousin this time."

"He was cute."

"Yeah, for the first five minutes. Try babysitting him the whole summer. He had a birthday party today, so I'm off the hook."

"Lucky you. What can I get you?"

"Purple Cow, small."

"Cool." I almost forget to offer our special flavor. "Hey, you wanna try the special? Becky and I are having a contest to see who can sell the most."

"Umm." Matt bites his lip and wrinkles his nose. "Will it help you win?"

"Yes," I lie.

"Then, okay."

I get him his ice cream, but the afternoon has finally started to slow down, and there's no one else in line, so Matt hangs around to talk with Becky and me. He takes a seat at one of the tables on the porch while Becky goes out to wipe them down. I stay inside, but near the window so I can still hear and in case any customers show up.

"Tell me something embarrassing about Sean," Becky says to Matt as she refills a napkin dispenser.

"Becky! I can hear you!"

She throws one of her cleaning rags at the service window.

"Something embarrassing?" Matt bites his lip in thought. "What about the time I caught him buying women's clothing at Walmart?"

"What?! I did not!" I sputter, sticking my head through the service window and hitting it on the sash.

"You did, too," Matt says.

"Sean, what did I say about buying your clothes at Walmart?" Becky says. "No good can come of it."

"But I didn't—"

"It was for the drama club. Remember when Allison was sick at dress rehearsal for *The Butler Did It?*"

And then I remember. "You were there?"

Matt turns to Becky. "Sean was the student director for that show, and when Allison got sick, he was the only one who knew all her lines on short notice. He thought he was going to have to play Miss Maple for her."

"But how did you see me? I made my mom drop me off and wouldn't even tell her why I was there. I told her I needed to pick up some last-minute props."

"I was there picking up some supplies for a science project. I saw you trying to pick out a woman's dress and pantyhose. I didn't say anything though."

I can feel my cheeks start to burn.

"I didn't know you were a cross-dresser!" Becky lets out a high-pitched laugh. "You'll have to do a drag show for us!"

"I didn't even end up wearing it. Allison got better just in time to play the part." My face is so hot, I'm about ready to go sit in the deep freeze for ten minutes just to cool down, but I'm smiling anyway. I can't believe Matt saw me.

Becky has finished wiping down all the porch tables and returns to help me clean the back when Renée walks in the back employee entrance.

"Fabulous. I like to see smiles. I'll be in the back restock—"

She stops next to the freezer, her eyes wide. "What...is... that?"

Becky puts on her two-hundred-watt smile. "What is what?"

Renée pulls the tub of raspberry latte out of the freezer and tilts it toward us.

"Oh, that. That's raspberry latte?" Becky asks as if Renée is testing her on flavor identification like she did at orientation.

"And since when do we sell raspberry latte?"

"Um, two hours ago." Becky keeps smiling.

"It looks like shit. This is fabulous, just fabulous." Renée slings the tub back into the freezer. It bounces with a rubbery thunk.

"Customers love it; just ask Matt," Becky says, pointing.

Renée crosses to the window and glares at Matt. He looks at me and then back at Renée.

"It was really good. You should put it on the menu. And I don't even like coffee ice cream."

"You don't like coffee?" I say.

"Enough!" Renée's voice is sharp, but low and dangerous. "Go get changed into your street clothes. You've worked enough today."

"Uh, are we fired?" I ask. I can already hear my dad's voice telling me how much fun I'll have spending the rest of the summer in Georgia.

"No, but don't tempt me."

Becky and I don't stick around to let Renée change her mind. We have a race back to the break room.

It's only been two minutes, and I'm waiting for Becky to find her purse when Renée walks in.

"We're going! Becky's just grabbing her purse," I say.

But Renée is smiling, and I notice she has a dish of ice cream in her hand. She holds it up. "You two are brilliant. This is fabulous!"

Becky and I exchange a smile. Becky says, "So we don't have to leave?"

"No, I want to look at your faces about as much as I want to look at this ice cream. But I've decided to put raspberry latte on the menu. Now get!" We make for the door, barely holding in our laughter, but as we pass Renée, she stops me with a hand on my shoulder. "Sean'll be right there," she says over her shoulder to Becky. Her voice is serious. I swallow hard.

"Listen. I know a little something about growing up in a small town and not quite fitting in. I know it's not as easy as Becky wants to make it for you." I nod slowly. "If you ever need someone to talk to, not someone who will tell you what to do, but just to listen, *talk*. I'm here. Okay?"

I have to clear my throat to get my voice to come out. "Okay."

I start to leave, and Renée pats my shoulder. Then she says, "Have you talked to him?" I pause just a moment before I head out the door. Something tells me that Renée isn't just finding out that I'm gay. Did she know when I met her that day I came looking for a job? I feel oddly exposed, and yet knowing that Renée's on my side is also comforting. I'm finding allies in all sorts of places.

But who does she want me to talk to? Jay? My dad? Both?

Chapter 25

Becky is waiting by the back door for me. "What was that all about?"

"Nothing."

Becky tilts her head and looks down her nose with the *no bullshit* expression. She will make a very good mother someday.

"Renée just wanted to talk to me about Jay, okay?" I say. "Thanks for letting that one out, by the way."

"Oh, c'mon, Sean. Renée's known you were gay since orientation."

"She did not!" I say, even though she's probably right. "Why do you assume that everyone just knows? Why are we even talking about this again?"

Becky and I have rounded the corner of the Pink Cone, and before she can answer, we discover Matt has been waiting for us.

"Hey," he says.

Happy for the change of subject, I walk over to him and put a fist in the air. "Hey, it's cool you waited for us." We knock knuckles and Becky falls in beside us.

"You two aren't in much trouble, are you?" he says. "I hope I didn't . . ."

"Are you kidding?" Becky says. "You were great! Renée tried our ice cream and now it's going to be on the menu!"

"Really? That's awesome. You two are ice cream chefs!"

"Yeah, I guess we are," I say. "Hey, we're out early. Let's do something to celebrate!"

Becky and I look at each other and say in unison, "Gold House!"

I leave my bike at the Cone and the three of us walk together down Main Street.

We order a large cheese fries and take them to a picnic table by the water. Becky and I sit across from each other, and Matt sits beside me, straddling the bench seat, so he can face both of us. We take turns pulling out long strings of greasy potatoes dripping with yellow-orange cheese sauce. Petrochemical goodness, Becky calls it.

"What should we do with our sudden extra free time?" I ask.

"I wish we had a boat. This is the perfect day to be on the lake," Becky says. She slaps her hand over her mouth almost as soon as she says it. "I'm sorry, Sean. I didn't mean . . ."

I smile with thin lips. "It's okay. I wish we had a boat, too."

Matt looks from Becky to me. "What?"

No one says anything.

"I don't get it. What's the big deal about a boat?" Matt says.

"Nothing," I say.

Becky opens her mouth to speak, but I cut her off.

"It's nothing." I shoot lasers from my eyes into Becky's skull. She closes her trap and gives me a slight nod. I mouth the words *Thank you.*

"Well." Matt interrupts our moment. "I have a boat."

Becky and I both turn. "You do?"

"My dad's boat, but I'm sure he would let us use it. You guys ever water-ski?"

"Water-ski? Does that require balance or coordination?" Becky asks.

Matt laughs. "A little."

Becky snags the last french fry. "Not my strong suits." And as if to make her point, a glob of half-congealed cheese sauce drops from the fry onto the middle of her shirt. "I hate breasts! They are always getting in the way." She grabs a napkin and starts dabbing at the spot, but the grease stain isn't going away.

"You'll have to change into your bathing suit anyway," Matt says. "C'mon." Matt punches me in the shoulder and jumps up from the table.

Becky starts to gather our trash, but Matt stops her. "I'll get it."

"What a gentleman," Becky says, sticking her tongue out at me. "Sean, you should take lessons."

I roll my eyes.

"I don't charge much," Matt says, returning from the trash can. Then he holds out his hand to Becky to help her from the table. Once she is on her feet he gracefully bends over her hand and kisses it. Becky giggles.

"I think I'm going to vomit," I say.

"Lesson number one," Matt says, "vomiting is so *not* gentlemanly." He turns back to Becky and sweeps his arm in a broad arc. "M'lady."

"Did I mention that Matt is in the drama club?" I say.

"I think it's cute," Becky says. "Let's go."

Chapter 26

After a quick stop to grab Becky's bathing suit, we get to Matt's house. Becky has to scrape my chin off the ground. "Nice mansion," I say.

Matt laughs. "It's not a mansion, but thanks."

I wonder how I could have known Matt for so long without realizing that his family was so well-off. I think about this for a few minutes and realize that Matt never does anything to let on that he has money. He doesn't wear designer clothes (although he does dress well); he doesn't have expensive toys like the flashiest new cell phone or MP3 player, and he doesn't throw money around. He even has a normal summer job babysitting his cousin.

His parents are home, even though it is still the middle of the day. "My father is an investment manager," he explains, "and he works from home most of the time. My mother is an artist and a writer."

In fact, we find his mom in her studio working on a painting. The studio looks like a paintball tournament just ended; besides the splotches of paint, which seem to have landed on every surface, the room is filled with canvases, paint tubes rolled up like used toothpaste, and brushes in mason jars. I stop to look at one painting leaning near the door. It's a water-color of Bell Cove, looking from the water. In the painting the sun is setting and the buildings are reflected in shades of pink, orange, and purple. I must have seen this same view a thousand times, but it's not just a quaint lakeside tourist town in her painting. It's pretty, sure, but the watercolors aren't precise, and if you look closely, the splotches of color blend together and the details are blurry. It's almost like the town in the paint-ing is hiding something, and you wish you could get closer to find out what it is. For the first time that I can remember, I find myself wanting to see more of Bell Cove.

Apparently, Matt has introduced us to his mom, because Becky kicks me in the shin, bringing me back to the chaotic stu-dio. "Nice to meet you, Sean," Matt's mom says. "Call me Jo Anne."

"You're a really good artist," I say, looking around the rest of the studio.

"Thank you."

I realize that most of the paintings in the studio are scenes from around Bell Cove. "You must really like it here," I say.

"I draw a lot of inspiration from my surroundings, yes, but I think you can be inspired anywhere." She starts digging in a pile of canvases near the window and pulls out a small oil paint-ing of a city street. "This was the view from our first apartment when Matt's dad and I were just married. It was only a one-bedroom and I had to go out on the fire escape to paint be-cause there wasn't room in the apartment."

She hands me the painting. It shows brick buildings along a strip of city street. There are people on the sidewalks and cars lining the curb Vibrant squares of green and red are the awnings of shops, where the pedestrians are window-shopping. I start to imagine what they might be buying: fruits and vegeta-bles at a small market, a gauzy sundress in a seamstress's shop.

"I keep this painting to remind me where I've come from, and that sometimes you need to look beyond the surface to find what you're searching for."

I hand back the painting. "I think I know what you mean," I say, looking back at the painting of Bell Cove by the door.

"Sean's a really good artist, too," Becky says.

"I'm okay."

"That's great," Jo Anne says. "I'd love to see some of your work."

"Yeah, me too," Matt says.

"Maybe," I say.

Jo Anne nods her head, and gives me a smile.

"You'll have to invite me to your house next time," Matt says and turns to his mom. "Where's Dad? We wanted to use the boat to go water-skiing."

"That sounds like fun; maybe we can all go. I think he's up in his office."

Matt's dad seems only too eager to get away from his office. As soon as we walk in, he's out of his chair and over to shake Becky's and my hands.

"Hi, guys! Call me Nathan," he says, pumping our hands in a firm grip. He's very tall, with gray hair in a stylish cut that didn't come from Stan the Barber on Main Street. It's hard for me to imagine Matt's dad in a suit; he looks so relaxed in khaki shorts and a light blue golf shirt. He's very fit, and I notice he has a tattoo on his left forearm of a rose and a cross. He also has a small diamond stud in his left ear.

"Absolutely," Nathan says after Matt asks him about water-skiing. "I'll meet you guys at the boat."

Matt lends me a bathing suit, and I change in one of what I imagine are several bathrooms in the Maguires' house. I find my way to the back deck where Becky is flirting with Matt. She snaps her towel at his chest, but he refuses to retaliate because she's a girl. This only makes her snap her towel at him more. I have to grab both her arms and wrestle the towel from her hands to make her stop.

"Your parents are so cool," Becky says as we walk down to the boathouse. Matt has an actual boathouse, so I know the boat must be amazing, and I am not disappointed. A thirty-foot Baja Islander floats majestically in front of us. It's white with a sleek blue, yellow, and green stripe curling around the engine housing.

"Whoa."

"My mom calls her my dad's midlife crisis," Matt jokes, pulling down a couple of life jackets for Becky and me. We climb in the boat to wait for Matt's parents.

"This thing has a toilet!" Becky squeals. "Do you think your parents would mind if I moved in? This boat is better than our cottage."

A few minutes later Matt's parents show up. His mom has changed into a turquoise bathing suit and a multicolored serape wrapped around her waist. Her jet-black hair is tied into a youthful ponytail. She could easily pass for early thirties, even though I know she must be at least ten years older.

Nathan backs the boat out of the boathouse, and we are speeding out onto the lake in no time at all. "Who's going first?" he says when we're a good distance from shore.

Becky and I smirk and both look at Matt.

"Sean, you live on the lake and you've never been water-skiing?" Jo Anne asks, smiling.

"We have a twelve-foot fishing boat."

"Well, don't be afraid. All it takes is a little balance."

"That leaves me out," Becky says.

Matt crosses to me. "Put on your life jacket. It's time to get wet."

The next thing I know I am in the water struggling to get my feet inside the rubber "boots" attached to the water skis. I imagine I look like an injured seal, thrashing around helplessly, waiting for a shark to put me out of my misery, but finally I do manage to get the skis on. Matt throws me a rope with a foam-covered handle at the end, instructing me to keep the rope between my skis.

"Hold on tight!" Before I can think, Nathan has started the boat, and the slack line is pulling away in a rapid snaking motion. It goes taut, and I am yanked forward with a sudden lurch. Somehow I manage to hang on, and in the next instant I am gliding above the water. At first all I can think is to hang on for dear life. The water is rushing by so quickly, I'm terrified. Becky is kneeling in the back of the boat with her hands in the air. Her screams of encouragement float back to me from the speeding boat. I start to realize that I am not mere seconds from certain death, and I take the time to look around. What a rush. Flying across the water on a couple of boards is liberating. It's like coasting down Mann's Hill at top speed on my bike, only with the real sense that I am flying. I imagine myself as a lake bird, skimming across the water's surface. The spray that hits my face is dried instantly in the rushing wind. I look around in the afternoon light. It is a calm afternoon, and the lake surface is glassy, reflecting the shoreline in perfect symmetry. I wonder how Jo Anne would paint the picture.

Finally, my arms start to get tired, and I run a finger across my neck, the signal that Matt showed me to tell the driver to kill the engine. After the cool air, the water feels warm as I sink back down. Nathan circles the boat around to pick me up, and I lift the skis into the boat first. I didn't realize how tiring waterskiing is, and my legs don't fully cooperate when I try to climb back in the boat. I trip trying to climb over the stern, and I practically tackle Matt when I fall into the boat.

"Sorry!" I roll off him, and Becky helps me to my feet.

Matt is laughing. "It's okay, but now that you got me all wet, I guess it's my turn to get in the water." He peels off his T-shirt, and I realize that skinny Matt actually has a pretty nice body.

We spend a few hours on the boat taking turns on the skis. We even get Becky in the water. After three or four tries, she makes it to her feet, and gets a tour of the lake. I can tell from her smile, she enjoys it just as much as I did.

When the sun starts to sink, we turn back toward town. As we near Bell Cove, the setting sun reflects off the water and tints the buildings on Main Street into a kaleidoscope of pink, orange, and purple. Jo Anne is sitting next to me, and she puts her hand on my shoulder.

"Just like your painting," I say.

Chapter 27

When I get home, I find a note from my mother on the kitchen table. *Out to dinner with Helen. Here's twenty for dinner. Mom.* I almost miss the P.S. scribbled at the bottom of the paper, *P.S. Jay called.*

My heart somersaults into my throat. He called. He actually called. I race to my room and find the phone on my desk. This time I have no hesitation in dialing.

I listen to the digital ring for one, two, three, four rings. Halfway through the fifth ring, Jay's voice mail cuts in.

"It's Jay, leave it."

"Uh, it's me. I mean, it's Sean. I got your message. You're probably still at work, but if you get a chance, you can call me back if you want. I'm not doing anything tonight so I should be around. Maybe we could go out when you're done or something. Anyway, yeah. Call me back. Thanks. Bye."

I hit the talk button on the phone, knowing I sounded like a fool. I'm never any good with answering machines, a trait I get from my mom, who has been known to have full conversations for minutes on end with voice mail. She once took four minutes to inform me she was going to be home late, even going so far as to tell me what exit she was passing on the highway and how much the upcoming toll was going to cost her (seventy-five cents).

I decide to order Chinese delivery and wait for Jay to call me back. I turn on the radio and hop online to kill time.

An instant message box pops up on my screen with a familiar beep.

LuvBug922:	Hi!
NHBeachBoi:	Hey, how's ur ankle?
LuvBug922:	Almost better. I can walk on it again, but I have one more day
NHBeachBoi:	that's good ☺
LuvBug922:	what r u up 2
NHBeachBoi:	nuthin
LuvBug922:	Brad says hi.
NHBeachBoi:	He's there?
LuvBug922:	yeah, he stopped by to bring me dinner. He's soo sweet ☺
NHBeachBoi:	awwww
LuvBug922:	I was thinking about our last convo
NHBeachBoi:	?
LuvBug922:	and I'm really glad you decided to tell me
LuvBug922:	I mean, I'm sad we can't be together but I think it's more important that u can be urself.
NHBeachBoi:	thx. I really mean that
LuvBug922:	Hey, tell me about the guy.

LuvBug922:	Don't worry, Brad left. He said he's glad you're on his team now.
LuvBug922:	so tell me
NHBeachBoi:	his name is Jay. He works with me at the Pink Cone
LuvBug922:	Wait! The tall one with the perfect tan and amazing blue eyes?
NHBeachBoi:	that's him
LuvBug922:	He worked there last year! He's GORGEOUS!
NHBeachBoi:	☺
LuvBug922:	OMG, I can't believe he's gay!
LuvBug922:	So have you kissed or anything?
NHBeachBoi:	yes
LuvBug922:	and?
NHBeachBoi:	It was AMAZING! We were on his boat the first time and I was cold and he wrapped his arms around me and we just . . . kissed
LuvBug922:	I'm so happy 4 u! ☺

The doorbell rings. Chinese.

| NHBeachBoi: | brb, my food is here |

I run to the door and pay for my food, thinking about Jay. I grab a fork and a couple of paper towels from the kitchen and head back to my room. I stare at the phone before finally typing again.

NHBeachBoi:	ok.
LuvBug922:	This guy sounds so amazing
NHBeachBoi:	He is
LuvBug922:	How old is he?
NHBeachBoi:	just turned 18
LuvBug922:	did he graduate yet?
NHBeachBoi:	yeah
LuvBug922:	what is he doing in the fall
NHBeachBoi:	college I guess
LuvBug922:	where
NHBeachBoi:	idk
LuvBug922:	eh, no biggie.
LuvBug922:	Hey, I gtg. It was fun chatting. Get me some pics you can send me of Jay! TTYL
NHBeachBoi:	Bye!

I turn my attention to my beef with broccoli, but I'm distracted by the phone on my desk. I look at the clock. It's still another forty-five minutes until Jay is off work, although I had hoped he would call on his break. I look back at the IM with Lisa. I click the box to close the window. On the radio an old Savage Garden song comes on: "Truly Madly Deeply." It makes me think of the first night with Jay on his boat, lying in his arms and falling asleep. I climb into my bed with the phone next to me on the pillow.

I wake up like that the next morning.

Chapter 28

When I get to work in the afternoon, Becky is already there.
She sees me coming in the back door.

"He's here."

I catch my breath. She has answered the very question I had
been asking myself all the way here. I take my time changing
into my work shirt, unable to decide if I am excited to see Jay or
worried about what he might have to say. I walk out to the
front.

"Hey, boy," he says when he sees me, a smile creeping across
his face.

"Hey."

"I got your message."

"Yeah."

"But it wasn't until really late."

"Okay. I was up though."

"Not waiting for me?" Jay raises his eyebrows.

"No, I was just messing around online."

He hands me his scoop. "Let's go out after work, okay?" Jay
smiles at me, but is it me, or does the smile not quite reach his
eyes? *You're being paranoid,* I tell myself.

"Okay." I nod.

"I need to refill this freezer. Can you and Becky handle the customers?" He doesn't wait for an answer and heads to the deep freezer to pull out some flavors to warm up.

"Well, that sounded good," Becky says, looking up from the freezer.

"Did it?"

"Well, yeah. You don't think so?"

"I guess." I just can't quite shake the idea that Jay isn't being completely truthful with me. Was Becky right when she said there might be someone else?

The rest of the night is uneventful, just the regular collection of families, evening walkers, and local teenagers. Matt stops by with his parents, and his dad compliments me on my shirt, but I'm pretty sure he's joking. It's just about my break time when they get there, so I decide to join them while they eat their ice cream.

I sit next to Matt on one side of the picnic table out in front of the Pink Cone, while Matt's parents sit on the other side. They're so cute; they lick each other's ice creams as if they are teenagers and when Jo Anne shivers in the night air, Nathan wraps his sweater around her shoulders.

Matt sticks a finger down his throat and makes puking noises, but I hit his shoulder.

"I think your parents are adorable."

"Thank you, Sean," Jo Anne says.

"You don't have to live with them." Matt returns my punch with a finger to my chest.

"Watch where you're putting that finger," I say. "If you want to keep it."

"I'll put this finger wherever I want." And the next thing I know Matt is tickling me underneath my ribs. I can barely stand it, and I fall over backward off the picnic table trying to get away.

"Stop!" I gasp between bursts of laughter. "Stop it!" We're all laughing, Nathan and Jo Anne included, when I hear Jay calling my name.

"Sean!" I look up to see Jay standing by the door to the Pink Cone. It's too dark to read his expression for sure, but he almost looks angry. "Sean, it's starting to get busy. I need you back from break."

"Thanks for stopping by," I say to the Maguires. "I gotta get back to work."

"I hope you'll be able to come water-skiing again soon," Nathan says to me. "You can invite Becky as well."

"See ya," Matt says.

I give a wave and head back inside the store.

"Who was that?" Jay asks me as soon as I get inside.

"The Maguires. Friends."

"No, who was the guy?" Jay's tone is sharp.

"Matt Maguire. I just said. He's a friend of mine from the drama club at school. The other two are his parents."

"Okay." I start to head back to the front to help with the rush, but Jay grabs my hand. The next thing I know, he's pulled me into the storage room and his lips are on mine in a kiss that I couldn't break away from if I wanted to. It's almost like he's marking me with the kiss. I belong to him. It only lasts a few seconds, but I am left completely breathless. Where did that come from? And why was I so worried? "Back to work," Jay says.

And then I am back at work. But I can't stop thinking about that kiss. And I can't wait for the next one like it.

Eventually, the clock creeps toward ten P.M.

"All right, kids, wrap it up," Jay says, closing the deep freezer.

"Way ahead of you, chief," Becky says. "We've already got everything put away and cleaned off. It was pretty slow tonight."

"Great. Sean, we still on?"

"Of course."

Fifteen minutes later, Jay is locking the back door.

"Call me in the morning," Becky says to me. "Tell me how it goes."

I nod, and Jay comes up behind me and puts his hands on my shoulders. He leans in and gives me a kiss on the neck. At first I stand stiff, but I let his arms pour around me and soon I've dissolved into his embrace. I turn my head, and he kisses me on the lips. The electricity that I remember flows through me, every point of contact between us like an electrode.

I let my lips part, and I feel his tongue slide between my lips, warm and soft. I breathe in, and I can smell his cologne; he must have put some on just before we left. It's spicy and sweet and a little smoky, like a freshly lit campfire. We stand in the shadows behind the Pink Cone for several minutes. I let my hands caress his body, down his thin cotton T-shirt to where it is tucked into his military canvas belt. I tug at the shirt until it comes loose, and slide my hands up under his shirt. His body is warm and firm beneath my hands. My fingers feel the contours of his chest and abs.

He takes a breath. "I'm sorry I didn't call."

"It's okay," I whisper back.

I don't know what I was worried about. A phone call? A skipped work shift? I'm worse than a soap opera character, jumping to conclusions. Jay is here in front of me with his arms around me. He's not with someone else. And I was foolish to think otherwise. Becky means well, but she doesn't always know. Finally, we break our embrace, and Jay takes my hand and leads me toward the dock and his boat.

"Still wanna go out? It's pretty late."

"Yes."

"Your mom won't be mad?"

"My mom will live."

We climb into Jay's boat in silence. Then he starts the motor with a chugging roar, and we're off. Jay squeezes over on the driver's seat and pats the space beside him. I sit on the edge, and he puts his left arm around me, holding me in, while he rests his right arm lightly on top of the steering wheel.

*   *   *

We're in the middle of the lake when Jay kills the engine. The wake slaps the boat as we slow to a drift, and then it is quiet. There is only the occasional musical splash against the hull to break the silence. Jay pulls me up from the seat.

"Where are we?" I ask.

"Nowhere," Jay says. "Are you scared?"

There is no moon tonight, and the darkness has closed in. There is an occasional twinkling light near where the horizon should be, but it is impossible to tell how far away it is. "A little," I say.

"Come here." Jay pulls me close and leads me to the bow of the boat, where there is a U-shaped section of seats. He holds me tightly from behind for a minute, then whispers, "Is that better?"

My heart has actually started to speed up, but I nod. Then we are sitting on the seats, our lips touching, our bodies close and hot. I let my hands slip under Jay's T-shirt again, but this time he pulls it off, and his skin is against me.

"Here," he says, and pulls at my shirt, helping me to shed the unnecessary layer. Skin against skin, we lie in stillness a moment. I can feel his heart beating beneath me. We kiss, long, slow, and deep.

I feel Jay's hand slide beneath me and start to play with the waistband of my shorts. He lets his fingers dip down to find the elastic band of my boxer shorts, playfully snapping it against my skin, just like I did to him that night after our escapade at Camp Aweelah. I am surprised, but excited, the small shock shooting through my entire body. He begins to unbutton my shorts. I know what he is doing, but I don't want him to stop, and a tingle of pleasure snakes up my spine when I hear him pull the zipper. I lean back and let him slide the material over my hips. The shorts fall to the floor of the boat with a soft crumbling sound.

Jay takes my hands and guides them to his own cargo shorts, and I work on the button. It's much trickier than I expected to unbutton someone else's clothes, and I fumble for a few seconds before slipping the button through the hole. I slide the shorts onto the floor and lean in to kiss him again. He frees an arm to pick up his shorts and finds his wallet in a pocket. He produces a condom.

"Is this okay?" Jay says in my ear.

It takes me a second to understand. Is this why Jay was distant? Was he frustrated that we were moving too slow? I don't want to disappoint him. I think of the kiss at the Pink Cone, the passion that I felt from him in that kiss, and then I know that I want more of that. I'm ready to have all of that.

"Yes," I say.

"Are you sure?"

"Yes."

His lips tickle my ear. "I love you."

My heart soars. And I believe him. Because I feel it, too.

"I love you."

The next forty-five minutes are everything I had imagined and nothing I could have predicted. First, his hands are everywhere, and I had no idea a touch could be so electric. He slides a finger up my chest and another down my leg. I can't help but gasp as the competing sensations send my brain to a place of light and magic. Jay's words echo in this place and as his tongue glides from my neck to my nipples and then down to my stomach, their meaning is magnified in my mind. Soon, there isn't a doubt left in my head. I've been transported off his boat, and I'm floating in a place of pure emotion where Jay's touch goes deeper than the surface. I'm ready to give every piece of myself to him. I trust him not to hurt me.

And he doesn't hurt me. We go slow. There's a pressure and a pain, but soon it's an ecstasy that I never want to stop. My lips are on his, and then on his neck. My hands grip his shoulders and I do everything I can to pull him as close to me as possible. When it does end, we don't move for a very long time. I can't move. Every sense in my body has been turned up so that every sound, every touch, every breath surges through my body and threatens to overload it. Jay and I have come as close as possible to becoming one. And I never want it to stop.

The lake breeze wakes me up with a chill, and I can feel the exposed skin of my arm puckered in goose bumps. I am spooned in Jay's arms, but his heat isn't enough to keep me warm. I wait for a few seconds, but I can't stand it, and I gently lift Jay's arm so I can look for my T-shirt.

Jay doesn't stir, and I look at him in the darkness. The boat's single white running light glows just enough for me to make out my surroundings. Even in this light, Jay's beauty is unmistakable, his body sculpted and smooth. I let my eyes wander over his body, stopping between his legs. Despite his limp state I am impressed by his size, even intimidated. I am suddenly, almost painfully, aware of my own nakedness, and I turn to find my discarded clothes, my need to cover my own inadequacies even more pressing than the cold breeze that has started to blow harder.

I find my shirt by the steering wheel and pull it over my head.

"Where'd you go?" I hear Jay stir in the front of the boat. "It's cold."

"What time is it?" I say.

More movement and then Jay's face is lit up by the blue glow from his cell phone. "Uh, twelve forty-eight." He snaps the phone shut, and I hear him sit up. I can feel his eyes on me in the darkness. I can't seem to find my underwear.

"Are you okay?" Jay asks.

"I'm good." I step into the bow of the boat to look for my underwear. "I'm really good," I add, thinking I didn't sound convincing the first time.

Jay reaches out from the bench seat and grabs my T-shirt in his fist. I pull away, but his grip is strong, and instead I overbalance and end up falling toward him. He leans over me and kisses me lightly.

"Good," he says, and kisses me again.

Even though I am wearing my T-shirt, I still feel naked in front of him, and I am tense in his arms. He is fluid and relaxed, but I am ashamed. I can't explain it. All I want to do is find my clothes and cover up. How can he be attracted to someone who is so inferior physically? I try to get up.

"Hey." Jay pulls me back. "Relax. What's wrong?"

"I don't know."

"I didn't hurt you?"

"No." Actually, it did hurt, but not in a bad way. He kept asking me if I wanted him to stop, and even though there was pain, I didn't want him to. Instead the pain was like electricity pulsing through me, and it made me lightheaded and warm, like holding your breath for too long. Now I feel slightly empty and slick, as if my legs move too easily and I might lose control. A question itches in the back of my head, but I'm afraid to ask it. "I think I need to get home."

Jay's hands snake around my waist, dipping dangerously low. His fingers send sparks into my skin. "Already?"

"Well . . ."

"A little longer," he whispers in my ear before gently tugging on my earlobe with his teeth. His hand dips lower, and I feel myself start to get hard, against my will.

I take a sharp breath and hold it. Jay kisses my neck and pulls me tighter. I can feel him pressing into my back.

I can't hold it any longer, and air shoots between my lips and the words come out with it. "Did you mean what you said?"

Jay freezes, but only for a second. He lifts his head from my neck, his lips only a fraction from my ear. "I love you."

The words curl into my ear and hit my brain like a shot of morphine. I feel my muscles loosen, and I let Jay work his magic. I twist and lean into him. We fall back onto the seat.

Chapter 29

"Hellooo!" Becky snaps her fingers in front of my face. "Earth to Sean!"

"Oh, hey."

"What is up with you?"

"Just tired. I was up late." I grab a plastic ice cream scoop from the water-filled bucket by the freezer. I stare at it for a second. What was I doing?

"With Jay?" Becky asks.

I can't keep a straight face. I stifle a giggle.

Becky narrows her eyes. She tilts her head as if something has just occurred to her. "You didn't . . ."

My shoelaces are suddenly very interesting, and my eyes involuntarily shoot downward.

"Were you planning to tell me?" Her eyes are wide in disbelief.

"It was like, I was dreaming."

Becky shoves a waxy paper bowl at me, but it crushes under the force of her hand. "Why don't you dream up a small vanilla with hot fudge?"

"I'm sorry," I say. "I just didn't know how you would react."

"Well, now you know." Becky turns back to the window, her

jaw clenched. I can see a muscle twitching just below her ear. I know I should have told her. Becky has been my best friend all summer. I open my mouth to . . . say what? I don't know. It's not like there's anything I can say that'll make her understand. I turn back to the freezer and start scooping vanilla.

Becky doesn't give me the cold shoulder for long. Her curiosity gets the better of her, and when we get off at six o'clock, she practically drags me to the Gold House for a plate of cheese fries.

"So, did you do it? I mean, did you—" Becky waves her hands in front of her chest, a makeshift sign language to fill in the words she doesn't say.

I stick my tongue out in an embarrassed smile.

"Omigod! You did!" Becky grabs a fry and points it at me. "Sean Jackson, please tell me you were safe!"

"Yes, Mom!"

"Thank God for that. So, what was it like? I want details."

I roll my eyes. "A gentleman never kisses and tells."

"Since when are you a gentleman?"

"Shut up."

I tell Becky everything. She eats up my words as if they were the fries in between us, which she does a pretty good job on, too. I get to the end and punctuate my story by snatching the last fry before Becky can snag it. I pop it in my mouth before she can protest.

"What did your mom say?"

"I didn't tell her."

"Well, duh, I mean, when you got home so late."

"She didn't say anything."

"Really?"

"She left me a note on the kitchen table."

"And?"

"It said, 'We have to talk.'" I shrug to say I'm not worried about it.

Becky leans back on the plastic bench seat and lowers her chin so she can look down her nose at me. She holds her gaze for a few seconds, then snatches the empty fry plate and gets up to return it. I watch her scrape our trash through the little swinging door below the counter and then leave the plate on top for someone to grab later. She turns back, and I read her T-shirt. IT'S ALL FUN AND GAMES UNTIL SOMEONE GETS HURT . . . THEN IT'S HILARIOUS! Where does she find them?

"C'mon, Matt said he would meet us down at the marina," she says.

"Right. What time is it?"

"Almost seven. Remind me again why your town has fireworks in August?"

"It's like the anniversary of some Revolutionary War battle. Supposedly the Bell Cove militia stopped the British reinforcements from crossing the lake and getting to the real battle on time. The way the Historical Society puts it, if it weren't for Bell Cove we'd still be under British rule."

"So, basically, this is the one day a year when Bell Cove gets to pretend it isn't some insignificant speck on the globe?" Becky skips ahead of me a few feet and turns around with an impish grin, inviting me to fight back.

I surrender. "That's not fair. You're from New York."

We walk out onto the series of wooden docks that serves as the Bell Cove marina. The docks are crowded tonight with boats from across the lake. Their owners are probably enjoying dinner on Main Street or grabbing an ice cream before night falls and the show begins. The town sets off the fireworks out on the lake, and by dusk the public beach will be carpeted with towels and picnic blankets. Many of these boats will be anchored out on the water for an even better view. That's why we're meeting Matt. He invited Becky and me to watch the fireworks with his parents out on their boat.

"I hope Matt could find a place to dock," Becky says, scanning the marina.

"I wish Jay was around," I say. I was hoping to watch the fireworks with Jay. Maybe even have a repeat of yesterday, but with fireworks in the background. Now that our relationship has moved to the next level, I want to make our feelings more public. I feel like I might be ready to take the next step out of the closet.

"You're not going to be one of those codependent boyfriends, are you?"

Do I sense a hint of disgust in her voice?

"No." But I do miss Jay. It's been eighteen hours since I was with him on the boat. Feels like much longer.

"Where is he, anyway?" Becky asks.

"Said he had family stuff."

"Matt?"

"No, Jay. Wait, I see Matt!" I point to the right, and Becky follows my finger to where a sleek boat is drifting up to the docks. Matt is leaning over the side getting ready to tie up. Nathan is standing at the wheel, and Jo Anne has her arm around his waist, her long black hair pulled back with a colorful scarf. We hurry over to help Matt.

"Hey!" he shouts when he sees us approaching. "Sorry we're a little late."

Jo Anne holds her hand out to me, and I help her out of the boat. She's wearing paint-spattered cutoffs and a gauzy white peasant top. "Nathan and I are going to pick up some veggie and hummus wraps at the Bread Board. Can we get you anything?"

Behind her, Becky puffs out her cheeks as if she is holding back a mouthful of vomit.

"No thanks," I say. "We just ate."

"Matt?"

"Extra pickles."

Nathan steps up onto the dock and takes Jo Anne's hand. We watch them head toward Main Street.

"Your parents are so cute," I say.

Becky puffs out her cheeks again, and this time adds sound effects. She's very convincing. "I'm not sure which is worse," she says, "your parents or your sandwich. Hummus?"

"It's all part of growing up hippie." Matt smiles at me. "I'm glad you two could make it."

"Because there's so much else for a kid without a car to do in Bell Cove."

Becky steps between us and throws her arms around our necks. It's a very Kodak moment. "Let's walk around the marina while we wait for your parents to get back. C'mon."

Becky pretends like she's a yoke, and Matt and I are stubborn oxen in need of guidance. She drags us down the wooden dock with her arms still around us. We have no choice but to obey.

The Bell Cove Marina is a series of six docks jutting out from the shore, connected by a seventh dock parallel to Main Street. Normally, there's space for five or six boats on both sides of each dock, and the marina is rarely even half full, but tonight it's operating beyond capacity. Boats of every shape and size are crammed in and tied up two or sometimes three to a mooring ring. There are V-bottomed fishing boats, canopied pontoon boats, twenty-year-old outboard speedboats, and brand-new swanky cruisers. We walk up and down each dock looking for our favorites.

Matt spots a classic wooden cigar boat. The high-gloss lacquer reflects pink light from the sinking sun.

"Sharp," I tell him.

Becky likes a slick black powerboat with a teal slash running down its side. Gold letters on the stern proclaim it *Deus ex Machina*. We covered that during mythology in English; it means "god from a machine."

Matt laughs at her. "I'm pretty sure that God doesn't need a boat. Parting the Red Sea and all."

"But he's got good color sense," Becky says, hitting Matt in the shoulder.

"Ow!" Matt rubs his arm.

"Yeah, she does it to me, too," I say.

"You let her?" Matt turns and hits my shoulder. "No wonder. You're easy!"

"Hey! That hurts!" But I can't help smiling. "And I'm not easy." I lunge across Matt's path to try and get Becky's shoulder, but she dodges out of the way.

"That's not what I hear," she says, laughing.

I open my mouth and let out a short gasp. The air comes out in a high-pitched hiccup, and I hear how gay I sound. I try to cover it up by doubling over in a coughing fit.

Becky stands over me and rolls her eyes, but Matt slaps me on the back and asks, "Are you okay?"

He is so earnest that I just can't take it. I start laughing one of those laughs that starts like a small grinding in the back of your throat but slowly builds until it starts to come out through your nose, and you can't hold it back anymore, and it shoots out in high-pitched squeaks that sound so ridiculous they just make you laugh harder. The terrible thing about that kind of laugh is that it also sounds like you could be crying, and Matt puts his arm around my shoulder, and he is really concerned.

"Are you okay? Sean?"

At this point I am laughing so hard I am losing my breath. I try to nod to reassure him, but the movement just makes me light-headed and suddenly I am going down—with Matt on top of me.

"Oops!" I make a pathetic attempt to catch myself, but only succeed in twisting around so Matt falls across my lap. I'm laughing so hard I'm crying, but Matt seems to have figured out I'm okay because he is laughing, too. Becky just stands over us shaking her head. She has a smile, though.

"Maybe it's time we head back to the boat. I'd go by myself, but clearly you two can't be left alone."

Matt crawls over me and manages to get to his feet. Still laughing, he pulls me up, and we start to head back toward his boat. Suddenly, I stop short. Did I just see what I thought I saw? I wheel around and look toward the end of the dock. There it is, a beautiful blue-and-white twenty-foot Craftsman tied up and gently bobbing alongside all of the other boats in the crowded marina.

"Is that . . . ?" I break away from Matt and Becky to investigate. I tell myself that it's just another, similar boat. But as I get closer I see a familiar hot-pink T-shirt in a ball under the windshield. I don't need to get any closer to know it's a Pink Cone T-shirt. Jay's Pink Cone T-shirt.

"What's wrong?" Becky asks as she catches up to me.

"That's Jay's boat."

"I thought you said—"

"He had other plans."

"Maybe his parents are here?"

"His plans were with his family."

Matt had kept a few feet behind us, but now he puts his hand on my shoulder. "Hey," he says, "we should get back."

I nod without saying anything and let Becky and Matt lead me back to Matt's boat. My mind is racing, trying to find an explanation, but I keep pulling blanks. Jay had specifically said he had to hang out with his parents. He had specifically *not* said they would be hanging out in Bell Cove. So why is his boat here? And more important, why did Jay lie to me?

Becky and Matt do their best to keep me from thinking about Jay for the rest of the evening. We find a great spot out on the water to watch the fireworks. Matt's dad produces a deck of cards, and the five of us start a game of bullshit. It doesn't surprise me when Becky wins, but who knew Matt's mom was such a good liar? Matt, on the other hand, is a terrible liar. Every time he tries to lie, he clears his throat first. All four of us laugh and call him on it. Needless to say, Matt ends up with all of the cards.

The fireworks start about nine thirty. Matt, Becky, and I take seats in the front of the boat while Matt's parents sit in the back. The display is nonstop, and there is too much to try to look at all at once. As soon as one blossom of red sparks explodes over our heads, a series of white pinwheels shoots out directly in front of us, and then twin threads of green twist and shoot their way into multicolored chandeliers.

"I love those," I say after one of the chandeliers twinkles toward the water.

"Me too," Matt says over the boom of a red, white, and blue explosion.

"I like the loud ones," Becky says.

"No surprise there," I say. Becky pushes me and I fall over into Matt's lap. Laughing, I look up at him.

"Sorry," I say. Matt's face is lit blue by another round of fireworks.

He smiles down at me. He shakes his head and sticks out his tongue. I sit up and push Becky back.

"Feeling any better?" she asks.

"A little."

We watch the rest of the fireworks in silence.

Chapter 30

I get home a little before eleven. The house is still dark; my mother isn't home yet. I lie down on my bed, but I'm not tired, and I'm not really thinking about sleeping. Actually, all I can think about is Jay. I was able to forget him for a few hours out on the boat, but in the silent house, my mind inevitably drifts back to my favorite subject.

After the fireworks, we took the boat back to Matt's house and his dad drove Becky and me home, stopping to pick up my bike from the Pink Cone on the way. I didn't get a chance to see if Jay's boat was still docked in the marina.

But why had it been there in the first place? Jay lives across the lake. He only comes to Bell Cove for work, and I had heard him say more than once that if it weren't for the Pink Cone, nobody would come to Bell Cove. I know there must be some logical explanation. I refuse to believe that Jay would lie to me.

I'm still not sleepy, but I decide I might as well get ready for bed. I pull off my cargos and flip them over the back of my computer chair. I stare at the little white light in the corner of the monitor. Out of curiosity I grab the computer mouse, waking the computer from sleep mode. After a few seconds, my

desktop appears. I click the instant message icon and wait for
the computer to sign me on. In a moment a long, thin box appears showing which of my friends are signed online. I scan the
list for Jay's screen name and double click to open a new chat.

NHBeachBoi: r u there?

There's an instant reply.

Jayman814:   Out. Leave me one for when I get back.

His away message. I wait for a few seconds, but nothing else
appears. He must really be away. I think about leaving him a
message saying I saw his boat at the marina, but what should I
say? Every time I try to type it sounds like I'm accusing him of
something. I start and delete a message four times, and I'm in
the middle of my fifth attempt when I hear the front door
open. Whatever. I wasn't getting anywhere trying to leave a
message anyway. I click the "X" and the message box disappears
from the screen. With a sigh, I decide I might as well get the
"talk" with my mother over with.

I'm halfway down the stairs when I hear my mother's voice. I
know my mother's crazy, but she doesn't usually talk to herself.
She's not alone. I take the last steps more carefully and follow
her voice into the kitchen.

He's sitting there, a man I haven't seen before, at the
counter, while my mother is twisting a corkscrew into a bottle of
wine. Two glasses sit on the counter between them. My mother's
back is to me, and the man is watching her closely, so he doesn't
see me at first. She's wearing a pink spaghetti-strap tank top,
and her shoulders are bare. She usually wears a blouse over this
particular top, and I notice that a white cotton button-down is
draped over one of the kitchen stools. My mother pulls the
cork from the bottle and begins to pour the wine. It's dark pur-

ple, almost black. She's leaning on the counter, and her hand is a little unsteady while pouring; this isn't her first glass of wine tonight.

I shift my weight, and the floorboards let out a low groan. My mother turns quickly to face me. She grips the wine bottle with both hands as if the sudden movement threatens to dislodge it.

"Sean!"

I don't speak, and an awkward five seconds pass between us. My mother's eyes are wide, and she seems confused by my presence. Finally, the man clears his throat, bringing my mother back to reality. Her head gives a quick jerk, and she places the bottle on the counter.

"Sean, this is Steve."

Steve stands up and reaches an arm across the counter to shake my hand. I stay in the doorway. For the first time, I really look at Steve closely. He's compact and wiry and not unattractive for someone dating my mother. At least my mom hasn't lost her touch. He's wearing a black polo shirt with a little alligator on the breast, and jeans. A lightweight corduroy blazer is hanging on the back of a dining room chair. It's the perfect trying-without-trying-too-hard outfit. His wire-rimmed glasses make him look distinctly professorial, especially when he puts that blazer on, I'm betting. All he needs is leather patches on the elbows and a nasal British accent.

When Steve figures out I am not about to shake his hand, he forces a smile that says, *I understand. I wouldn't shake my hand either,* and sits back down. If my mother is aware of my rudeness, she doesn't show it.

"We were just having a nightcap." She grabs the wine bottle again and holds it up to me, proving her point. "I thought you were out watching the fireworks."

"I thought you were, too." I can't help letting a little teenage impudence sneak into my tone. "So you should know they ended almost two hours ago."

She cocks her head. "Of course."

"I just came down because I thought we 'needed to talk.' " I do finger quotes. "But clearly that isn't an option tonight."

My mother's mouth opens slightly, but no words come out. She doesn't want to show anger in front of a guest so she's choosing her words carefully. "Maybe . . ." She trails off and looks at Steve. I can tell she's contemplating asking him to leave. She tightens her lips into a forced smile, and she stares down at the wine bottle in her hands.

I look at her hands, too, and I notice that they are not the hands of a young woman. My mother has always aged gracefully, as they say, and so I often forget that she is nearly fifty. Her hair is not gray, she has kept her figure, and she goes out on school nights. But her hands give her away. I can see blue veins protruding slightly on the backs of them, and her knuckles are small knobs in the middle of her bony fingers. My mother's face and body may pass for ten years younger, but not her hands. And I realize that I can't remember the last time my mother had a boyfriend. She and my dad have been divorced for five years, and my father has moved on and is starting over with a new girlfriend. But my mother is still single. Part of me likes it that way; I get her all to myself. But a smaller, less selfish part of me understands how unfair I'm being.

"Forget it, Mom. We can talk tomorrow. I didn't mean to interrupt your date." I turn to go, but stop and turn back. "It was nice to meet you, Steve." There's a moment of awkwardness, and I book it out of there before any more weirdness takes place.

Chapter 31

I'm anxious to see Jay when I get to work the next day. I didn't sleep well, and it would do a lot to ease my mind if I could just talk to him. But when I walk in the back door and see the fabulous Renée, I know something's up.

"Sean, fabulous." Renée dumps a tub of mocha chip in my arms before I even have a chance to say hello. She's in nonstop mode, and in her Pink Cone T-shirt, she reminds me of the Energizer Bunny. She heads into the storeroom and begins tearing it apart. I can barely hear her over the sound of boxes being thrown from shelves. "Jay called in sick. Harleigh sprained her ankle horseback riding, and I can't find the cherries. I called Ashley, but she's not answering her phone. I sent Becky out to buy cherries. We open in fifteen minutes. Where is she?"

"I'm right here!" Becky is pushing through the back door with a brown shopping bag full of jars of maraschino cherries. "They didn't have any of the bulk jars at Porfido's Market, so I just bought all of the little jars."

"Fabulous!" Renée steps out of the storeroom. Her face is red, and the hair on one side of her head is sticking out where she's been pulling at it. "Jay was supposed to order cherries, and now he's not even here. No Jay. No cherries. No Harleigh.

No Ashley. What else don't we have? Do we have spoons? This is an ice cream shop; we're supposed to have spoons. Where are the spoons?!"

Becky shoves the bag of cherries onto the warming table and grabs Renée by the shoulders. "Breathe. Sean and I can handle this. There's spoons for everyone."

Renée's eyes are wide, and they keep sliding from side to side like she expects a SWAT team to come bursting through the doors at any moment. I grab a container of plastic spoons and hold it up to reassure her.

Finally, after several deep breaths, Renée has calmed down. She waves her hands in front of her face like she is brushing away a mosquito. "I'm sorry. You guys must think I'm crazy."

"We already knew that," Becky says.

"It's just that Hannah's parents are in town this weekend and . . ." Renée clenches her hands into fists, searching for the right words. "We . . . don't . . . see eye to eye. They still blame me for turning Hannah into a lesbian."

Becky and I just stare. What do you say to a forty-year-old lesbian with in-law problems?

Renée closes her eyes and shakes her head. "Why am I even telling you this? You two are, what? Sixteen? Seventeen?" She snorts in disgust and goes back in the storeroom. We hear boxes being slammed around again. We have been dismissed.

Renée finally leaves the Pink Cone an hour later after completely reorganizing the storeroom in alphabetical order, which is not necessarily a good thing. Now the pineapple topping is next to the paper dishes and pint containers, while the chocolate chips are next to the condensed milk. It takes Becky and me almost ten minutes to figure out that the coconut is on the shelf with the strawberries and sprinkles because it is called "shredded coconut."

"People who organize things when they are stressed out," Becky says, standing in the storeroom doorway, "stress me out."

It's a slow day for customers, most people having met their ice cream quota last night during the fireworks, so Becky and I have plenty of time to talk.

"Where do you think Jay is?" I ask during one of the lulls.

"Probably hungover."

"I really wanted to talk to him."

"What would you say?"

"I just want to know why his boat was here."

Becky is crouching down, restocking a cabinet with bowls and spoons, and she doesn't look up to answer. "You're still on that? If it's that important, why don't you just call him?"

There's a good reason for that. "He doesn't pick up."

Becky lets out a short laugh. She finishes stocking the cabinet and admires her work for a second before standing to face me.

"Sean, I hope you're not getting the wrong idea."

"What do you mean?"

"It's just—" Becky takes a breath. "It sounds like you hooked up."

"Yeah?"

"I mean, like, you hooked up. Just hooked up."

I don't understand, and my face must show my confusion because Becky explains.

"I don't think Jay ever wanted to be your boyfriend."

"What?"

"Think about it. I mean, what kind of boyfriend doesn't answer his phone when you call, or at least call you back?"

"We work together. I see him, like, every day."

"Okay, then where is he? What about his other friends? The ones he goes clubbing with? What about the guy I heard him talking to on the phone?"

"Friends."

"Sean, he's eighteen."

"So?"

Becky sounds like a doctor giving bad news to a patient. "Jay just wanted you for one thing."

"What about Camp Aweelah?"

"He was having fun. He said himself his plans were canceled."

"We had sex." I don't want to believe Becky, but a gnawing in the bottom of my stomach is growing. I feel my gut twisting, and I take deep breaths to keep from throwing up. "He said he loved me."

"Oh, babe." Becky pulls me to her and pushes my head into her shoulder.

My eyes are hot with tears. "I don't want to be a cliché."

I let Becky stroke the back of my neck, thankful for a friend like her. After a minute, my nose is running, and I sniff to clear it. I pull away from Becky to wipe my face. She hands me a napkin from the dispenser by the window and gives me a look of pity. Her eyes are shiny, and I can tell she feels bad for me, but she's also enjoying her role as comforter. And then I realize, Becky has every reason to sabotage my relationship with Jay. She's just jealous. It's not that Jay lied to me, it's that Becky wants me to think that Jay lied to me. The gnawing in my stomach turns to an icy certainty, and I take a step away from Becky.

"No."

"No?"

"No. I don't believe you."

"Sean?"

"I don't believe you. Jay does love me. You're just jealous because I want to spend time with him." If Jay didn't love me, then why would he spend so much time with me? Take me out on his boat, flirt with me at work, kiss me the way he does? Why would he say he loves me? Jay wouldn't say it without meaning it. He just wouldn't.

"What?"

"Why? Why would you say that?"

"Don't get upset."

"I'm already upset. You almost convinced me that Jay didn't love me. That he used me for sex. I thought you were my friend."

"I am."

I clench my jaw, and I barely open my lips. "Not anymore." I turn and walk out of the Pink Cone. Becky doesn't say a word.

Chapter 32

I don't go straight home. I ride my bike to Mann's Hill and sit for a long time on top of my favorite rock. I go over every moment I've spent with Jay until I am convinced that I am right. I can't believe I almost listened to Becky. Jay has been nothing but sweet to me since my first day at the Pink Cone. Why would I ever think he didn't love me? Just because his boat wasn't where he said it would be? It's late afternoon before I finally head back to my house.

My mom is in the kitchen when I get home, but I go straight to my room to change. I pull off my work shirt and throw it in a ball in the corner of my room. I spilled hot fudge on my shorts, so I slide them off and kick them in the corner, too. Looking around for clean clothes, I realize my room is a mess. I haven't cleaned it all summer, and it shows. How am I supposed to find anything in here? I pull out the second drawer in my dresser for a new pair of shorts. It's empty. When was the last time I did laundry?

I'm suddenly very tired. I collapse into my desk chair. I sit there in my boxers, not sure of what to do next. There's a pile of dirty clothes spilling out of my closet; maybe I can find a wearable pair of shorts. I spin around in my chair, relaxing my eyes and letting my room turn into a blur until I'm so dizzy I can't take it anymore. I fall over onto my desk. The sudden movement wakes up my computer and the screen comes to life. I focus my eyes. There he is in my instant message buddy list: Jayman814.

NHBeachBoi:	Hi

I wait a few seconds. There's no away message this time.

Jayman814:	sup?
NHBeachBoi:	you weren't at work
Jayman814:	so hungover ☹
NHBeachBoi:	feeling better?
Jayman814:	yea
NHBeachBoi:	I was hoping to see you
Jayman814:	sry man
NHBeachBoi:	tonight?
Jayman814:	not relly up 2 it
Jayman814:	Hey, gtg
Jayman814:	ttyl

Before I can reply, Jay's screen name disappears from my buddy list. I notice I have goose bumps on my arm. I get up and start to dig through the pile of laundry. I need to put on a shirt.

I pull a yellow T-shirt from under the pile and hold it up to my nose for inspection. It passes. Barely. I turn it right side out so I can put it on and I realize it's the sign language shirt that Becky and I bought at the thrift store at the beginning of the summer. I smile at the memory. I almost throw the shirt back in the pile, but I change my mind. I pull it over my head.

I find a pair of cargo shorts I'm pretty sure I only wore once and pull them on, too. I'm just doing the button when there's a knock at my door.

"Honey?"

"It's open."

My mom walks in and lets her eyes scan the room.

"I know. I'll clean it this weekend."

She nods. She shifts a pile of rejected T-shirts from the end of the bed and sits down. She reaches out a hand and guides me to the spot next to her. I swallow. I can sense that she's about to cash in on that talk I owe her.

"After last night, I thought a lot about how I've been treating you."

I keep quiet. I don't know where she's going with this yet.

"And I realized that I haven't been fair. How can I be upset with you for staying out late and not telling me where you've been when I'm doing the exact same thing to you?" She puts a hand on my knee and squeezes it. "I guess what I'm trying to say is I'm sorry. At school, I'm always telling parents that the 'Do what I say, not what I do' method of parenting never works. And here I am, not following my own advice."

I still don't say anything. I'm afraid if I agree it'll sound like I'm saying I told you so.

"From now on, let's be honest with each other. I'll tell you about Steve, and you tell me about Jay." She turns to look at me and then slides an arm around my shoulders. "Is it a deal?"

I nod my head. "Yeah. I'd like that."

She squeezes me in a one-armed hug. After a while she pulls me up from the bed, and we head downstairs.

At the top of the stairs, my mom says, "There's someone else you might think about telling about Jay."

"Who?"

But she doesn't answer. She doesn't need to. We get to the bottom of the stairs, and my dad is sitting on the living room sofa. He's facing the picture windows that look out over the lake, but he turns around when he hears us on the stairs.

"Sean! I was thinking you might want to go out fishing with me tonight."

"Tonight?"

"You have other plans?"

I want to say yes, but in this whole new spirit of honesty, I just shake my head.

"Great! I have to head back to Georgia next week, and I thought we could go out on the lake one last time."

I look at my mother, and I am angry. I feel ambushed. She feeds me a story about our new open-and-honest policy and then lures me downstairs to my waiting father. "I don't think so."

"What?"

"I don't want to go fishing. I don't even know why you came up here. Don't you understand? I went out of my way to get a job here in Bell Cove so I wouldn't have to spend the summer with you. Just because you traveled a thousand miles doesn't change that."

My mother puts a hand on my arm, but I shake it off. "And you! 'Let's be honest with each other'? This is bullshit."

"Sean, don't talk to your moth—"

"BULLSHIT!" I storm back up to my room and slam the door so hard it sounds like a gunshot.

My knees are sliding beneath me as I sink to the floor with my back against my bedroom door. It wasn't that long ago I found myself in this position because I didn't know how to tell my mom about Jay. And in a strange way, that's why I'm here again. If I'm honest with myself, I'm not really mad with either of my parents. I'm mad because everyone keeps telling me that my boyfriend isn't who he says he is. And they're all wrong. It's true that I've let Jay have a little piece of my emotions, and instead of taking care of that like a rare gift, he's tossed it away like a prize from a Cracker Jack box. But that doesn't mean he doesn't love me. I *know* he does.

Chapter 33

I make it out of the house the next day without seeing my mother and head to the Pink Cone for an opening shift with Jay and Becky. I'm prepared for a showdown and am surprised and relieved that Becky isn't there. Jay tells me that since Becky ended up working half her shift by herself yesterday, Renée gave her the day off today. Yeah, I feel a little guilty about that. But only a little.

And any guilt I have is quickly forgotten when I realize I will have Jay all to myself for the whole shift. This will give us a chance to talk, and if it's slow, who knows?

I have a lot of fun shamelessly flirting with Jay all afternoon. I take every chance I get to tickle him, tousle his hair, and basically be in constant contact. Of course, I don't do anything in front of customers, but there are long stretches where it's just us, and I love it.

I keep making excuses to go get things from the storeroom, hoping that one time Jay will suddenly "remember" something that he needs also, and we can sneak a kiss, but he never catches on. Finally, we run low on plastic spoons while I am helping a customer, and Jay goes to get them. Of course, since plastic spoons are on the "p" shelf it takes Jay a while to find them, and I am finished with the customer before he returns. I decide that he must need help looking.

I find Jay in the storeroom and come up behind him. I snake my arms around his waist and try to kiss his neck. He shrugs me off.

"What are you doing?"

"I'm giving my boyfriend a kiss?"

"We're at work."

"There aren't any customers." I start to put my arms around him again, but he catches my hands. His grip surprises me.

"Cool it. Out on my boat, that's one thing,"

"I'm only your boyfriend on your boat?"

"I'm just saying I like my space. You're a little clingy."

"Clingy?"

"The constant contact thing. Just because we're together, doesn't mean we have to always be together." He crosses his fingers and holds them in front of my face to emphasize his point. Then he snaps them apart. I get the picture.

"Fine." I set my jaw and turn away, but when I reach the doorway, he stops me.

"We can go out tonight, if you want."

"Woohoo, on your boat again?" My sarcasm drips like a sugar cone in mid-July.

"Don't be like that. No, let's get dinner. Like at a real restaurant, where they bring you menus?"

"Yeah, okay." I smile just a little. I turn around to leave.

"Sean?"

"Yeah?"

"Do you have any idea where the spoons are?"

"Try looking next to the pineapple topping."

The rest of my shift goes by quickly, and I am looking forward to our date. Jay is actually scheduled to work a couple of hours longer than me, so we make plans to meet up after he gets out. When my shift is over, I'm in the break room changing my shirt before I head home when I hear a high-pitched cell phone beep. Jay's sweatshirt is on a hook on the wall, and I reach in the front pocket and find his cigarettes and his cell phone. The front screen on the phone says he has a new text message.

I think about bringing the phone out to Jay, but curiosity gets the better of me. I flip open the phone.

You have a new text message

I press the read button and the screen changes.

R we still on 4 2nite?

Apparently, Jay had plans for tonight. But Jay made plans with me. I tell myself that his plans aren't that important since Jay is going out with me. I wonder who the text message is from. I select "keep as new" so Jay will see that he has an unread message, and I head out the door.

"See you tonight," I call to Jay on my way out.

He gives me a smile and a wave and turns back to the customer at the window.

Chapter 34

Jay holds the door for me at the Rattlesnake Grill. It's not busy, and in a few minutes we have a booth to ourselves near the bar. The Rattlesnake Grill is one of those western-themed restaurants where the servers all wear oversized belt buckles and occasionally start line dancing while your food is getting cold in the kitchen.

Jay grabs a handful of peanuts from the aluminum bucket on the table and starts cracking them open, tossing the shells on the floor. Apparently, this is accepted behavior here because peanut shells cover the floor like beige snow. I look around at the piles and wonder who is in charge of sweeping. It's worse than when my father last dragged me to a baseball game.

Jay hands me a menu from the rustic wooden holder at the end of the table. "Hey, sorry about today," he says.

"It's okay."

He reaches across the table and takes my hand. I look up from my menu and into his eyes. He's smiling.

From out of nowhere, a perky waitress appears at our table. I instinctively pull my hand away. I study my menu.

The waitress is oblivious. "Can I start you off with something to drink?"

"Diet Coke," Jay says, "with a lime."

I'm still hiding behind my menu. My face is hot, partly from embarrassment at what I think the waitress might have seen, and partly out of shame for pulling my hand away. Aren't I the one who wanted to go out with Jay somewhere other than his boat?

"And for you?" The waitress isn't much older than Jay, but she treats us like we're a middle-aged couple enjoying a night away from the kids.

"Sean?" Jay reaches over and pulls my menu down.

"Iced tea," I mumble. The waitress leaves, and I put my menu down.

"You okay?" Jay's eyebrows scrunch together, and he smiles with mock concern. Again he reaches for my hand, but this time his phone interrupts with its high-pitched text message beep.

Jay reaches into his pocket. He opens the phone and studies the message for a few seconds, then flips it closed with a plastic snap. He places the phone on the table and focuses his attention on me again.

"Who was it?" I ask.

"Nobody. A friend. Wants to know if I can go out tonight."

"Later?"

"Yeah."

"Oh."

"I don't know, I might go."

"Where?"

"This club in Manchester."

I nod like I've been there, even though I have never been to a club in my life since I'm only sixteen. I wonder if it's a gay club.

"Is that okay?" Jay says.

"Are you asking my permission?"

"No. But you seem upset."

"No."

"You just seem . . ." He's searching for a word, and he purses his lips together. If we were on his boat I would kiss him. The thought makes me smile.

His phone beeps again. He flips it open, and this time he types a return message. While he is typing, the waitress brings our drinks. She pulls two straws from her apron and slides them across the table, then waits patiently for Jay to finish his message.

"Ready to order?"

We place our orders—Jay gets a steak, and I get a Sidewinder Burger, which is just a normal hamburger with bacon and sautéed mushrooms on it.

After the waitress goes, Jay says, "Sorry about that."

"No biggie."

"What's with all the one-word answers?"

"What do you mean?"

"You just seem kind of quiet tonight."

"I guess I just don't have much to say."

Jay is about to say something else, but his phone goes off again. He picks it up and starts to type a reply.

"I'm sorry I'm not as much fun as a club," I say. Wow, that sounded bitchy. But I guess I got Jay's attention, because he stops in mid-text.

"Sean, I have other friends."

"I know."

"I'm sorry. I wish I could take you to the club, but you're not eighteen."

"My mom wouldn't let me go anyway. I'm already in trouble for staying out so late with you."

Jay finishes off his text and flips his phone shut. "Your mom must hate me."

"No. Well, maybe a little." I think back to the night she met Jay at the Pink Cone. "She's just being a mom."

Jay nods. "My parents aren't around that much. I pretty much get to do what I want."

"How come?"

"My dad's a lawyer and he works a lot, and my mother's a nurse and she does a lot of overnight shifts, so . . ." He shrugs. "It's not like I want to hang out with them anyway."

"Right. I get that," I say, even though I don't. My mom and I have always been close. Maybe not so much lately, but it's not like I'm ready to move out or anything.

"I basically have my own apartment in the basement. It's cool. I even have a separate entrance. Comes in handy."

The waitress appears with our food. "Can I get you guys anything else?" she asks.

Jay reaches across the table and steals one of my fries. "Ketchup," he says.

The waitress points to the wooden rack that holds the menus. The condiments, including ketchup, are stuck in holes on either side.

"Oh, right. Thanks," Jay says, chewing on my fry. The waitress leaves. Jay grabs the plastic ketchup bottle and squeezes out a red pool onto the edge of his plate. He grabs another one of my fries.

"Help yourself," I say.

"Thanks. Do you mind?"

"No, that's okay. You could have ordered fries, you know."

"I like mashed potatoes. Besides, I knew I could steal yours."

"Whatever."

We don't talk for several minutes while we eat our food. I think about whoever keeps texting Jay and whether he'll meet them at the club later on. The burger is pretty good, I guess, although I'm concentrating too hard on Jay's cell phone to notice much. Sure enough, his phone beeps again.

"You sure are popular tonight," I say.

Jay gives me a closed-lip smile, since his mouth is full, and picks up his phone. I grab a bottle out of the holder, Rattlesnake Grill Steak Sauce, and study the label. The "S" in *Steak* is a cartoon rattlesnake wearing a cowboy hat. Jay puts his phone down again.

"Sorry about that," he says.

"It's okay. I thought we were on a date."

"We are."

"It feels more like you and your phone are on a date." There's that bitchy tone again. I don't want to fight. Part of my purpose tonight is to prove Becky wrong, and fighting won't help my case.

"What do you want to talk about?"

"I don't know."

"How's your burger?" Jay says.

"Good. How are my fries?" I force a smile. I can make myself have fun.

Jay laughs and takes another fry off my plate. He dips it in ketchup. "There's a smile," he says. "You're cute when you smile."

I roll my eyes, but I keep smiling, and this time it's genuine. Maybe this date isn't going too badly after all.

Chapter 35

Jay gives me a ride home after dinner. We pull into my driveway about eight thirty, and Jay puts the car in neutral.

"So," I say, breaking the silence.

"So," Jay says.

I keep looking straight ahead. There are no lights on, so my mother must be out, probably with Steve. Jay puts his hand on my thigh. I look down and then put my hand over his. He has a yellow rubber bracelet with words imprinted on it. I run my finger over it, feeling the depressions the letters make in the rubber. Finally, I look over at Jay.

He is smiling at me, and then he is leaning over, and then he is kissing me. His lips spark against mine, and a surge of adrenaline fires through my body. This is the moment I've been thinking about all night. After what Becky said, I was worried that I wouldn't feel anything anymore. My eyes are closed, but colors flash through my brain. I see a kaleidoscope of reds, blues, and yellows; this is better than any club dance floor. Jay's hand slides up my thigh. If he doesn't love me, how can he make me feel like this?

I push forward, into his kiss. I move so I can reach across

with my right hand and feel his body. My hand moves over his thin cotton T-shirt; his biceps shift beneath my fingers. My hand moves up his arm and past his shoulder. He's wearing a necklace, a thin silver chain, and I run a finger under it, feeling its surprising weight and warmth. Finally, I cup his cheek in my palm. I can feel a day's worth of stubble under my fingertips, each prickle sending more sparks shooting through me. I let my hand just barely graze across his skin, so lightly it tickles, and I almost can't stand it. I breathe him in, through my nose, through my mouth. His smell is sweetly spicy, like chai tea, and faintly smoky. I fill my lungs, and for a moment I believe he is my oxygen, necessary for life.

But then Jay pulls back. His hand comes up and takes mine from his face. He smiles at me.

"You better get going," he says.

"I don't think anyone's home."

"Tomorrow?" It's half a question, half a command.

I bite my lower lip. I can still taste him. "Are you sure?"

Jay smiles, and as an answer, he reaches down and puts the car in reverse. I exhale through my nose, making a soft rushing noise, and then breathe in deeply, trying to savor the moment. I pull the door handle and climb out of the car. Jay blows me a kiss, and maneuvers the car back down the driveway. I stand in the dark and watch him go until his lights have disappeared from view.

The house is empty, as I suspected, so I head up to my room. It's still early, and I'm not tired. I sit down at the computer to see who is online. Lisa.

NHBeachBoi:	hi
LuvBug922:	SEAN! {{{HUGS}}}
NHBeachBoi:	how r u

LuvBug922:	good. I can't believe this is my last week! It went by so fast
NHBeachBoi:	i no
LuvBug922:	whats up with u?
NHBeachBoi:	nothing much. Just seeing who's online
LuvBug922:	cool cool. how's ur guy?

I'm a little surprised that Lisa would ask, but also relieved. Lisa and I might not have been meant for each other romantically, but we were always good friends and could talk about anything. I guess after a summer with Becky, it's easy to forget who you used to talk to about stuff.

NHBeachBoi:	I'm not sure. good I guess
LuvBug922:	u guess?
NHBeachBoi:	well, I thought so. He told me he loved me.
LuvBug922:	that's great!
NHBeachBoi:	but my friend Becky said he was using me
LuvBug922:	oh
LuvBug922:	well, is there any reason to believe her? Maybe she's just jealous
NHBeachBoi:	I thought so too. We had a date tonight
LuvBug922:	and?
NHBeachBoi:	okay. Hold on.
NHBeachBoi:	so he picks me up and we went to Rattlesnake and he was all cute and stuff and we ate dinner and it was good. but all through dinner he kept

> getting texts, and I was like, that's so rude, and he was like, i have other friends. and yesterday he told me i was to clingy cuz i tried to kiss him at work. and then he got a text at work and I looked at it—i no i suck—and it said he had plans with somebody, and anyway Becky says she overheard him making plans with some guy one night when he was supposed to hang out with me,and since he won't answer his phone that means he really isn't into me, and he just wants sex.

NHBeachBoi: sorry that was like a novel

There's a long pause while she reads what I wrote. I look around my room. I really do need to clean it. I decide to start by making my bed. I pull off all the blankets and sheets. My computer beeps.

LuvBug922:   wow

LuvBug922:   the text thing is really rude. if I was with a guy who did that, I'd be pissed

NHBeachBoi: yeah

LuvBug922:   I mean, if it's a date, he's supposed to be focused on you.

NHBeachBoi: yeah

LuvBug922:   well, what do u like about him?

NHBeachBoi: what do u mean?

LuvBug922:   u said he was hot, but what do u guys talk about? What do u have in common?

My fingers hover over the keyboard, but I don't type anything. I don't know what to type. The truth is Jay was the first gay guy I had ever met, and meeting him felt like winning the lottery, like a once-in-a-lifetime thing. I went out with Jay because I thought I had to; I might not get another chance.

NHBeachBoi:	we're both gay and we both work at the pink cone
LuvBug922:	But what about the stuff u like? Movies, and drama club, and drawing?
NHBeachBoi:	idk
LuvBug922:	maybe u should find out
NHBeachBoi:	yeah
NHBeachBoi:	u have any plans for next week?
LuvBug922:	no
NHBeachBoi:	wanna hang out, just friends?
LuvBug922:	absolutely. Maybe I can introduce you to Brad
NHBeachBoi:	that would be cool.
LuvBug922:	yeah, he's helping to start a PFLAG chapter in Bell Cove. Maybe you can get your mother to go.
NHBeachBoi:	PFLAG?
LuvBug922:	Parents, Families, and Friends of Lesbians and Gays. It's like a GSA but for the real world. Not school, you know?
NHBeachBoi:	GSA?
LuvBug922:	Gay-Straight Alliance. It's a club where gay and straight kids talk about tolerance and how to make the school a safer place.

LuvBug922:	Maybe we can start one at BCHS!
NHBeachBoi:	idk. U think there r other gay kids at BCHS?
LuvBug922:	It's for straight kids too!
NHBeachBoi:	idk. I'll think about it. The PFLAG thing sounds cool though. My mom might actually do that. She used to be pretty cool.
LuvBug922:	yeah. Well, I gotta go. I can't wait to see you next week. I miss you! {{{HUGS}}} TTYL!
NHBeachBoi:	ttyl

I close the IM window and just sit for a few minutes in front of the computer screen. Talking with Lisa reminds me why we were so close to begin with. She always seems to know what to say. Maybe Jay isn't the only gay guy out there. If Lisa can find a gay guy at a Christian summer camp, then they can't be that hard to find.

I turn away from my computer. My bed is stripped bare, and my old sheets are on the floor in a ball. My closet is overflowing with dirty clothes. My desk is littered with soda cups from the Pink Cone, and the carpet might have been blue, back when I used to be able to see it, before it was covered with newspapers and shopping bags and clothes hangers, and who knows what else. Might as well get started. I grab an empty plastic shopping bag off the floor, and I start filling it with trash. By midnight, my room is spotless.

Chapter 36

As it happens, I have three days off in a row after that, and I have no desire to be anywhere near the Pink Cone. Between fighting with Becky, wondering about Jay, and a boss having a mental breakdown, it feels good to get away for a bit.

When I return to work three days later, I already have a plan. I stopped up on Mann's Hill and sat on my rock to work it all out in my head. Now I'm ready to go. Jay is already there when I walk in. Harleigh is manning the window. Becky isn't there, and that's part of my plan. I don't want Jay to know that Becky and I are fighting.

"Hey Jay," I call into the freezer where Jay is retrieving a container of vanilla.

"Hey, babe. It's payday!"

"Awesome. How was the club?"

"It was all right. Saw a couple people I know."

"Cool. What kind of music do they play?"

"Mostly house and reggae." Jay comes out of the freezer with a plastic container in his arms. He sets it on the warming table.

"Is that what you like?" I ask.

"Yeah."

"What else do you listen to?"

"I don't know. Some rap, some hip-hop. That kind of stuff."

"Any pop?"

"If it's on the radio," he says. He heads back into the freezer for another flavor, and I go out front to join Harleigh.

It's a slow day, and we spend most of the afternoon cleaning. We clean the store every night, but not thoroughly. It's more like wipe down all the surfaces and mop the floor. It's amazing where ice cream manages to get when you aren't looking, and even more amazing how sticky it is.

Harleigh has one of the big mixers pulled out and is scrubbing it down from behind while I wash the windows. I stand on a chair to reach the top.

"How does ice cream get up here? This looks like strawberry," I say.

"You don't want to know what this looks like," Harleigh says.

Jay comes out of the storeroom. "I think I finally got it back to normal," he says. "I can't believe she put the sugar next to the cherries because the package says cane sugar."

Both Harleigh and I shake our heads. Luckily, Renée's in-laws have left town and she's mostly back to normal. Normal for Renée, that is.

"Sean, when you're done with that, can you refill the napkin dispensers?"

"As you wish, my dearest Buttercup."

"What?"

"*The Princess Bride.* It's one of my favorite movies."

"Never seen it."

"Seriously?" I can't believe what I am hearing. "What's your favorite movie?"

Jay thinks for minute. "I don't know. I like action movies. I liked *Independence Day.*"

"What about *Indiana Jones?*"

"Yeah, that was okay."

"Okay? *Okay?*" Time for a real test. "Hey, after Becky goes back to New York, you want to plan a road trip down to visit her?"

"Definitely," Jay says. "They have great clubs in New York."

"Yeah. Maybe we could see a show on Broadway. I've always wanted to see *The Lion King*."

"Maybe," Jay says. "If you're into that."

"You're not?"

Harleigh speaks up. "Sean, weren't you the lead in the spring musical?"

"I wasn't the lead, but I did have a pretty important part."

"My friend Stephanie was in it. I remember you. You were good." Harleigh smiles.

"Thanks." I turn back to Jay. "So you really don't like musicals?"

Jay just shrugs.

"What about art? If we go to New York, would you go to any of the museums with me?"

"What's with all the questions?"

"I'm just curious."

"Yeah. Just curious." Jay goes back into the storeroom and comes out with some bundles of paper napkins. They are wrapped in brown paper, but the ends are open, showing the white paper insides. He tosses the bundles to me. "Here. Go be curious about the napkin dispensers." He's smiling, but I can tell I've annoyed him.

I'm just about finished with the napkins when Jay sticks his head through the window. "Hey, babe, wanna go home early?"

"How early?"

"Now."

"Why don't you send Harleigh home?" I say.

"I asked her, but her ride won't be here till four."

"Fine. Whatever."

"Are you mad?"

"No. It's just too bad. We could have had the afternoon to-gether."

"I know." He drums the counter with his hands. "Space is a good thing." Jay pulls his head back through the window. I fin-ish filling the last dispenser and head back around to the inside of the shop.

"Are you sure you don't need me?"

"No. Get out of here. I'll catch you online tonight."

"Yeah. Later then."

I head out the back door and unlock my bike from the metal railing on the steps. I swing my leg over the seat, but I don't ride away. Jay is a different person to me today. He doesn't like the same music as me. Not the same movies. He's not into the-ater, and definitely not into art. I tell myself people can learn to like these things. I'm sure he would love *The Princess Bride* if he saw it. In fact, that would make a great date. But still. Lisa was right. Maybe I do like Jay for the wrong reasons.

But that's just it. I *do* like Jay. When I'm with Jay I feel more alive, like I can do anything. I think back to the stars on his boat, and the night at Camp Aweelah, and the first day at the Pink Cone. I sit up on the bike seat and push down on the ped-als. In a few moments, I'm heading home. Lisa might be right, but I know Becky was wrong. Jay does love me. And I love Jay.

I'm halfway home, when I realize I forgot to pick up my pay-check.

"Damn it!" I yell loud enough that I startle a squirrel and send it scurrying through the brush. I'm not scheduled tomor-row, so if I want my check, I need to get it now. I glance over my shoulder to check for traffic and make a wide U-turn back the way I came.

There are more uphills going back into town so it takes me more than twenty minutes to get back to the Cone, plus I'm not rushing. I pull in the driveway and ride around back. I leave my bike propped against the stairs; I don't bother to lock it. I take the steps two at a time, and throw open the back door.

"I'm baaaaaaack! Did you miss—" I stop short. I feel like I've been punched in the gut. I have no air left in me. Jay is standing just inside the doorway—with another guy. Kissing.

The guy is tall and thin with dark curly hair that hangs to his chin. He has an eyebrow piercing, and his eyes are very green. I don't have to ask. I know this is the text messager.

"Sean." Jay doesn't say anything else. He just stares at me. Then, in slow motion, he raises a hand to his forehead and slides it back through his short, sun-streaked hair. Green-eyes leans against the break room doorway, his hands limp at his sides. He's skinny, but his wife-beater is tight enough to show off well-defined abs. He looks a little older than Jay, nineteen or twenty. Probably a college kid from Manchester.

"Is this the kid you're fucking?" He says it without inflection, no malice or irony. Just matter-of-fact.

Jay turns to look at him and whisper-yells, "Cody!" His eyes are back on me. He turns his palms upward and reaches them out, like a minister asking for a blessing at church. My eyes sting with tears, and I blink to hold them back. A sound is bubbling up inside of me; I can feel it rising unevenly inside my chest, an explosive, boiling heat I don't think I can control. And then my knees are bending, collapsing beneath me; the raw surge of emotion pulsing from my lungs to my throat is draining me of everything else. I don't have much time; I stagger back out the door and down the stone steps. I barely make it to the grass. Then I am doubled over, and my stomach heaves, and I vomit.

I throw up my lunch first. And then my breakfast. And then it's my pride. My stomach is still pumping like an engine piston, but there's not much left. Quick jump cuts of the summer skip through my brain: Lisa leaving for camp, Jay arriving in Bell Cove, Becky on a bench eating a Slim Jim, buying new clothes downtown, dinner with my dad, Jay's boat at night, his lips on mine. And then there is nothing.

I end up on my knees with my eyes closed, too exhausted and too humiliated to move. I don't know how long I'm there, but I feel a hand on my shoulder.

"You okay?" It's Jay.

I want to sit up and scream, "No! Of course I'm not okay. I was in love with you!" but I can't. I don't have it in me, so I just shake my head. I rock back and sit on my heels, with my head between my knees. Jay leaves his hand on my back for a few more minutes, and then he kneels down beside me.

"I know it doesn't mean much right now, but I am sorry."

I can tell he means it. His voice is cracked and has the quality of a wounded animal. Maybe he really did love me, at least, a little.

"We had fun," he says. "But ask yourself, did you really think this was going to be more than a summer fling?"

Finally, I gather my strength to lift my head, and I look him in the eyes. I don't answer him. It seems so obvious now, and I don't want to admit that I ever thought it might be more than it was. Finally, I shake my head.

"Listen. He went out the front. But he's waiting for me."

"Okay." I barely manage a whisper, but when Jay starts to stand up, I catch his arm. "Why?"

"Why?"

I clear my throat. "Why him?"

"He goes to UNH. I'll be there next month. I see him at the club all the time." Jay lets out a sigh. "Sean, you're sweet, cute, I mean . . . you're the perfect guy for someone. But. We're not made for each other. You've got to know that."

I think back to what Lisa said last night, and what Becky said, and I know. I know. I nod my head.

"I'm going to go," Jay says.

Chapter 37

I sit on the steps and try to catch my breath. I'm there for only a minute or two when Renée shows up.

As soon as she sees me, she's next to me, throwing an arm around my shoulders. "Oh, honey, what's wrong? You sick?"

"Is it that obvious?"

"What happened?"

"Jay."

"Oh." Renée takes her other hand and pulls my head onto her shoulder. "Did you two break up?"

"Yeah."

"Tell me what happened." She rubs my back and doesn't say anything else. She's waiting for me whenever I'm ready.

Harleigh pops her head around the back door. "Renée?"

"Not now! Can't you see I'm busy being a mom?" Harleigh opens her mouth to say something, but Renée stops her. "Go!"

I can't help myself. A smile creeps to my lips. Before I know it, I have told her everything.

"Jay has worked for me for three summers now," she says, "but there's no excusing what he did."

I look at Renée with wet eyes.

"But listen. Every guy has the potential to be a jerk, and if you don't protect yourself, you're going to get hurt again."

"Protect myself?"

"I mean don't fall in love so quickly. Get to know a guy first. Ask questions. Talk to him."

I'm reminded of a day when Renée asked me if I had talked to Jay. Now I think I understand what she meant. I was so excited to have a boyfriend, I didn't stop to figure out if I had found the right boyfriend. I realize now that Jay and I had almost nothing in common. But finding Jay was hard enough. How am I going to find someone who shares my interests . . . and is gay?

Renée can read my mind because she pats my back lightly and says, "Don't try so hard. You'd be surprised where guys'll turn up. Sometimes they're right in front of you."

"Thanks."

"Don't mention it. I know it's going to take some time to get over this. Broken hearts don't heal overnight. Why don't you take a couple of days off? I'll see you next week." Renée pats me on the back one more time and then gets up. When I look up to thank her again, she's already through the door.

I can hear her talking to Harleigh. "Okay. Fabulous! What was it you wanted?"

When I get home, my mom is in the kitchen making dinner. Normally, this would be a golden opportunity to make fun of her for trying to be domestic, but I just don't feel up to it. I head up to my room.

I stand in the doorway to my room. It's nice that it's clean, but there's also something foreign and uncomfortable about the smooth surface of the neatly made bed and the vast expanse of blue carpet that is usually littered with clothes. Looking at all the order makes me tired, but I don't have the heart to untuck the blankets to sleep under them. My grandmother's quilt is folded across the foot of the bed. I unfold it. I lie back on my pillows and pull the blanket up to my chin. I'm asleep almost instantly.

My mother knocks on my door. "Honey, you want some dinner?"

"Huh?" How long have I been sleeping?

She cracks open the door. "You feeling okay?"

"Not really."

"Can I come in?" She doesn't wait for a response. Instead she enters the room and sits next to me on the bed. She strokes my forehead and then rests the back of her hand across it. "You don't feel warm."

"I'm not sick."

"What's wrong?"

"Nothing."

She's quiet for a long time. She just sits and continues stroking my forehead. Finally, she says, "I made lasagna."

"I'm not hungry."

"I'll wrap up a plate in the fridge in case you feel like eating later." She gets up and moves to the door. She starts to leave, but then she turns back. "I'm here," she says, "if you need to talk."

I don't want to talk. I don't want to eat. I don't want to sleep. I don't want to do anything.

I try to tell myself that I shouldn't be so hurt. I was already coming to the realization that Jay and I might not be a perfect match, but to have it thrust in my face, it stings.

Two and a half months ago, everything was different. I was looking forward to summer vacation. I was going to lie around the house all summer, ride my bike, watch some movies, go swimming. I never got in fights with my mother. My father was way off in Georgia. I had a girlfriend.

How did I end up here, trying to smother myself in my own bed, unable to face the mirror, let alone the world? Becky almost had me convinced that being gay was okay, that I could be happy, that being myself wasn't a death sentence. She was wrong. Jay was wrong. I was wrong.

Bright light wakes me up. I open my eyes to a sun-filled room. It looks like my room, only cleaner. Out of the window, the sky is so bright, it appears painted on, like a movie set. From my view, there are no clouds, only clear, perfect blue. Somehow, I have slept through the night—and much of the day. There's a hollow feeling in my stomach, and I realize it's more than just the understanding that Jay and I are over; I'm hungry. I'm not sure that eating will make me feel better, though.

I roll over to find my alarm clock: 11:37. I wonder how long I can stay in bed. How long before my mother comes to investigate? My answer comes sooner than expected. There's a knock on my door, and it opens just a crack.

"Sean?"

"Yeah," I mumble. No use pretending to be asleep.

"There's someone here to see you."

Jay? For a moment I think that maybe I've overreacted. There's an explanation. Jay has come to apologize. I sit up. "Yeah?"

"Should I send her up, or are you coming down?"

"Huh?" It's not Jay?

"Should I send Becky up, or ask her to wait downstairs?" My mother's voice has an edge to it.

"I don't want to talk to Becky." What will she say? She told me so? That's the last thing I need right now.

There's a good five-second pause, but the door stays cracked open, and I know my mother hasn't left. Eventually, I hear her sigh, and I think that will be the end of it, but the door opens and she walks in. Her jaw is set, and her lips are compressed into thin pink lines. I think she's angry with me until I realize her eyes are shiny. She crosses to the foot of my bed and stands there. She wipes her eyes with the back of a hand, first one and then the other. Finally, she sits down on the end of the bed. She pulls one leg up so she can twist around to face me. She stretches out a hand and finds my foot under the quilt.

"Sean." Her voice is barely above a whisper, and it has a pinched, throaty quality, like if she tried to speak normally she might lose control and begin to cry. "I need you to tell me what's going on."

"It's nothing."

"It's not nothing. I've never seen you like this. You've been locked in here for a day. You won't come out to eat; you'll barely talk." She takes a deep breath and holds it for a second before letting it out in a rush. Her eyes roll up to the ceiling. Is she saying a prayer? Then they're back on me. "Becky has been your best friend all summer. Why won't you talk to her?"

"Because."

"Did you have a fight?"

"Sort of."

"What did you fight about? What could be so bad that you won't talk to her?"

I just shake my head. I don't think she would understand.

"I think she's come to say good-bye."

"Huh?"

"Her family is going back to New York."

"Oh." The thought of Becky leaving forever is like a slap in the face. I mean, we did fight and she was right, but that doesn't mean I never want to see her again. "Maybe I'll come down."

"All right. I'll ask her to wait." She pats my foot again, but she doesn't get up. She turns her body like she's going to stand, but then, without looking at me, she says, "Does this have to do with Jay?"

When she says his name, it's as if she's unlocked a secret compartment inside me, and suddenly tears are pouring out of my eyes, the tears that I tried so hard to hold back last night. I can't stop them, and my breaths start to come in staccato little huffs of emotion. There's no use denying it. "Yes," I force out between gasps.

As soon as she realizes I'm crying, my mother turns around again and climbs up on the bed. She holds me in her arms, and pulls my head onto her shoulder. Suddenly, my mother is psychic. She knows everything that's happened without my saying anything. Since when did my mother know me so well?

"You and Jay broke up?" My mother's voice coos in my ear. I nod. "Becky tried to warn you? Jay found someone else? But you didn't believe her?"

"How did you . . . ?"

"Because I've had my heart broken, too." She holds me tighter in her arms until my tears have stopped. Finally, she says, "I know you don't feel like it, but talking to Becky will help. Get yourself together, and we'll be waiting downstairs when you're ready." She pushes up off the bed and leaves the room, shutting the door behind her.

It takes me half an hour before I'm ready to venture downstairs, but Becky is still waiting for me. She and my mom have cups of tea at the kitchen table. A plate of cookies is between them. When my mother sees me, she stands up and takes her tea into the living room without saying anything.

"Hi," I say to Becky.

"Don't you know Jewish girls don't like to wait?" Her smile is genuine, and it's contagious.

"I thought that was New Yorkers."

"I'm both. I can barely wait two minutes for a Hot Pocket in the microwave. What makes you think you're so special?"

"I'm not."

"Honey. Yes, you are." She gets up from the table and pulls me into her. I put my arms around her, too, and we stand together for a long minute. Finally, I try to pull away.

"Not yet," she says.

"I can't breathe."

"Fine." Becky lets me out of her grip, but she's still smiling. "I'm sorry I was such a bitch."

"You were right, though."

"Of course I was, but I didn't have to be so bitchy."

"You were just being Becky. I should have listened to you."

"Nah. You had to find out for yourself."

I grab a cookie from the plate on the table. I take a bite and realize I'm starving. I grab two more from the plate.

"Hey," Becky says, "I made you something."

"You did?" I say with my mouth full.

"You don't have to wear it." Becky reaches into her pocket and pulls out a strand of colorful beads. "It's a necklace."

I take it from her and hold it by one end. I pull it through my fingers, letting the translucent plastic beads catch the light. The beads are arranged by color in groups of five, so that they make a rainbow. The pattern repeats several times. "I love it," I say. I try to put it on, but I've never worn a necklace before, and I have trouble with the clasp.

"Here." Becky comes around behind me and helps me get it on.

I walk into the hallway where there's a mirror on the wall. It's just a small change, but I feel like I'm looking at a whole new person. A gay person. A happy gay person.

I turn back to Becky and give her another hug. "Thank you."

"Here's something else." She hands me a folded piece of paper. It says *JewTalkin2U*. "It's my screen name," she says. "Use it."

I stare at the paper for a few seconds, and then stuff it in my pocket. "I will." I smile at Becky. "I'll use it every day and twice on Sundays."

"Let's not get carried away." Becky slaps me on the back. "Hey, your mom said it would be okay if you came down to visit me in New York this fall. We can go see a show on Broadway."

"She said that?" Could this really be the same mom who freaked out at the beginning of the summer because I got in a canoe? And it hits me exactly how much has changed in the last two and a half months. "I'm already voting for *Avenue Q.*"

"It's a date." And I know that even after Becky leaves today, this is not really good-bye.

Chapter 38

Later that night, I'm eating leftover lasagna at the kitchen table with my mother. "I'm glad you and Becky made up," she says.

"Yeah, me too." When I think about how much I almost lost because I was too focused on Jay, I can't believe it. I never thought I was someone who would act like that, letting my feelings for someone get in the way of my friendships and my family.

But Jay wasn't all bad either. If it hadn't been for him, I might still be pretending to be someone I'm not with Lisa, and that wouldn't be good for me or for her. But next time, I'll be more careful, especially since next time I might not have Becky there to warn me.

I think about how supportive Becky was from the very beginning. She pulled me out of my shell, and there was never any question about giving support. I was afraid to come out to my mother, but Becky gave me the strength I needed to do it. If only she was still around so I could come out to my dad.

But I don't need Becky to come out to my dad. I have my mom now, and besides, if there's one thing I've learned this summer, coming out is always easier in real life than you imagine it to be in your head. Sure, my dad might not be happy, but it's not really his happiness that matters to me.

I finish my lasagna. It will still be light out for another hour or two. I make a decision.

"I'm going out," I say to my mother.

"By yourself?"

"I have something I have to do."

It's a perfect evening for a bike ride, and I enjoy the trip over to the Lakeside Cottages. Lights are starting to come on in windows. I take a detour up Mann's Hill so I can look at my little town peppered along the shoreline. I used to make fun of Bell Cove because it's so small, but I'm starting to realize that it's only small in my mind. I shouldn't be so eager to escape. There's plenty here left for me.

I cruise down the hill toward my destination, but the closer I get, the more anxious I feel. Twenty minutes ago, at the dinner table, everything was clear in my mind, but now sweat beads on my forehead despite the cool evening air. I must tell my father. I need to tell my father. But what will he say?

I play the scenario over and over in my head. "Dad, I'm gay." I repeat it to myself. *You can do this, Sean.* I remember how I felt sitting with Becky on the bench by the lake. It's such a simple sentence, and yet the uncertainty behind it is paralyzing. What will he say? What will he do?

But it doesn't matter. It doesn't matter what he does or says. It's about me. I want my father to know who I am.

I take a deep breath. I am ready. My bike bounces over the dirt driveway that leads down to the cottages. *You can do this, Sean.*

But the cottage is dark. This late in the season, only a few cars are parked along the driveway. Most people have returned to their normal lives somewhere else, my father among them. When did he leave? Was he gone when I dropped Becky off earlier? He didn't say good-bye?

I stop the bike in front of my father's cottage. There are no fishing poles leaning by the door, no coffee cup left sitting on the porch railing. The cottage is empty. My father is gone.

Conflicting emotions swirl in my chest. My lungs loosen and I can breathe, realizing I don't have to do it now, but something hard and cold slides down my stomach. I can't do it now.

I had worked myself up for this. I *knew* it was what I had to do. I was going to come out to my father, look him in the eyes. But he's gone. Back to Georgia.

"FUCK!" A surge of anger erupts inside me. I yell it loud, and it echoes across the lake like a rifle shot. A screen door squeaks open a few cottages down, and in the failing light I can see a man watching me from his front steps. He doesn't say anything. Neither do I. I climb back on my bike and ride home.

"He left last night." My mother is sitting in the living room with a book when I come in. "You were asleep."

"I thought he wasn't leaving until next week."

"Did you know your father's girlfriend was pregnant?"

"What?"

"Apparently." My mother puts her book down. "She went into labor last night. Six weeks early."

"Nice of him to tell me."

She looks at me over her reading glasses. "There's a lot of things we should tell each other."

The news isn't shocking to me. I always knew my father had a new life in Georgia, and since our conversations rarely go deeper than who's hitting cleanup for the Red Sox, I had no reason to find out. It's not like I ever asked what was going on in his life. I think back to our fishing trip. He had something important to talk to me about, and I had assumed it was about me being gay, but maybe this was what he wanted to say. Maybe it was as hard for him to tell me as it was for me to tell him.

"Will he call?"

"I'm sure he will."

The idea of a new brother or sister is funny to me. I'm sixteen. I'll be in my thirties by the time the kid is in high school. And my dad's not exactly young. I shake my head, and a dry laugh comes out of my mouth. I'm surprised that I could find it funny, but I do. And suddenly I'm laughing harder. My mother looks at me for a moment longer, and then she is laughing, too. I fall on the couch next to her, and we laugh until it starts to hurt.

Finally, between breaths I ask, "Do you think it will be okay to visit?"

My mother takes my hand and squeezes. "Your father would like that."

"Maybe over Christmas vacation. I can tell him then."

"That's a good idea."

"Thanks, Mom." I get up from the couch. I head up to my room. I'm tired, but also full of energy. My head spins with everything that's happened today, happened this summer. And I realize, my mom has been there the whole time. Even when she was mad at me, she was there. When I thought I was alone, that there was no one to tell about how I was feeling, no one to tell about being gay, my mom was always available. And I know that's not going to change. When this summer started, I didn't think there was anywhere or anyone to turn to. How wrong I was.

I wonder if maybe I've been selling my dad short, too. That day out on the lake, he said I could talk to him about anything. I think about his new family, and how much my dad has changed in just the past year: moving to Georgia, a girlfriend he's probably going to marry, a new child. Is it too much to believe my dad could change in other ways, too? I lie on my bed and think about my father and his new family. I know I'll have a second chance.

Chapter 39

Lisa comes back on Saturday. I want to meet her at the dock, but we both decide that explaining things to her father would be awkward, so I hang out at my house waiting for her to call. Now that Becky's left, there's not much to do, and I'm pretty anxious to get back to school. The Pink Cone won't close up for another month or so, and I'll keep working there once school starts. But I've decided to take a little break until Jay leaves for college in a week. Renée is very understanding. I never did pick up my paycheck, and Renée told me Jay wouldn't be working this afternoon. I figure I can stop in after Lisa calls.

She doesn't call until after three. I'm waiting by the phone, and I pick up on the first ring.

"It's about time!"

"Hello to you, too." Lisa is laughing on the other end.

"When are we hanging out?"

"Whoa there, cowboy. My mother's acting like I've been gone for three months, which I kind of have."

"What about tonight?"

"I'm going out with a bunch of people from camp. We're having an end-of-summer bonfire. It'd be awesome if you can come."

I had planned on having Lisa to myself, but the idea of making some new friends isn't so bad either. I have a thought.

"Is Brad going to be there?" I ask.

"He's the one that's planning everything. You would so love him. You have to come!"

"Okay," I say, trying not to sound too eager. I want to see Brad again almost as much as I want to see Lisa. Other than Jay, I don't know any gay people my age. My mom's been great, and Becky was awesome, and Lisa seems really supportive, but none of them really know what it's like. Having just one person to talk to would make all the difference.

We make plans to meet up later that night. In the meantime, I head down to the Pink Cone.

Renée comes out to meet me when I get there, and she gives me a hug.

"How you doin', hon?"

"Okay."

We sit on the stone wall along the front of the store. "It's been quiet around here without you and Becky."

"Yeah?"

"It'll be fabulous when you come back." We sit for a minute in silence. I understand now that Renée knew more about me than I did when she hired me at the beginning of the summer. I wonder if that's how Jay started working here, if he was ever confused and scared. Did Renée help him, too?

"Thanks, Renée," I say.

She checks her watch. Even her watchband is pink. "You're welcome, hon." She stands up to go back inside, but I catch her hand.

"I mean it. Thank you."

"I know. You're welcome." She gives me a knowing look, and then her attitude shifts abruptly. She starts up the walk to the store. "I've scheduled you for three days next week. Don't be late."

I smile after her. I'm just now realizing how much of a friend Renée is to me. I still don't like the pink shirts, though.

I sit on the wall and look out at the lake. It's late afternoon, and the sun has dropped so that the light has that indirect quality that makes everything look like a postcard. There is no wind today, and the lake is glassy. The boats moored at the docks float above perfect mirror images of themselves. A jagged line of ducks paddles along the edge, sending ripples out into the water. It's one of the last Saturdays of summer, and Bell Cove is quiet. I'm so absorbed by the scene, I don't notice when someone sits down next to me.

"What are you looking at?"

I jump, just a little. I'm embarrassed to be snuck up on, but then I see it's Matt. I haven't seen him since Becky left.

"Nothing. Just the lake."

"It's beautiful."

"What brings you down here?"

"I was hoping you'd be working. Felt like a scoop of Purple Cow."

"Not raspberry latte?"

"I like Purple Cow better."

"I'm not working, but I could probably snag us both a scoop if you want," I say. He nods and I jump up to get us the ice cream.

He's still sitting on the wall when I get back. We eat in silence for a few minutes, before Matt says, "So, uh, how's Jay?"

He takes me by surprise. I didn't realize he knew I was gay. "We broke up," I say.

"I'm sorry."

"Don't be. He was a jerk. Becky tried to warn me."

"Was he your first boyfriend?"

I nod.

"Everyone has to have a jerk boyfriend sometime. You got yours out of the way."

We eat the rest of our ice cream and talk about the summer. Neither of us can believe how quickly it went.

"It was too fast. I didn't get to do half of what I wanted," Matt says.

"I know," I say.

"What's one thing you wish you could have done this summer that you didn't get a chance to do?"

I don't even hesitate. "Tell my dad I'm gay."

"He doesn't know?"

I shake my head. "I tried to tell him, but I couldn't seem to find the right moment."

"Do you think he'd be okay with it?"

"Yeah. Yeah, I do. It's just hard, you know?"

"Yeah, I do," he says.

"I mean, my mother's like the most accepting person on the planet, and she had a hard time. It's scary. She's still got lots of questions."

"Yeah?"

"She's started reading books about it."

"Maybe she should go to a PFLAG meeting."

PFLAG is that group that Lisa told me Brad wants to start. How does Matt know about that? He must have seen my confused look, because he adds, "My parents are starting a chapter."

"They are?"

"You know what it is?"

"Yeah, Lisa told me about it. She said some guy from her summer camp is starting one."

"That must be Brad."

"You know Brad?"

"He's a wicked-cool guy. He's having an end-of-summer bonfire tonight."

"You're going?"

"Yeah, you should come."

"I am. Lisa already invited me." I look at Matt in his cargo shorts and T-shirt. I have to ask. "Why are your parents starting a PFLAG chapter?"

Matt doesn't answer. He just gives me a half smile and raises his eyebrows.

"Are you . . . ?"

"Gay?" Matt says.

"Are you?"

"I've had a crush on you since freshman year. Why do you think I kept eating your ice cream?"

"What?"

"I don't even like coffee ice cream. I only ate your raspberry latte because, well, because you made it."

"What?" My brain keeps replaying the last thirty seconds in my head like a TiVo. I really did hear what I think I heard.

"I'm pathetic, I know," he says.

"No, you're not. I'm the one who's pathetic. I thought I was the only gay guy in school, the only gay guy in Bell Cove."

"Surprise."

We throw out our ice cream bowls, and I suggest we take a bike ride before we meet Lisa for the bonfire. There's still at least an hour of light left so I lead us up to Mann's Hill. We climb up on my favorite rock to watch the sunset. I never noticed how much room there was up here.

We talk about school, and what plays we might do this year in drama club, and what books we like (mysteries) and movies (horror and action). We talk about friends we have in common and teachers we like.

"I really like you, Sean," Matt says.

He catches me off guard. I know he doesn't mean as in friends.

"I like you, too," I say.

"But?"

"But, I don't know if I should jump into anything right now."

"I get that." Matt looks off over the lake. Above us, long tendrils of clouds create pink and orange and purple bands across the sky. They're reflected as long tongues of color over the water.

I watch him in the evening light, and suddenly I find myself leaning over, and I give him a kiss on the cheek.

Matt turns to me in surprise. He bites his tongue between his teeth in embarrassment, and even in the fading light I can see that he is blushing.

I take his hand. We can take this slow. He laces his fingers between mine and squeezes. I squeeze back. We don't say anything. We don't need to. We just watch the sun set.

IF I TOLD YOU SO

Timothy Woodward

ABOUT THIS GUIDE

The suggested questions are included to enhance
your group's reading of Timothy Woodward's
If I Told You So.

DISCUSSION QUESTIONS

1. Before Sean meets Becky he has led a very sheltered life growing up in a small town. How might growing up near a city have changed Sean's life? Would it have made coming out any easier for him?

2. Sean describes his relationship with Lisa as very tame, which makes it easier for Sean to be Lisa's boyfriend. How is this relationship mutually beneficial? Is it possible that Lisa suspects that Sean is gay? Why would she stay with him if this were the case?

3. Sean admits to enjoying kissing with Lisa. How is it possible that he can enjoy kissing a girl while claiming to be gay? Is Sean being hypocritical in his relationship with Lisa?

4. Sean is surprised when Lisa tells him that Brad, a fellow camp counselor, is gay. Why is this so surprising to Sean? Sean also admits that he'd like to talk to Brad about coming out. What insights could Brad offer to Sean? How would Brad's coming out story differ from Sean's? How would it be similar?

5. Sean says his mother is a school counselor and he's pretty sure she'll be accepting of him as gay, but he's still reluctant to share his sexuality with her. Why would Sean be unsure? What incidents from Sean's past may have created his doubts? Why is it important for adults or those in positions of authority to speak up when they hear anti-gay language or bullying?

6. What is Sean's mother's initial reaction to his coming out? Does the circumstance of Sean's announcement affect her reaction? Would she be more accepting if Sean had broken the news in another way? How does she let Sean know that she will be supportive?

7. Why does Sean have such a hard time coming out to his father? What does his father do or say that keeps Sean from opening up? Does the fact that Sean's father lives in Georgia affect Sean's willingness to come out to him? Does distance make staying in the closet easier?

8. Why is Sean's relationship with his father so difficult? Why is it hard for them to communicate? Does Sean feel his father abandoned him by moving to Georgia? If so, why isn't he happier for his dad to show up in Bell Cove? How do Sean's father's actions show his true feelings for his son?

9. Becky gives Sean "Gay Culture 101," teaching him about gay movies, clothing, and music. Why wouldn't Sean have discovered these on his own? Why does Sean need someone like Becky to help him experience gay culture when he has the resources of the Internet available to him? Why, do you think, is Sean so sheltered? Is it by choice or by circumstance?

10. Why does Sean fall for Jay so quickly? Even though she encouraged Sean to pursue Jay, Becky also warns Sean to take things slowly. Why does she give Sean this advice? Did Becky see Jay's betrayal coming? What does Jay do that would make Becky suspicious? What warning signs did Sean have that may have saved him from heartbreak?

11. Sean admires one of Jo Anne's paintings of Bell Cove and says that "for the first time that I can remember, I find myself wanting to see more of Bell Cove." What is it about the painting that intrigues him? How has the summer changed Sean's attitude toward Bell Cove? Jo Anne then shows Sean a painting from her first apartment in New York City and tells him "that sometimes you need to look beyond the surface to find what you're looking for." How does that apply to Sean's life in Bell Cove? How does it apply to his life as a gay man?

12. Sean says he thought he was the only gay person in Bell Cove, but he discovers this isn't so. How many gay people does Sean meet? Are they all surprises to him? How do you think these discoveries will change Sean's feelings toward his hometown? How important is it for gay youth to be able to see themselves in their surroundings? Why are events like Gay Pride important for this purpose?

13. How will Sean's life change as he heads back to school after the summer? Do you think he will come out to the rest of the school? What difficulties might he encounter? What resources will he have to rely on?